CARNIVAL MASTER

SELENA WINTERS

Carnival Master Copyright © 2024 Selena Winters

All Rights Reserved.
No part of this publication may be reproduced, stored, or transmitted in any form or by any means, electronic, mechanical, photocopying, recording, scanning, or otherwise without written permission from the publisher. It is illegal to copy this book, post it to a website, or distribute it by any other means without permission.

This novel is entirely a work of fiction. The names, characters and incidents portrayed in it are the work of the author's imagination. Any resemblance to actual persons, living or dead, events or localities is entirely coincidental.

Warning: the unauthorized reproduction or distribution of this copyrighted work is illegal. Criminal copyright infringement, including infringement without monetary gain, is investigated by the FBI and is punishable by up to 5 years in prison and a fine of $250,000.

CONTENTS

Playlist	v
Author's Note	ix
1. Tyson	1
2. Sofia	9
3. Tyson	19
4. Sofia	25
5. Tyson	31
6. Sofia	39
7. Tyson	45
8. Sofia	51
9. Tyson	57
10. Sofia	65
11. Tyson	71
12. Sofia	75
13. Tyson	83
14. Sofia	89
15. Tyson	99
16. Sofia	107
17. Tyson	113
18. Sofia	125
19. Tyson	131
20. Sofia	139
21. Tyson	147
22. Sofia	153
23. Tyson	159
24. Sofia	167
25. Tyson	173
26. Tyson	181
27. Sofia	191

28. Tyson	203
29. Sofia	215
30. Tyson	223
31. Tyson	233
32. Tyson	243
33. Sofia	257
34. Tyson	265
35. Sofia	271
36. Tyson	277
37. Sofia	285
38. Tyson	291
39. Epilogue	301
About the Author	311

PLAYLIST

CARNIVAL MASTER PLAYLIST

"You Put A Spell On Me"—Austin Giorgio
"Beggin For Thread"—BANKS
"Church"—Chase Atlantic
"Intoxicated"—Aaryan Shah
"Body (Slowed & Reverb)"—Rosenfeld
"Fire Up The Night"—New Medicine
"Bite Marks"—Ari Abdul
"Heartbeat"—Isabel LaRosa
"Dirty Mind"—Boy Epic
"All Mine"—Plaza
"Whisper"—Able Heart
"Gangsta"—Kehlani
"Sex, Drugs, Etc."—Beach Weather
"Solo"—Prismo
"Don't Blame Me"—Taylor Swift
"Self Love"—Jason Lyric, Nevaeh

You can find the playlist on Spotify here

To all the depraved little book sluts who fantasize about being stripped bare and broken by a man who knows exactly how to make you scream his name...

AUTHOR'S NOTE

Author's Note

This story explores dark romance and contains explicit content that may not be suitable for all readers. It includes themes of dominance, psychotic behavior, possessiveness, and explicit mature scenes presented alongside delicate subject matters that may be distressing or triggering for some individuals.

Please refer to the comprehensive list of warnings on my website for detailed information on this book's triggers.

I advise reader discretion and recommend only proceeding if you're comfortable with the mentioned themes. Rest assured, the story ends in a HEA with no cliffhanger or cheating between the main characters.

1

TYSON

We're in the city of Dawsbury. The perfect pit stop for what I've got planned. As soon as the crew starts setting up the rides and tents, I slip away to make some calls.

My phone buzzes with messages from clients eager to restock their supplies. "Easy, fellas, I've got you covered," I mutter. Twenty kilos are packed tightly in the Ferris wheel trailer's hidden compartment, and more are coming from our supplier on Friday. We'll have more than enough to keep my clients happy.

I punch in the number for Jimmy Moretti, the boss running this city.

"Ty, my man!" Jimmy's gruff voice booms through the phone. "You got my shipment all squared away?"

"I always come through for you, Jimmy." I lean back against the trailer, keeping my voice low. "Twenty-five kilos, as we discussed. It should keep you and your crew satisfied for a while."

Jimmy grunts in approval. "That's what I like to

hear. I'll be there tonight after your show to discuss pickup. You know the drill—keep it on the down-low."

"Goes without saying," I assure him. "The carnival's just a cover. You won't have any issues on my end."

As I disconnect the call, I can't help but smirk. Jimmy may take over half the shipment, but the rest will keep my regular customers in this region nicely stocked. Guys like Tommy Valenti, Paulie Gambino, and Frank Scarpelli—rely on my steady supply to keep their operations running smoothly.

With that settled, it's time for me to slip back into my other role—the ringleader of this traveling circus. I head for my trailer to get changed. Being the ringmaster isn't just about putting on a show. It's about keeping everyone in line. Making sure the rides run smoothly and the crowds are entertained. But right now, I need a damn break.

I step inside, locking the door behind me. A moment of peace before the chaos unfolds. That's when I hear moans. Fucking Cade and his girl—the diner waitress he stole from Willow Creek.

I shouldn't be surprised. They've been like rabbits since they met. But fuck, the sounds they're making have my cock hardening. It's been too long since I've had a decent lay. My balls are bluer than a Wookiee's ballsack.

I pace the confines of my trailer, running a hand through my hair. I need to find some action in this town, or I'll lose my mind. The memory of the last woman I bedded, a curvy blonde, flashes in my mind. But that was weeks ago, and my body craves release.

I yank open a drawer, grab a bottle of whiskey, and

take a long swig. The burn soothes my restless thoughts momentarily. But the sounds of Cade and Lily's passionate fucking filter through the wall, mocking my pent-up desires.

I take another swig of whiskey, reveling in the burn as it trails down my throat. My thoughts drift to the curvy blonde from a few weeks back. The memory of her soft, round ass and the feel of her full breasts against my palms stir something deep inside me.

My cock is throbbing now, demanding attention. With a slight smirk, I pull it out, relishing the sensation of freedom. I wrap my fingers around it and start stroking slowly. My pierced cock glistens with a bead of pre-cum.

I angle my ear toward the wall, their rhythmic grunts and moans filling the room. It fuels my strokes, each one firmer and faster than the last. The pleasure builds, my breath quickening as I imagine the curvy blonde's mouth wrapped around my cock, her tongue playing with the piercing.

My eyes drift shut as I lose myself in the fantasy. I can almost feel her soft lips trailing down my chest, her fingers gently scraping against the rough hair on my legs. As my strokes become more urgent, I adjust my stance, one hand against the wall for support.

Their pace quickens next door, the headboard banging against the wall. The sound of their passion fuels my desire. I imagine the blonde I'd fucked a month ago riding me, her full breasts bouncing with each movement, her fingers raking down my chest.

My free hand roams over my chest, tweaking a

nipple as my hand moves in more frenzied movements. I bite my lip, not wanting to alert Cade that I'm jerking off while listening to them. Not that he'd mind. He's fucked her in front of guys here while they jerked off. The piercings send sensations throughout my body, heightening the pleasure.

The sound of their fucking gets louder, their cries signaling their impending release. My strokes become more urgent, my body tensing as I feel myself reaching the brink.

As their voices peak in unison, my body convulses. I bite down hard, tasting the coppery tang of blood as I spill over my hand.

I lower myself to the ground, my body sated, yet my heart still pounding in my chest. I take a moment to catch my breath, the room now quiet as Cade and Lily likely lay sprawled and satisfied next door. The fucker should be working, but he never sticks to the rules. With a slight head shake, I chuckle, enjoying the post-orgasmic buzz.

"Well, hell," I mutter, straightening up and tucking myself back into my pants.

I move to the kitchen and wash the evidence from my hand. "Might as well go put on a show."

With a satisfied grin, I crack open the door, the sounds of the carnival outside filtering in. I step out, ready to join the fray and see if any new distractions or delights have arrived with our stay in this town. My eyes scan the crowd, eager for a fresh pursuit.

Walking toward the main tent, I straighten my jacket and plaster my most charming smile.

Here we go, showtime. I stride into the big top with an extra swagger, basking in the crowd's roar. This is my domain, my kingdom.

"Ladies and gentlemen!" I boom into the microphone, my voice carrying over the excited murmurs. "Welcome to the greatest show on Earth!"

The crowd erupts in cheers and applause. I can feel the energy crackling in the air, a live current that only I can harness and control. With a sweeping gesture, I direct their attention to the center ring.

"Prepare to be amazed as we bring you feats of daring and displays of unparalleled talent!"

On cue, a spotlight cuts through the dimness, illuminating the graceful figure of a lithe acrobat ascending the silk ropes. It's Nash, executing his routine with flawless precision, twisting and spinning high above the ground.

I pace the perimeter, playing the role of ringmaster to perfection. "Marvel at the artistry! The flexibility. The raw courage required to perform such gravity-defying stunts!"

The crowd is transfixed, oohing and ahhing in sync with Nash's every move. He's putting on a show, just like he trains to. Nash and Colt always start with a solo show, then bring in the big guns and do their ridiculously talented duo show, tossing each other up in the air on the trapeze.

Once Nash sticks the dismount, I whip the audience into another frenzy of applause. "Incredible! But that's just the beginning, my friends! Hold onto your hats because you haven't seen anything yet!"

The rest of the show goes off without a hitch, and when it's finished, the crowd's roars are deafening as I take my final bow. These people live for the spectacle, the thrill of witnessing death-defying stunts right before their eyes.

And I love to give it to them.

As the tent empties, I go backstage to congratulate the crew. Nash is already there, grinning from ear to ear as he towels off the sweat glistening on his chiseled body.

"You were on fire out there tonight, man!" I clap him on the back, matching his infectious energy. "The crowd was eating out of the palm of your hand."

Nash flexes his biceps with a cocky smirk. "What can I say? They just can't get enough of this."

I chuckle and shake my head. His talent matches his arrogance. "Don't let it go to your head, pretty boy. We've got another show tomorrow night."

I go to Colt, who's methodically packing the rigging equipment. He's focused, his brow furrowed in concentration as he coils the ropes with practiced efficiency.

"Colt, my man," I say, clapping him on the shoulder. "Solid work out there tonight. Great show."

He looks up, his steely gaze meeting mine. "Thanks, boss. Just doing my job."

"Keep up the good work." I turn and stride out of the main tent, still riding high on the rush of another successful show. The roar of the crowd, the electric atmosphere—it's a feeling like no other, and I thrive on it. With a satisfied grin, I loosen my tie and roll my shoulders back, ready to slip into my other role for the night's dealings.

That's when I slam right into her.

The impact knocks the breath out of me, but not because of the force—no, the beauty standing before me leaves me stunned. Fiery red hair frames a heart-shaped face with delicate features and full, rosy lips. But her eyes ensnare me the most. Twin pools of emerald green pierce right through me.

"Well, hello there," I drawl, recovering my composure with a grin. I take a step back, giving the woman an appreciative once-over. "Fancy running into you like this."

She arches one perfectly sculpted eyebrow, clearly unimpressed by my attempt at charm. "Oh, I'm so sorry," she deadpans, sarcasm dripping from her words. "I'll be more careful next time."

Undeterred, I lean in closer, dropping my voice to a low rumble. "No need to apologize, baby girl. I'd run into you again any day." I flash her my most disarming smile, which usually has women melting at my feet.

But this fiery vixen doesn't seem fazed in the slightest. She regards me with an amused look as if I'm some pesky insect she could swat away without a second thought.

"You've got some nerve, don't you?" She eyes me up and down with thinly veiled disdain. "Sorry, but I don't go for the whole 'carnie' look."

With that scathing remark, she brushes past me, the sway of her hips and the scent of her vanilla perfume lingering in her wake. She's curvy in all the right places, and fuck, I love a curvy girl. For a moment, I'm rendered speechless—an incredibly rare occurrence.

As I watch her disappear into the crowd, I can't help but feel a spark of intrigue ignite within me. This woman is different, immune to my usual tactics and unaffected by my charisma. And strangely, that only makes me want her more.

A slow, predatory grin spreads across my face.

You can run, baby girl, but you can't hide from me. I'll show you why you should be totally into the carnie look when you're bouncing on my cock later.

2

SOFIA

I search for my father through the carnival grounds, my nose wrinkling at the smell of grease and sweat mingling in the summer heat. This place gives me the creeps—too many shady characters lurking about, their eyes lingering too long.

That ringmaster is the worst of them all. Who does he think he is, undressing me with those dark eyes and giving me that wolfish grin? The nerve of him flirting so brazenly after literally slamming into me. I don't care how ripped he is under that stupid ringmaster costume, with those intricate tattoos snaking across his muscular arms.

Ugh, I can't be thinking about him like that. I'm spoken for, thanks to dear old Dad setting up this ridiculous arranged marriage. To a mobster—because that's just what a girl dreams of. Marrying into the family business of extortion and violence.

My aimless wandering leads me right to the freak show tent. Of course. I peek inside, grimacing at the strange human oddities on display. A woman with a beard thicker than most men, contortionists folding themselves into impossible knots, and... is that a guy hammering a nail into his nose? I stumble back, hand over my mouth to stifle my revolted gasp.

"There you are." Dad's gruff voice makes me jump. He grabs my arm, yanking me away from the tent flap. "C'mon, we gotta meet Tyson about that shipment."

Tyson.

Isn't that the ringmaster's name? My heart stutters in my chest. I don't want to see that arrogant, inappropriately flirtatious jackass again.

But I don't have a choice. Dad's already dragging me toward the main tent, his beefy hand clamped around my wrist like a vise.

I steel myself as Dad yanks open the tent flap, the heavy canvas parting to reveal a dimly lit space that reeks of cigarette smoke and cheap beer. A few burly men lounge around a rickety card table, their laughter rough and grating.

In the center of it all is the ringmaster himself—Tyson. He's shed the gaudy red jacket, wearing a tight black tank that strains against his muscular frame. Those intricate tattoos I noticed earlier wrap around his bulging biceps, disappearing beneath the fabric. A cold sweat prickles my neck despite the heat as his dark gaze lands on me.

"Mr. Moretti." Tyson rises to his feet, that insufferable grin playing at the corners of his lips. "I wasn't expecting such lovely company."

Dad grunts, oblivious to the way Tyson's eyes roam over me. "You got those supplies we talked about?"

"Of course." Tyson's focus shifts back to my father, all traces of flirtation vanishing as he launches into logistics about weights, quantities, and drop-off points.

I try to tune it out, my cheeks flushing with embarrassment and anger. The way he looked at me like he wanted to devour me right there. Surely, if he knows anything about my dad, he knows I'm in an arranged marriage. Not that I want to marry that slimeball Paulie Gambino, but still. I have my obligations.

Tyson's deep voice cuts through my thoughts. "Everything'll be ready by midnight like we discussed. You're good for the payment?"

Dad huffs out a laugh, slapping a thick envelope on the table. The sound of it smacking down makes me cringe. "You know I'm good for it. Now, are we done here? I got places to be."

"That's it, Mr. Moretti. Good doing business with you." Tyson scoops up the envelope, tucking it into his waistband.

I avert my gaze, refusing to meet his eyes again. But not before catching the briefest glimpse of the bulge in his pants and how it strains against the fabric.

No. I don't want to think about the bulge in his pants. I turn on my heel and storm out of the stifling tent, leaving Dad and his goons behind. The carnival has officially lost all its charm. Not that it had much in the first place.

I storm away from the tent, my face burning. The

nerve of that Tyson guy, looking at me like a piece of meat right in front of my father.

Heavy footsteps sound behind me, closing in fast. Before I can react, a strong hand clamps down on my upper arm, wrenching me backward into the shadows between two tents.

"Let go of me!" I cry, struggling against him while he pins me against the faded canvas.

Tyson's face looms in front of mine, his eyes glittering with an intensity that makes my breath catch. Up close, I can see a faint scar over his eyebrow, remnants of past fights or troubles with the law. He's terrifyingly attractive in a rough, dangerous way.

"You shouldn't have run off like that." His voice is a deep, gritty rasp that sends a shiver down my spine. "We weren't finished talking."

"Get your hands off me, you pig!" I snarl, pushing against his chest. But he doesn't budge, his body a solid wall of muscle trapping me in place. "If Paulie knew you were touching his future wife, he'd cut your filthy hands off."

A dark chuckle rumbles from Tyson's throat as he leans in closer, his lips brushing the shell of my ear. "Is that what you want? To be Paulie Gambino's little wifey, popping out babies and turning a blind eye while he fucks every piece of ass in the city?"

It's true—everything Tyson's saying about Paulie. The guy's a notorious womanizer, bragging to his goons about all the side pieces he's got stashed around the city. And I'm sure that won't change once we're married. It'll just be another way for him to flaunt his power and status, keeping his wife at home barefoot and pregnant while he philanders around.

But it's my duty. My obligation as the daughter of a mob boss is to make this arranged marriage work. To play the good little mobster's wife and keep up appearances, no matter how much it makes my skin crawl.

"It's my duty," I grit out, struggling against Tyson. "Something a carnie like you could never understand."

His eyes narrow to dangerous slits. But then that insufferable grin creeps back across his lips, and he leans in until our faces are inches apart.

"Oh, I understand duty just fine, baby girl." His raspy voice drips with contempt on that last word. "But I also understand when someone's trying to convince themselves they're okay with a shitty situation."

I open my mouth to protest, but he barrels on, his tone low and intense.

"You deserve so much better than being Paulie's latest possession. A woman like you needs a real man who can keep her satisfied, not some two-timing scumbag who'll be too busy sticking it in anything with a pulse."

My breath catches in my throat as Tyson's hands grip my hips. An unwelcome spark of desire flares in my core at the raw hunger in his gaze.

"You should be mine, Sofia." His lips ghost my jaw, his beard scratching deliciously against my skin. "I'd treat you like a fucking queen, not some glorified baby maker. You'd never want for anything. I promise you that."

Part of me wants to slap him, to knee him right in

the balls for daring to speak to me that way. But another part—a deeper, more primal part that I've denied for far too long—is thrumming with excitement at his bold words and even bolder touch.

This is so wrong. So utterly inappropriate, not to mention insulting to my family's honor. I'm not some cheap piece of ass to be leered at and grabbed by a shady guy.

My body betrays me, instinctively arching into Tyson's solid frame as his calloused palm skims up my rib cage to cup my breast through the thin fabric of my blouse. A ragged gasp escapes my lips before I can stop it.

"That's it, princess," he murmurs, his thumb grazing my peaked nipple. "Let me show you what a real man feels like."

I yank myself free from Tyson's grasp, stumbling backward as fury burns through my veins. Who does this piece of trailer trash think he is, grabbing me and spewing that filth?

"Get your hands off me," I snarl, shoving him hard in the chest. He staggers back a step, that infuriating smirk never leaving his face. "The only man who'll be showing me anything is Paulie. My fiancé."

Tyson lets out a harsh bark of laughter, raking an appraising gaze over my body that makes me want to squirm. "Let me guess—you're a virgin, saving yourself for marriage like a good little girl?"

Heat floods my cheeks as I straighten my spine, glaring defiantly into his mocking eyes. "That's none of your business. But for your information, I'm not some blushing innocent. I lost my virginity years ago."

The words tumble out before I can stop them. Tyson's brows shoot up, that shit-eating grin widening as he takes a deliberate step forward, crowding my space again.

"Is that so?" His voice drops to a low, gravelly purr. "Do tell, baby girl. Who was the lucky guy?"

I open my mouth to tell him where he can shove his condescending attitude. But the memory rises unbidden—a drunken night in some frat guy's basement, stumbling through the motions with a sloppy, impatient idiot who couldn't be bothered to make sure I enjoyed myself.

The humiliation still stings all these years later. I shake my head, forcing the memory away.

"None of your damn business," I repeat, mustering every ounce of venom I can. "Just some loser in college who couldn't find a woman's clit with a map and a flashlight."

Tyson throws his head back with a roar of laughter, the unexpected sound making me flinch. When he meets my glare again, his eyes are bright with amusement.

"Well, damn. Guess the poor bastard didn't do a very good job showing you how it's supposed to be." He takes another deliberate step forward, his body a solid, scorching presence against mine as he leans close. "Let me demonstrate that I know exactly where your clit is and how to make you scream with my tongue."

I gasp at Tyson's filthy words, my core clenching. The rough timbre of his voice, coupled with the blazing intensity in his eyes, has me struggling to maintain my composure.

Part of me wants nothing more than to give in and let this rugged man devour me right here in the shadowy alley between the tents. To finally experience the white-hot passion I've been denied for far too long.

But I can't. I'm the daughter of Jimmy Moretti, one of the most powerful men in Dawsbury. I have to marry well and produce heirs to continue the family legacy. As distasteful as the idea is, Paulie Gambino is my best option, even if he is a womanizing scumbag.

Squaring my shoulders, I summon every ounce of defiance I can muster and meet Tyson's gaze head-on. "Keep your filthy promises to yourself." My voice thankfully emerges stronger than I feel as I shove him away. "I'm not some cheap carnival whore you can leer at and grab whenever you want."

Tyson's eyes roam over me in a way that makes me feel stripped bare. "Whatever you say. But you can't fool me—I saw that hunger in your eyes. That aching need for a real man's touch."

My breath catches as he leans in close again, his raspy voice a low, gravelly purr in my ear. "When you finally get tired of playing the good little mobster's daughter and want to scratch that itch, you know where to find me."

With that, he turns on his heel and strides away, disappearing between the tent and trailers and leaving me flushed and flustered in his wake. I press trembling fingers to my flushed cheeks, struggling to steady my ragged breathing.

That arrogant, insufferable prick.

And yet a tiny, treacherous part of me can't quite silence the thrill that shot through me at his crude words, at the scorching promise in his eyes. It's been so long since I've felt raw, primal hunger for a man. Too long since I've allowed myself to embrace my desires instead of burying them beneath duty and obligation.

Suddenly, the carnival feels stifling, the air thick and cloying with grease, sweat, and desperation. I need to escape this place and the unsettling effect Tyson seems to have on me. Smoothing my hands over my rumpled blouse, I straighten my spine and stride toward the exit, leaving the carnival behind.

My heels click determinedly against the pavement as I walk across the sprawling parking lot. I search for my keys in my purse, my hands only shaking slightly as I accidentally drop my credit card and bend down to pick it up.

I scan the rows of cars for my cherry-red Mustang. There it is, a welcome beacon amidst the sea of minivans and beaters surrounding it. I lengthen my stride, unable to shake the feeling of eyes burning into my back as I hurry toward my car's comforting familiarity.

Just a few more steps, and I'll be safe inside, able to crank up my favorite trashy pop music to drown out the lingering echoes of Tyson's sinful promises. I can pretend this whole encounter never happened, that I didn't come perilously close to betraying everything I've been groomed for.

With a shaky exhale, I hit the button on my key fob to unlock the doors.

I'm almost there. Just a few more steps to the driver's side door. I can escape and put Tyson out of my mind for good.

That's when I hear a powerful engine's low, rumbling growl approaching from behind. My pulse skyrockets as I whip around, clutching my keys like a makeshift weapon.

The sleek, matte-black Suburban roars through the parking lot, its tinted windows glinting menacingly in the late afternoon sun. It peels around the corner with a squeal of tires, heading straight for me with no signs of slowing.

3

TYSON

She thinks I left, but I can't fucking stay away as I turn back around and follow her. Her red hair bounces with each angry step toward the parking lot. Damn, that girl's got fire. The way she stood up to me, refusing to be charmed, only makes me want her more.

I trail behind at a distance, keeping my eyes locked on the hypnotic rhythm of her stride. Her jeans hug those curves and thick thighs in all the right places. I lick my lips, imagining peeling them off.

I hang back as she reaches the parking lot, hiding behind a rusted pickup truck. Sofia digs through her purse, no doubt searching for her keys. She drops something and bends over to pick it up, and I drink in the view, my jeans growing tighter.

She unlocks her little red Mustang—proving to me she has taste, even if it is a new one and not a classic like mine. As she's about to open the door, something in my periphery catches my eye—a black SUV barreling through the parking lot straight toward her.

"Sofia! Watch out!" I yell, my body reacting before my brain can process what's happening.

In long strides, I've closed the distance between us. I wrap my arms around her waist and yank her backward with all my strength. Sofia lets out a startled yelp as I pull her off balance, tumbling us both to the hard asphalt.

The SUV blows past, the rush of air ruffling my hair. It barely misses clipping Sofia's car as the driver slams on the brakes, tires screeching in protest.

I roll off Sofia and scramble to my feet, my heart pounding. What the hell was that about? I scan the area, my fists clenched.

Sofia pushes herself to a sitting position, her eyes wide with shock. "What... what just happened?"

I don't answer, my focus locked on the SUV as it peels out of the lot in a spray of loose gravel.

The SUV's taillights disappear around the corner, and my jaw clenches tight. Someone just tried to run down Sofia Moretti in my damn carnival. This won't stand.

I pull out my cell and punch in Phoenix's number. He picks up on the second ring.

"Boss?" His voice crackles through the speaker.

"I need you to pull the security footage from the parking lot cameras. Now. Some asshole in a black SUV just tried to flatten Sofia."

"You mean Jimmy's daughter?" Phoenix asks.

"Yeah, that Sofia. I want the plates on that vehicle. And I want the owner's name."

"On it, boss."

I end the call and turn back to the fiery redhead. She's on her feet, brushing dirt off her jeans with shaky hands.

"You okay?" I ask, stepping closer.

Her green eyes are filled with fear when she meets my gaze. "No, I'm not okay! Someone just tried to kill me!"

I place my hands on her shoulders, feeling the tension thrumming through her body. "I won't let that happen. Whoever's behind this, I'll find them."

She shrugs off my hands, taking a step back. "Why do you even care? Aren't you just some carnie drug dealer?"

Her words sting, but I don't let it show. I close the distance between us, holding her gaze steady. "You're on my turf now. That means you're under my protection whether you like it or not. And your father is one of my clients. I can't have his daughter murdered at my carnival."

She opens her mouth to protest, but I cut her off. "I know you don't trust me. Hell, you probably don't even like me. But I saved your life and am on your side."

Conflict plays out across her face, the desire to tell me off, warring with the knowledge that I'm right. Finally, she lets out a heavy sigh. "Fine. But if you try anything funny, I'll make you regret it."

A smile tugs at my lips. "Wouldn't dream of it, baby girl."

My phone buzzes in my pocket, and I fish it out, glancing at the screen. It's a text from Phoenix with the license plate number, address, and owner's name.

Game on, you son of a bitch. I'm coming for you.

I turn to her. "Listen, I know you don't think much of me. But this whole situation? It'll allow me to prove I'm more than just some carnie."

Sofia rolls her eyes, but I catch the hint of a smirk playing at the corner of her lips. "Well, I should thank you for saving my life."

Before I can respond, Jimmy clears his throat behind us. "What's going on here?"

I turn around, meeting his gaze head-on. "Jimmy, someone just tried to kill your daughter. Came tearing through the lot in an SUV, aiming right for her."

Jimmy's face contorts with rage, his fists clenching at his sides. "What? Who the fuck would dare?"

I hold up my hands, trying to calm him down. "I don't know yet. But I've got my guys looking into it. We'll find out who's behind this."

Jimmy turns to Sofia, his expression softening. "Are you alright, sweetheart?"

Sofia nods, but I can see the tension in her shoulders. "I'm fine, Dad. Tyson pulled me out of the way just in time."

Jimmy looks at me, surprise flickering in his eyes. "You saved her?"

I shrug, playing it off. "Just doing what any decent person would."

Jimmy clasps my shoulder, his grip firm. "I owe you, Tyson. Anything you need, you say the word."

I nod, my mind already racing with possibilities. Having Jimmy Moretti in my debt could open up a lot of doors.

But right now, all I care about is keeping Sofia safe and finding the bastard who tried to hurt her. I'll make them pay for even thinking they could touch her on my watch.

I watch Jimmy's face closely, gauging his reaction. The attempt on Sofia's life has shaken him. I can see the wheels turning in his head, trying to figure out who would dare cross him like this.

An idea flickers through my mind—a way to turn this situation to my advantage. Jimmy said he owed me and would give me anything I wanted. What if I asked for Sofia? To have her as payment for saving her life?

The thought sends a dark thrill through me. To possess her body and soul and make her mine in every way possible. I imagine her in my bed, that fiery red hair spread out across my pillow as I—

No. I can't go down that road. Jimmy's daughter isn't some prize to be won or bartered. And even if she were, Sofia would never agree to it. She's made it clear she wants nothing to do with me. At least not yet, but I want to find a way to change her mind.

4

SOFIA

I sit across from Paulie at the restaurant, pushing my salad around the plate. My mind keeps drifting to the carnival, Tyson's intense gaze, and how he saved my life. I can't shake the feeling that there's more to him than meets the eye.

Paulie's voice snaps me back to reality. "Babe, you're not even listening to me." He scowls, stabbing his steak with unnecessary force.

"Sorry, I'm just... distracted." I take a sip of wine, trying to focus.

"Yeah, well, snap out of it. I'm trying to tell you about the new club opening downtown. We're going tonight." It's not a question but a demand.

I sigh, setting down my fork. "Paulie, I'm not in the mood for a club. I almost died yesterday, remember?"

He rolls his eyes. "Oh, come on. You're fine. Besides, it'll be good for you to get out and have fun."

"Fun? You think getting drunk and grinding on

strangers is fun?" I can't keep the disgust out of my voice.

Paulie leans back in his chair, smirking. "Don't knock it 'til you try it, babe. You might surprise yourself."

I shake my head, pushing my plate away. "I think I'll pass. I have some things I need to take care of anyway."

"What things? Shopping for more designer handbags?" He laughs, but there's an edge to it.

"No. I'm going to visit my grandmother. She's been sick, and I want to check on her." It's a white lie since she's not sick, but I don't care. I need an excuse to get away from him.

Paulie's face darkens. "You're choosing some old lady over me? I'm your fiancé, Sofia. You should be making me your priority."

I stand up, grabbing my purse. "She's not some old lady. She's family. And right now, she needs me more than you do."

Walking away, I feel Paulie's eyes boring into my back. But for once, I don't care about his anger or his threats. I can only think about how Tyson looked at me as if he noticed something special that no one else did. And I can't help but wonder if maybe, just maybe, he's the one who can save me from this life I never wanted.

I hail a cab outside the restaurant, eager to put some distance between myself and Paulie. As I slide into the back seat, I give the driver my grandmother's address on the other side of town.

Nonna Maria is my favorite person in the world. She's always been there for me, offering a shoulder to cry on. I can tell her anything without fear of judgment.

The cab weaves through the busy streets, and I feel lost in thought. Yesterday's events swirl in my mind—the attack in the parking lot, Tyson's unexpected rescue, and the strange pull I feel toward him despite my better judgment.

Before I know it, the cab pulls up in front of Nonna's house. I pay the driver and make my way up the familiar steps, knocking on the door.

"Sofia, my darling!" Nonna exclaims as she opens the door and pulls me into a warm hug. The scent of her perfume and the warmth of her hug instantly calm my nerves.

"Hi, Nonna," I say, the tension draining from my body. "I hope I'm not interrupting anything."

"Nonsense, you're always welcome here." She ushers me inside, leading me to the cozy living room. "Now, tell me what's troubling you."

I sink onto the sofa, fiddling with the hem of my skirt. "It's just ...everything. The wedding, Paulie, and..."

Nonna's eyes widen with concern. "Sofia, are you okay? Your father told me about the attempt on your life. I was so shocked and worried about you."

I nod, taking a deep breath. "I'm okay, Nonna. It was terrifying, but that's not what has me so conflicted."

She tilts her head, studying me. "What is it then, my dear?"

I bite my lip, unsure how to explain my desire for Tyson. "It's... the man who saved my life. The ringmaster of the carnival."

Nonna raises an eyebrow. "The ringmaster? What about him?"

I fidget with my hands, trying to find the right words. "He's just... different. When he looked at me, it was like he saw through to the real me. And the way he saved me, without hesitation... I can't stop thinking about him."

She reaches out, taking my hand in hers. "Sofia, it's natural to feel a connection to someone who saved your life. But you need to be careful. You don't know anything about this man."

I nod. "I know, Nonna. But there's just something about him. I can't explain it."

She squeezes my hand. "I understand what it's like to be drawn to someone, even when it doesn't make sense. But you have to think about your future, Sofia. You're engaged to Paulie."

I sigh, the weight of my impending marriage heavy on my shoulders. "I know."

"Come," Nonna says, rising from her seat. "Let me fix you some of my famous lasagna. I made it fresh this morning."

The smell of garlic and herbs wafts from her kitchen, making my mouth water. "You always know exactly what I need."

She makes herself busy preparing our plates while I lean against her counter, watching her practiced movements. "A good meal can heal many troubles," she says, sliding a generous portion onto a plate.

"I wish everything was simpler." I take a bite of the lasagna, savoring the rich flavor. "Like your cooking. It's straightforward, honest, perfect."

She sits across from me, her wise eyes studying my

face. "Life is rarely simple, my dear. But that doesn't mean we can't find joy in the complicated parts."

I try to focus on my food, but Tyson's face keeps appearing in my mind—his intense gaze, the way he moved confidently. I shake my head, attempting to dispel the thoughts.

"You're thinking about him again," Nonna observes.

"I'm trying not to." I take another bite, letting the familiar taste of her cooking ground me. "It's just whenever I close my eyes..."

"Some people leave an impression on our hearts, whether we want them to or not." She reaches across the table, patting my hand. "But remember who you are, Sofia. You're strong."

"I know." I manage a small smile. "This lasagna helps. Everything seems clearer when I'm here with you."

"Then stay for dessert, too. I made tiramisu."

I laugh. "You're spoiling me, Nonna."

"That's what grandmothers are for." She stands to get the dessert, and I try once again to push thoughts of Tyson from my mind. But even surrounded by the comfort of Nonna's kitchen and her incredible cooking, his image lingers like a shadow I can't quite shake.

5

TYSON

I pace my office trailer, unable to focus on tonight's carnival preparations. My phone buzzes with a message from Phoenix, including a video link. My breath catches when I click it.

There she is. Sofia. Sprawled across her bed in tiny sleep shorts and a tank top, completely absorbed in her book. Her red hair fans out on the propped-up pillow like liquid fire.

"Fuck." I adjust my stance, already hard just looking at her. The camera angle from her iMac gives me a perfect view of those curves. Her full chest moves up and down with each breath, and how her teeth catch her bottom lip when she reaches an interesting part.

My fingers trace the screen, imagining touching her soft skin. I shouldn't be watching her like this. It's crossing a line. But I'm already too deep, consumed by thoughts of making her mine.

She shifts position, stretching like a cat, and my grip tightens on the phone. Those little shorts ride up, revealing more thick, creamy thigh. I groan, picturing how it would feel to run my hands up those legs and hear her gasp my name.

"You're going to be mine, baby girl," I murmur to the screen. "Whether daddy dearest likes it or not."

I should be focusing on tonight's carnival. On the shipments coming in. On literally anything else. But I can't tear my eyes away from her. The way she absent-mindedly twirls that red hair around her finger. How she occasionally smiles at something in her book.

Phoenix came through with this feed. I'll have to thank him later. Sitting at my desk, I airdrop the feed link to my Mac and then open a new text message to Sofia.

> Baby girl, I've been thinking about you.

I press send, then watch as her eyes flick down to her phone. She furrows her brow, then picks it up.

Her confused expression turns to one of annoyance as she reads my message.

> Who the hell is this?

Her reply comes a few seconds later, and her voice carries a hint of irritation as she speaks aloud through the iMac microphone.

I almost feel bad for a second—almost. I type my response back.

> You know who this is. Your favorite carnie.

Her eyes widen at the response, and I hear her annoyed huff through the iMac. I want to see that flush on her cheeks, how her chest rises and falls faster with each message.

> I know you want me. Admit it, baby girl.

I send, then watch with a smirk as she hurries to respond.

> You've got the wrong idea! And stop calling me baby girl!

She fires back, and I can tell she's frustrated now. Good.

> Make me.

I send back in a challenge already texting my next message.

> Tell me you didn't feel something when I touched you the other day. Admit you liked it.

Her brow knits together as she reads and sets the phone on the bed. She folds her arms, clearly debating how to respond. Finally, she picks up the phone again.

> Fine. Maybe I felt something. Happy?

I laugh out loud, unable to help myself. This is too easy. I love a good chase, and Sofia's playing hard to get. Makes the game all the more fun.

Time to turn up the heat.

My smirk widens as I type out the next message, my gaze fixed on her beautiful form.

> Tell me something. Have you ever been with a guy who's cock is pierced?

I send the message and watch, knowing this will get her going.

Sure enough, her eyes widen as she reads, and she bites that damnable lip again. This time, though, it's not from concentration. It's from the building heat between her thighs, and I know it.

I steady my breathing as I watch her text back. Her reply comes in.

> Not interested in your dick.

It's a lie as I notice her thighs pressing together on screen.

My eyes lock on the way she shifts in her position, spreading those thick thighs. The thin fabric of her sleep shorts does nothing to hide the growing wet spot between her legs. Fuck, she's getting turned on despite her dismissive texts.

> Just imagine the metal sliding against your G-spot while I'm buried deep inside you.

Her next reply comes in.

> You're disgusting. Leave me alone.

But on screen, her hand trails down her stomach, fingers ghosting over her shorts. She starts rubbing slow circles right where that damp patch is spreading. My cock throbs painfully against my jeans.

I free my length, wrapping my hand around the thick shaft. The barbells of my magic cross glint in the office light as I stroke, imagining how it would feel sliding against her clit.

She's trying hard to be cool in her texts, but I've got a sneak peek into the truth. The way she grinds subtly against her hand makes her breathing heavier. When she adjusts again, legs falling wider apart, that wet spot is unmistakable.

"Fuck," I growl, pumping my cock faster. The metal of my piercings adds delicious friction with each stroke.

I knew I was getting to her, but I needed to see her reaction. Glancing down at my rock-hard cock, an idea forms, and I don't hesitate to act on it.

Grabbing my shaft, I angle the phone to capture the full length of my erection, the metal barbells glinting in the light. I snap a few photos, my heart pounding with anticipation.

Then, without a second thought, I send one to her.

On-screen, her eyes widen, and her fingers pause in their motion. Her tongue peeks out to wet her lips, and I know she's imagining that thick length inside her.

"Holy fuck," she breathes, and my cock twitches.

I can see the wheels turning in her head as she debates her next move. Her gaze flicks between her phone and her hand, rubbing her clit.

I bite back a groan as she shifts position again, dragging those tiny shorts down her thighs. Fucking hell, I'm about to lose it.

The sounds of her gasps and whimpers fill the room as her fingers dive between her legs. Sofia throws her head back, oblivious that I'm watching her every move.

"Keep going, baby girl," I mutter as she spreads herself open. Her pretty pink cunt is glistening from her arousal.

She's so fucking responsive, and I haven't even touched her yet. I stroke myself harder, loving how she loses herself in her pleasure.

> You have no idea how good it would feel to have my cock inside your tight pussy.

I send, my eyes locked on the screen as her eyes squeeze shut.

"Oh, fuck," she whimpers, and I know my words are getting to her.

Good.

I type more.

> Imagine me stretching you open. Filling you up with every inch.

Her fingers move faster, her hips lifting off the bed.

> You want this cock, don't you?

I text, adding another photo of my hard cock and pressing send as I watch her.

She reads the text and looks at the photo. "Fuck, yes. I want it," she breathes.

I smirk, knowing she wouldn't admit it in a text or out loud if she knew I could hear.

> You're an ass.

She sends, her chest heaving.

> That's not the part of me you're thinking about. 😉

Her mouth falls open as her fingers plunge in and out of her glistening cunt.

"Damn, you look so fucking sexy like that. Bet that pussy feels amazing." I growl to myself, typing another text.

> I'm going to plow into you so hard. Make you feel every inch.

And that does it.

She comes with a loud moan, hips bucking off the bed. Her eyes shut as she rides out the waves of pleasure, fingers working furiously.

"Fuck," I grunt, unable to hold back anymore. I come with a few more strokes, spilling my release onto the desk with a satisfied groan.

That was fucking intense. And we haven't even touched each other yet. I chuckle, shaking my head.

Sitting back in my chair, I use my dirty shirt to wipe

up the mess I made. My cock still twitching, sated but eager for more. Fucking hell, this woman is going to be the death of me. And I can't wait.

6

SOFIA

I clutch the bottle of Macallan 25 against my chest, weaving through the carnival crowd. The evening air crackles with excitement as families and couples stream toward the big top. I tell myself I'm just here to thank him properly for saving me, but my racing pulse suggests otherwise.

Finding a seat near the front, I settle in as the lights dim. The whiskey bottle's weight in my lap reminds me of my flimsy excuse to see the ringmaster again.

The music swells, and there he is—Tyson commands the ring in a deep burgundy coat that highlights his broad shoulders. His voice booms across the tent, introducing acts with such natural charisma that I can't take my eyes off him.

This isn't the rough carnival worker I first dismissed. He moves with practiced grace, timing each announcement perfectly with the performers' entrances. When he catches my eye, a knowing smile plays on his lips. Heat floods my cheeks, but I don't look away.

The way he works the crowd shows intelligence behind that raw sexuality. His jokes land perfectly, making children giggle while sliding in subtle innuendos that have adults smirking. I find myself laughing along, drawn into his magnetic performance.

Between acts, he prowls the ring's edge with lethal grace. Those muscled arms that held me during the attack now gesture dramatically, conducting the show like a master orchestrator. My breath catches when he does a backflip off the ring barrier, landing with catlike precision.

I squeeze my thighs together, remembering our heated exchange over text last night. The memory of the photos of his pierced cock makes my core clench. What started as a simple attraction has evolved into something more complex. This man is dangerous—not because he's a carnival worker who runs drugs, but because he's far more fascinating than I ever expected.

The final applause fades as families stream toward the exits. I stay glued to my seat, the bottle of whiskey warm from being clutched in my hands all evening. My heart pounds against my ribs as the crowd thins out.

Tyson stands in the center ring, that infuriating smirk playing across his lips as he watches me. Heat floods my cheeks at the intensity of his stare, but I refuse to look away first.

He knows what he's doing to me. The memory of our heated text exchange burns through my mind, making my thighs press together of their own accord. Those photos... God, I shouldn't be thinking about that here.

The last few stragglers file out, leaving us alone in the vast tent. The silence feels electric, charged with unspoken tension. Tyson's smirk widens as he takes a deliberate step in my direction, like a predator who knows his prey can't escape.

I grip the whiskey bottle tighter, reminding myself I came to thank him for saving my life. But how he's looking at me now makes it clear we both know that's not the only reason.

"That was quite a show," I say.

He steps closer, his eyes flicking to the whiskey bottle in my hands. "Is that for me?"

"Yes. I wanted to thank you." I lick my lips, my heart pounding as I stand, thrusting the bottle at him.

He closes the distance between us in two long strides, his tall frame hovering over me. My pulse quickens as he takes the bottle, his fingers brushing mine intentionally. "Getting me drunk isn't necessary. I told you, we're even."

"But I wanted to." I bite my lip, unsure how to say what's on my mind. "You saved my life, and I..."

"You what?" He leans closer, his warm breath tickling my ear. "You wanted to thank me properly?"

My breath catches in my throat as his lips brush my earlobe. "You... you know what I mean," I whisper.

"Do I?" His free hand slides onto my waist, pulling me closer, his lips still against my ear. "You want to get down on your knees and show your appreciation? Because I'm not gonna say no."

The pulse between my thighs throbs at his suggestion. "I-I wasn't..."

He chuckles, his hot breath sending shivers down my spine. "Don't play coy. I know what you want." His fingers dip into the back pocket of my jeans, squeezing my ass. "You want to see my cock in person, don't you?"

I gasp, my knees going weak. "I..."

"Yeah, you do." His voice drops an octave. "Admit it. Admit you want my cock."

His intoxicating scent fills my lungs, clouding my already muddled thoughts. I can't think straight, but my body screams, 'Yes.' "I..."

"Say it. Tell me how much you want my cock." His hand presses firmer against my lower back, urging me forward. "You like it when I talk dirty, don't you?"

My chest rises and falls rapidly as his words wash over me. I should be appalled, but the truth is—I do want him. More than I've ever wanted anyone. And something about his crass manner stirs a fire in me that I can't ignore.

"You want to know what I want?" I meet his gaze. "I want you to shut up and kiss me."

His lips crash against mine, and my world explodes into sensation. The kiss is nothing like the tepid pecks I've shared with Paulie. Tyson's mouth claims mine with a hunger that sets my blood on fire, his tongue sliding in and out in a dance that makes my toes curl.

My fingers tangle in his hair as he deepens the kiss, drawing a moan from deep in my throat. He tastes like danger and desire, and I want more. His strong hands grip my waist, and suddenly I'm airborne.

"Oh!" I gasp against his mouth as he lifts me. Heat floods my cheeks—I'm not some petite thing that men typically sweep off their feet. But Tyson doesn't notice or care about my few extra pounds, holding me steady as if I weigh nothing.

I wrap my legs around his waist, lost in the intoxicating feel of him, when a throat-clearing cuts through our passion.

"Boss." A man's gravelly voice sends ice through my veins.

I scramble out of Tyson's embrace to the ground, my heart pounding for a different reason. Oh God. What am I doing? I'm engaged. This can't happen.

"I should... I need to go," I stammer, unable to look at either man as shame and guilt crash over me. I grab my purse from where it fell and practically run from the tent, leaving my dignity behind.

7

TYSON

I slam my fist against one of the tent poles, my cock throbbing from Sofia's body in my arms. "What the fuck, Lars? You couldn't wait five fucking minutes?"

Lars shifts his weight, running a hand through his dark hair. "Boss, I'm sorry about the cockblock, but we've got bigger problems."

"Bigger than me getting somewhere with Jimmy's daughter?" The tension in my shoulders builds as I adjust myself, trying to get comfortable.

"The Friday shipment." Lars's voice drops lower. "Just got word twenty kilos went missing from our supplier's warehouse."

"Fuck!" I kick over a nearby chair, sending it clattering across the ground. "That's almost half our order. Jimmy's gonna have my balls in a vice if we can't deliver."

"That's not all." Lars crosses his arms. "Word is it

wasn't random. Someone knew exactly what they were looking for."

The implication hits me like a punch to the gut. We've got a leak somewhere in the supply chain, and now I've got to deal with this shit instead of pursuing Sofia. Between my blue balls and this clusterfuck, my mood turns darker by the second.

"Get Phoenix, Nash, and Colt. Meeting in my trailer in ten. And Lars?" I fix him with a hard stare. "Next time you interrupt me with a woman, it better be because the whole fucking carnival's on fire."

He nods and strolls out.

I rest my forehead against the cool metal of the tent pole, the same one that had supported Sofia's weight moments ago. Her scent still lingers—a mix of vanilla and something uniquely her. My dick throbs in my pants, though the urgency has faded since Lars's interruption.

"Fuck." I exhale, squeezing my eyes shut. The memory of her soft curves pressed against me, the way she melted into my kiss—it's all burned into my brain. The little whimper she made when I pulled her closer.

I straighten, adjusting myself in my jeans. My fingers trace the metal tent pole, remembering how perfectly she fit there.

"Get it together," I mutter to myself. I can't afford distractions, not with this shipment mess threatening everything I've built. But damn, if Sofia Moretti isn't the most delicious distraction I've ever encountered.

The tent feels empty now, hollow without her presence. The usual carnival sounds seem muted like they're coming from miles away. My skin still burns where she touched me, and my lips tingle from our kiss.

I push off the pole, rolling my shoulders back. Time to switch gears and deal with this situation. But as I turn to head toward my trailer, my cock gives another defiant throb, reminding me exactly what I'm walking away from.

Jimmy Moretti's daughter. Of all the women to get tangled up with, I had to pick her. And now I've got to figure out how to tell her father that his shipment's been compromised. Perfect fucking timing.

I storm into my trailer, the door banging against the wall. The usual suspects are already here—Lars leaning against the counter, Colt sprawled on my couch, Nash perched on the arm, and Phoenix pacing by the window.

"Someone better have answers," I growl.

Phoenix stops his pacing, his expression softer than usual. Ever since he met Tilly, he's lost that perpetual scowl. He's still a grumpy bastard half the time, but at least now he cracks the occasional smile.

"Got some leads on who might've hit the warehouse," Phoenix says, pulling out his phone. "Security footage shows three guys, professional job. In and out in under ten minutes."

"They knew exactly what they were looking for," Lars adds, echoing his earlier warning.

Nash leans forward, his grace evident even in that simple movement. "Inside job?"

"Has to be." Colt sits straighter. "No way they'd know which shipment to hit otherwise."

I rub my temples, the headache from earlier intensifying. "Show me the footage."

Phoenix hands over his phone. The video quality is shit, but I can make out three figures moving with military precision through the warehouse. They bypass other valuable merchandise, heading straight for our shipment.

"Any faces?" I ask.

"Masked," Phoenix confirms. "But check out how they move. Ex-military, maybe private security. These aren't street thugs."

"Great." I toss the phone back at Phoenix. "So we've got professionals stealing our shit, and I've got Jimmy Moretti breathing down my neck, expecting his order."

The memory of Sofia's kiss flashes through my mind, making this situation even more complicated. Her father is not just a client anymore—he's the father of the woman I can't get out of my head—a woman who is engaged to another one of my clients.

"Options?" I look around at my most trusted crew. These men have never let me down before. We'll figure this out. We have to.

I lean back in my chair, rubbing my jaw as Lars speaks up.

"I've been looking at the numbers, boss. If we drop Paulie or Frank's shipment, we can deliver it to Jimmy. Just put the smaller fish off for now."

"You want me to stiff either the future son-in-law of Jimmy Moretti or the guy who's been with us since day one?" I shake my head. "That's a powder keg waiting to blow."

"Frank's been getting cocky," Nash chimes in. "Acting like he owns us."

"And Paulie's a piece of shit," Colt adds. "Everyone knows it."

My mind drifts to the memory of Sofia and how she looked at me in that tent. The thought of her marrying that bastard Paulie makes my blood boil. But business is business. Isn't it?

"Either way, someone's going to be pissed," Phoenix points out. "The question is, who can we afford to have gunning for us?"

Lars crosses his arms. "Jimmy's the biggest player in Dawsbury. We lose him, we can't move the product."

He's right. Jimmy Moretti could crush us without breaking a sweat. But crossing either Frank or Paulie could start a war we're not ready for. Plus, there's Sofia to consider. One wrong move and I could lose any slim chance with her.

I drum my fingers on the desk, weighing our options. The numbers don't lie—we can only fully deliver to Frank or Paulie. Jimmy Moretti isn't the type of man who accepts partial shipments. But do I piss off his future son-in-law or his rival?

I grind my teeth and am about to make a decision when Phoenix clears his throat. "Boss, you might want to check out what I found about the SUV owner and who he works for."

"What?" I ask, walking over to the desk.

"He works for Frank. Frank tried to take out Jimmy's daughter here at the carnival."

"Motherfucker!" I growl, hands clenching by my

sides. "Well, that decides it then. Frank's out. He fucked up trying to kill Jimmy's daughter on my turf. Consider this karma."

Lars nods, a smirk playing at the corners of his mouth. "Want me to break it to him gently?"

"No. Not yet. I'll tell him at our usual meeting. He's lucky I don't tell Jimmy it was him."

Colt stretches his long frame on the couch. "Frank's been pushing boundaries for a while. This'll knock him down a few pegs."

"More than a few," Nash adds. "Without our supply, he'll be crippled in Dawsbury. Jimmy will eat up his territory within weeks."

"Exactly." I crack my knuckles, satisfaction coursing through me. "Two birds, one stone. We keep Jimmy happy with his shipment, and Frank learns what happens when you fuck with the wrong people."

The crew exchanges knowing looks. We've all been waiting for an excuse to cut Frank loose. His attempted hit on Sofia made the decision easier. Jimmy will crush him, and I won't have to lift a finger.

8

SOFIA

I fidget with the hem of my black evening gown, tuning out Paulie's latest critique about my weight as we navigate the crowded ballroom. The champagne in my glass remains untouched—my mind keeps drifting to Tyson's heated kiss in the big top.

"Are you even listening?" Paulie's fingers dig into my arm. "I said you should skip dessert tonight. That dress is looking a bit snug."

"I heard you the first three times." I pull away from his grip, earning a disapproving look from my father across the room.

"Watch your tone." Paulie's breath reeks of scotch as he leans in close. "You're making me look bad in front of potential business partners."

I force a smile as another couple approaches. Paulie launches into his rehearsed speech about our upcoming wedding, his hand possessively gripping my waist. I nod at all the right moments while my thoughts wander to strong arms wrapped around me, the intoxicating scent of leather and tobacco.

"My beautiful fiancée is just shy," Paulie announces to our latest audience. "Though she could stand to hit the gym more before the wedding, right honey?"

The couple laughs awkwardly. My cheeks burn as I take a large gulp of champagne, wishing I was anywhere else. Wishing I was back in that tent, Tyson's fingers tangled in my hair...

"Stop daydreaming." Paulie pinches my side. "You're embarrassing me again. At least try to look interested when I'm talking business."

I force another fake smile as he drags me to the next group, already launching into the same tired story about how we met—conveniently leaving out that it was an arranged marriage. My father catches my eye across the room and gives me a stern nod. I straighten my spine and play my part, all while my mind rebels against this gilded cage he's built around me.

Dad strides over, his presence commanding instant respect. Paulie's grip on my waist loosens, his demeanor shifting to that of the perfect gentleman. The transformation would be impressive if it wasn't so nauseating.

"Princess, you look beautiful tonight." Dad kisses my cheek. "Shall we head to our table? The first course will be served soon."

I catch Paulie's eye twitch when Dad uses his pet name for me. Good. Let him stew.

"Of course, Daddy." I slip my arm through him, grateful for the break from Paulie.

The crystal chandeliers sparkle overhead as we weave between tables draped in cream silk. Everyone who matters in Dawsbury is here tonight, dressed in their finest, playing their parts in this elaborate performance. I've been doing this dance since I was old enough to walk—charity galas, business dinners, and social events where alliances and deals are made behind practiced smiles.

But tonight feels different. As I sit between Dad and Paulie, my thoughts drift to rough hands and a piercing gaze that sees right through my carefully constructed facade. Tyson didn't care about my family name or social status. He wanted me—the real me, curves and all.

Paulie naturally orders my meal—a salad—while discussing business with Dad. I push lettuce around my plate, remembering how it felt to be truly desired and looked at with raw hunger instead of criticism.

Could I really walk away from all this? From the expectations, the criticism, the arranged marriage to a man who sees me as nothing more than an accessory to be used and bred?

The weight of my father's empire sits heavy on my shoulders as waiters glide past with plates of food I'm not allowed to eat. But for the first time in my life, I wonder if there might be another path leading away from these suffocating ballrooms and toward a life that's mine.

I stab another piece of lettuce, lost in thought. Sure, there are perks to being Jimmy Moretti's daughter—the weekly spa treatments, shopping sprees at Gucci and Prada, and my closet full of Louboutins. Just yesterday I dropped five grand on a handbag without blinking.

But what good is all that when I can't even order my meal? When every bite I take is scrutinized? When my future has been decided for me?

And when Paulie's not around I gorge myself on chocolate or pizza—something I never did before meeting him. Sure, I'd eat chocolate or pizza occasionally and not secretly. I feel so guilty afterward. I'm well aware I've got an eating disorder and use food as my coping mechanism, but I doubt I'd need it if I wasn't controlled constantly by my husband-to-be.

My phone vibrates in my clutch. Paulie is deep in conversation with Dad about some business deal, so I carefully slide it out, angling the screen away from prying eyes.

A message from Tyson makes my heart skip:

> Why'd you run? I was nowhere near finished with you.

Heat floods my cheeks as memories of his kiss flood back and the way his hands gripped my hips, how his tongue...

"Who are you texting?" Paulie's sharp voice cuts through my thoughts.

I quickly lock the screen and slip the phone away. "Just Sasha, about our spa day tomorrow."

He narrows his eyes but returns to his conversation with Dad. I release a shaky breath, pushing food around my plate while my phone burns a hole in my purse.

Tyson's message weighs heavy on my mind and thoughts of freedom beyond these suffocating walls. Freedom that is too far out of my reach to ever become a reality.

9

TYSON

I pace the office trailer, checking my phone for the hundredth time. No messages from Sofia. My jaw clenches as I toss the device onto my desk.

"Fuck this." I slam my fist against the wall, leaving a dent in the thin metal.

The door creaks open, and Lars steps in. "Boss, Phoenix found them."

My mood shifts instantly. "Where?"

"Dark web. Bunch of ex-military trying to flip our product." Lars hands me his tablet. "They had the skills to lift it but no connections to move it."

"How likely is it we can take them down?" I ask.

Lars shrugs. "We'd have the element of surprise and Phoenix can give us eyes inside their den. We should get it back piece of cake and be able to supply Frank if you still want to."

I scan through Phoenix's report, a cruel smile spreading across my face. "Get Gage, Remy, Nash, and Colt. Time to pay these fuckers a visit."

Two hours later, we're standing in an abandoned warehouse, surrounded by bodies. Blood pools beneath my boots as I retrieve our stolen twenty kilos from their van and load it into the trunk of my Mustang. The idiots thought they could steal from us and get away with it.

"Clean this up," I order, watching Nash and Colt drag the first body toward their truck. "Make sure nothing traces back."

Lars wipes his blade on one of the dead men's shirts. "What about the product?" He nods toward it.

"You and Gage can load it while Nash, Colt, and Remy deal with the bodies." I check my phone again. Still nothing from Sofia. "I've got somewhere to be."

"Leave it to us." Lars wipes his hands on a cloth. "We'll get it sorted. See you back at the carnival."

I nod, already heading for my car. My phone burns a hole in my pocket—still no response from Sofia. The memory of her curves pressed against me makes my blood run hot. I'm done waiting for a reply.

After punching the address Phoenix sent me for Sofia into my GPS, I turn the key and the engine roars to life. Downtown Dawsbury is fancy as fuck, starkly contrasting the warehouse district I'm leaving behind.

My fingers drum against the steering wheel at each red light. The need to see her claws at my chest. To hell with waiting for her to text back.

I park across from a sleek modern house with floor-to-ceiling windows. Her little red Mustang sits in the curved driveway—her car—the same one she drove away from the carnival in.

Killing the engine, I sit in the growing darkness. The

house glows from within, and through the windows, I catch glimpses of movement. My baby girl is in there, probably trying to forget about our kiss.

But I won't let her forget. Not when she sets my world on fire with just a look.

I slip through her back door, picking the lock with practiced ease. The house is quiet except for water running upstairs. My boots make no sound on the hardwood as I follow the sound.

Steam billows from the master bathroom. I catch glimpses of creamy curves through the glass door as Sofia showers, completely unaware of my presence. My cock strains against my jeans at the sight.

I open the door and lean against the doorframe, crossing my arms. "Quite a show you're putting on, baby girl."

Her scream pierces the air as she spins around, nearly slipping. Those gorgeous green eyes go wide. "What the fuck! Get out, or I'm calling the cops!"

"Go ahead." I prowl closer to the shower. "But we both know you don't want that."

"Stay back!" She opens the door and fumbles for her phone on the counter, but I snatch it first.

"Looking for this?" I dangle it just out of reach.

Her chest heaves, water running down her curves. Despite her fear, I notice how her nipples harden under my gaze. "You're insane. You can't break into people's houses!"

I press my palm against the glass, watching her press against the opposite wall. "I can do whatever I want, especially when you've ignored my messages."

"Because I'm engaged! And you're breaking and entering!"

I watch as panic flashes across her face. She frantically grabs at the shower door, water dripping down her curves as she tries to shield herself from my gaze with her arms.

"Don't." But she's already darting past me, snatching a towel from the rack.

My fists clench as she wraps the fluffy fabric around her body, hiding every inch of those luscious curves I've been dreaming about.

"Stop covering yourself." The words come out as a growl, deep and primal. "Your body is fucking stunning."

Her eyes snap to mine, and her lips part in surprise. A blush spreads across her cheeks and down her neck, disappearing beneath the towel. She clutches the fabric tighter, but I catch the slight tremor in her hands.

"I..." She swallows hard. "I'm not... I mean, I'm not exactly model material."

The self-consciousness in her voice makes my blood boil. Someone's been in her head, making her doubt herself and think she needs to hide.

"Who told you that bullshit?" I take a step closer, watching her breath catch. "Because they're fucking blind."

Her eyes flash with anger, cutting through her fear. Good. I love it when she shows her fire.

"Don't change the subject!" she snaps, backing away from me. "You broke into my fucking house. You're acting like a complete psycho!"

My lips curl into a smile as I stalk toward her. "Am I? And here I thought you liked it when I act like a psycho."

Her back hits the wall. I cage her in with my arms, breathing in the sweet scent of her shower gel.

"What are you talking about?" Her voice wavers, but her chin lifts defiantly.

I lean closer, my breath fanning across her neck. "You looked so fucking beautiful touching yourself after I sent that picture and dirty messages. The way your back arched off those silk sheets..."

Her eyes go wide. "What? How did you—"

"Your iMac camera gave me quite the show. The sounds you made..." I grip the wall harder, my cock throbbing at the memory. "Those little whimpers when you came..."

The color drains from her face before fury ignites in those green eyes. She shoves hard against my chest, breaking free from where I've caged her.

"Get the fuck out." Her voice is steel, that fire I love blazing in her eyes. "Now."

"Come on, baby girl—"

"Don't call me that." She grabs her phone from where I put it, finger hovering over the emergency button. "Get out of my house before I call the cops. I'm not playing games."

Even wrapped in just a towel, she radiates pure strength. Her jaw is set, eyes flashing with determination. No trace of the trembling girl from moments ago remains.

"Last warning," she says, voice deadly calm. "Get. Out."

"You think you're so tough, but you're not."

She takes another step back, clutching her phone. My blood pumps hot, desire ripping through me as I respond to her challenge.

I lunge forward, grabbing her wrist and twirling her so her back hits my chest. She drops the phone, which falls to the ground with a clatter. She struggles, but I tighten my grip around her wrists, holding them captive behind her back.

"Tough enough to bring the mighty Tyson to his knees, aren't you?" I growl, my lips hovering dangerously close to her ear. "Admit it. You want this as much as I do."

"No, I—" She bites her lip, eyes widening at the raw hunger in my voice.

"Don't lie." I slide my free hand down to her throat and angle her so she's looking at me in the mirror over the sink, applying just enough pressure to feel her pulse against my palm. Her breath catches, eyes fluttering shut as a soft whimper escapes her lips. "You like it when I get a little forceful."

"No, I—"

"You love it." My thumb strokes over her pulse, feeling her heartbeat quicken. I tighten my grip, cutting off her air. "A part of you wishes I'd take you here against this wall, show you what a real man can do."

She trembles, a soft moan escaping her lips. My entire body tenses, my grip tightening as I silently beg her to ask for it. To beg me to take her right here, right now.

"I..." Her eyes flicker open, chest heaving as she searches my gaze in the mirror. "I hate that I do."

Hearing her admit it makes my body coil even tighter. I ease my grip just enough so she can breathe, knowing I'll lose her if I push too far.

"But you do." My lips brush against her earlobe. "Admit it."

She opens her mouth to protest, but I twirl her to face me and cut her off with my mouth on hers, stealing her breath and her willpower. A muffled whimper escapes her throat as my tongue tangles with hers, a plea for more.

I want to devour her, brand her as mine. Mark every inch of her perfect skin and keep her with me forever.

But that's not our reality.

I reluctantly release her, her body sliding away. She sags against the wall, eyes dazed as she pants, watching me warily.

"See?" I grin. "You just needed a little persuasion."

She swallows hard, tucking a strand of hair behind her ear. "This changes nothing. My answer is still no."

My smile fades. "Why? You feel it, too. I know you do."

She lifts her chin, determination sparking in her eyes. "Because some things are worth resisting, no matter how tempting."

Her words strike me like a blow to the gut. Worth resisting. Am I so easy to turn down?

I straighten. "Guess I'll have to try harder, then."

Her eyes widen, breath catching. "Are you threatening me?"

"Never." I turn, heading for the back door. "I'd never force you, Sofia. But I will convince you. Someday, you'll beg me to finish what we started."

"In your dreams." But the breathlessness in her voice tells me she's not as unaffected as she pretends.

I grin, opening the door. "Sweet dreams, baby girl."

And with that, I leave, the memory of our kiss and her trembling body seared into my mind. My girl might be putting up a fight, but I live for the chase. And I always get what I want.

10

SOFIA

I sink into the plush spa chair beside Sasha, the warm water bubbling around my feet. My best friend's presence usually calms me, but my stomach churns with guilt today.

"Spill it," Sasha says, eyeing me over her cucumber water. "Your texts were cryptic as hell."

I stare at my feet. "I met someone."

"Not Paulie, clearly." She leans closer. "Who is he?"

"The ringmaster at the carnival." Heat creeps up my neck. "Tyson."

"A carnie?" Sasha's eyebrows shoot up. "That's... different for you."

My hands tremble as I consider telling her the whole truth. How do I explain that he spied on me using my webcam? That he broke into my house? Instead of calling the police, I kissed him?

"There's more," I whisper, "but you have to promise not to freak out."

"Girl, you're scaring me."

"He's intense. Like, stalker intense." The words tumble out. "He hacked my computer and watched me through my webcam. Then, showed up at my house uninvited."

Sasha's face drains of color. "Please tell me you called the cops."

I shake my head, shame burning my cheeks. "I didn't. I... I kissed him instead."

"What the actual fuck, Sofia?" Sasha grabs my arm. "This isn't some fictional dark romance novel. This is serious stalker behavior. Why didn't you report him?"

That's the question I've been asking myself. Why didn't I? The answer terrifies me more than Tyson's actions.

"I don't know," I admit, my voice barely audible over the bubbling water. "There's something about him. I know it's crazy, but..."

"But nothing! He's dangerous, Sofia."

I close my eyes, remembering the electricity of his touch, the thrill of danger in his kiss. "I know he is. That might be part of why I can't stay away."

Sasha's disapproving head shake cuts through me. "You're walking a dangerous line. Between your dad, Paulie, and now this carnival guy? It's like you're playing with matches in a powder keg."

I sink deeper into the spa chair, the warm water doing nothing to ease the knot in my stomach. "You don't understand what it's like with Paulie. Every time he looks at me, his eyes find something new to criticize. My weight, clothes, even how I hold my fork at dinner."

Sasha sets down her cucumber water with a sharp

clink. "Look, I get it. Paulie's an asshole. How he treats you makes me want to jam these pedicure tools somewhere unpleasant." She shifts in her chair to face me fully. "But trading one toxic man for another isn't the answer, babe. This Tyson guy? He's showing classic predator behavior. Stalking, surveillance, breaking and entering? That's not romantic—that's criminal."

I twist my hands in my lap, unable to meet her concerned gaze. "You don't know him like I do."

"Oh honey, that's what every woman says before appearing on the evening news." She reaches over and squeezes my hand. "I know Paulie's awful. The way he degrades you, making those snide comments about your body—it's emotional abuse, plain and simple. But jumping from his brand of toxicity to Mr. Stalker won't fix anything. It's like choosing between drinking alcohol or taking cocaine—they'll destroy you differently."

The truth in her words stings, but I can't deny the logic. Still, my heart races whenever I think of Tyson's intense stare and commanding presence. "What am I supposed to do, then?"

"How about choosing yourself for once?" Sasha's voice softens. "Instead of picking between two controlling men, maybe it's time to break free of both of them."

I can't help but laugh, the sound bitter even to my own ears. If only Sasha knew the whole truth. She's been my best friend since grade school, but there are parts of my life I've never shared with her. How could I?

"It's not that simple," I say, watching the water

ripple around my feet. "The marriage to Paulie... it's complicated."

"What's complicated about it? You said yes to that jerk. Just say no now."

My chest tightens. She thinks I had a choice—I actually agreed to marry him. In her world, women don't get handed over like property, sealed in marriage deals between criminal enterprises. She doesn't know that my father, Jimmy Moretti, isn't just a successful businessman—he's the most feared mob boss in Dawsbury.

"Sash, there are things about my family..." I trail off, unable to finish. How do I explain that my father's word is law? That refusing this marriage could get people killed?

"What things? Come on, Sofia. Your dad might be strict, but he loves you. He wouldn't want you marrying someone who treats you like garbage."

I smile, remembering the cold look in Dad's eyes when he announced my engagement to Paulie. Love had nothing to do with it. This was business, pure and simple. But Sasha sees my father as the generous man who helped fund her college scholarship and always had candy in his pockets for neighborhood kids. She needs to learn about the blood money that pays for his kindness.

"You're right," I lie, hating myself for it. "I'll think about what you said."

Sasha's warm fingers squeeze mine, her eyes full of concern. "I just want you to be happy and safe, girl. That's all I've ever wanted for you."

The genuine worry in her voice makes my throat

tight. Despite all my secrets, despite the dark world I can never tell her about, Sasha has always been my rock—my one true friend who wants nothing from me except my well-being.

"If you do see this carnival guy again..." She pauses, choosing her words carefully. "Just be careful, okay?"

I nod, knowing in my gut that crossing paths with Tyson again isn't a matter of *if* but when. How he looked at, touched, and spoke to me felt inevitable—like a magnet pulling two objects together, whether they wanted it or not.

"I'll be careful," I promise. However, I'm not sure what careful means anymore, not in my world, where danger lurks behind every smile, where trust is a luxury I can't afford.

The warm water swells around our feet, but I barely notice it now. My mind is drifting to piercing eyes and strong hands, to the thrill of forbidden kisses and the promise of something more dangerous than anything I've known.

Our paths will cross again, whether I want them to or not.

11

TYSON

I storm into Frank's office, my blood boiling. He lounges behind his desk, feet propped up, a self-satisfied smirk on his face. The sight of him makes my fists clench.

"Tyson, what brings you—"

I grab him by the throat and slam him against the wall. "You tried to have her killed."

"Who?" Frank chokes out.

"Don't play dumb. Sofia Moretti. The black SUV? Ring any bells?"

His eyes widen. I release my grip enough for him to speak.

"Jimmy and Paulie joining forces will destroy me. You know that."

"So you target an innocent woman?" I press harder. "His daughter?"

"Business is business." Frank wheezes. "Nothing personal."

I drive my fist into his gut. He doubles over, gasping.

"Here's what's going to happen. You're going to leave Sofia alone. If anything happens to her and you're responsible, I'll fucking kill you."

Frank straightens, rubbing his throat. "You're threatening me over some mob princess? One who's due to marry Paulie, for fuck's sake. What's it to you?"

I tighten my grip on Frank's throat, my knuckles white with rage. "What she is to me doesn't matter. You put a hit on her while she was at *my* carnival. That makes it personal."

"Come on, Tyson. Think about it. Jimmy and Paulie's alliance will squeeze out everyone else in Dawsbury." Frank's voice comes out strained. "I did us both a favor."

"A favor?" I slam him against the wall again. "You endangered my client's daughter. Do you know what Jimmy would do if he found out it was you?"

Frank's face pales. "You wouldn't tell him."

"Try me." I lean in close, my voice dropping to a deadly whisper. "And that's not even considering what I'll do to you if you try anything like this again."

"Fine." Frank raises his hands in surrender. "I'll back off. But you're making a mistake getting involved with her. She's Paulie's."

The way he says it makes my blood boil. I release him with a shove, watching him stumble.

"She's not anyone's property." I straighten my jacket. "And if I ever hear about another attempt on her life, our business arrangement is done. Permanently."

Frank rubs his throat. "You'd throw away years of partnership over some girl?"

"No, you would if you decide to go against me." I meet his gaze and don't back down.

He holds his hands up. "Fine. Since you're here, let's talk about our other business." He pulls out a briefcase of cash and clicks it open. "I want ten kilos, as discussed."

My jaw tightens. Part of me wants to tell him to shove his money where the sun doesn't shine, but business is business. It was the plan when we didn't have the product, but since we recovered it, I need to keep the cash flowing and the drugs moving. And keeping him as a client means I can closely monitor his movements.

"Same price as always," I say, watching him count out stacks of bills for me.

"Quality better be consistent," he replies.

"When have I ever disappointed you?" I gather the cash, doing a quick count. "Delivery will be Sunday night, usual spot."

Frank nods, lighting a cigar. "We good, then?"

"For now." I pocket the money. "But remember what I said about Sofia. I won't repeat myself."

"Message received." He blows out a cloud of smoke. "Loud and clear," he adds.

I head for the door, pausing with my hand on the handle. "One more thing, Frank. This is your only chance. Cross me again, and you won't like the fallout."

I stride from Frank's office, my boots echoing down the marble hallway. The tension in my shoulders eases with each step—nothing like putting an entitled prick in his place.

Behind me, Frank mutters something under his

breath. Probably cursing my name, but I couldn't care less. He got the message.

My black Mustang gleams in the afternoon sun as I slide behind the wheel. Turning the key in the ignition and revving the engine, I peel out of the parking lot, leaving rubber on the pavement. Let Frank stew over that, too.

My mind drifts to Sofia as I navigate through downtown Dawsbury. Those curves, that fiery red hair, how she tries to resist me but can't help herself. The memory of her touching herself while watching my photo makes my cock twitch.

Tonight can't come soon enough. I've got plans for my baby girl—I'm gonna make her scream my name until her throat's raw. Even if she's completely unaware, we've got a date. I've arranged a car to pick her up for the best night of her life.

The carnival comes into view, the Ferris wheel rising above the trees. Time to handle business before pleasure. But damn, if I'm not counting down the hours until I get my hands on Sofia.

I park behind my trailer, adjusting myself in my jeans. The memory of her moans against my mouth as I kissed her has me hard as steel.

Focus, Tyson. Work first, then play.

12

SOFIA

I'm curled up on my couch with a book when a sharp knock echoes through my house. The clock reads six. My stomach churns because I'm not expecting anyone.

I spot a burly man in dark clothes standing on my porch through the peephole. Against my better judgment, I crack open the door, keeping the chain lock in place.

"Can I help you?"

"I'm here to pick you up." His gruff voice matches his appearance.

"What?"

His jaw clenches. "I've got orders to collect you and take you to a location."

"Take me where exactly?" My fingers grip the doorframe.

"It's a surprise." A smirk plays across his face. "Boss's orders."

My jaw clenches. "If Paulie sent you, you can tell him I'm not interested in his surprises."

The man shakes his head. "Not Paulie. Tyson clarified that you might protest, but I should bring you anyway."

Ice floods my veins at the mention of Tyson's name. That arrogant ringmaster thinks he can just summon me whenever he wants?

"Well, you can tell Tyson I'm not some puppet he can control. I'm not going anywhere."

"Ma'am, with all due respect, this isn't a request." He places his foot in the doorway before I can slam it shut. "The boss was very specific about not taking no for an answer."

My hand trembles as I grab the pepper spray from the console table. The guy pushes against my door, the chain straining.

"Last warning. Back off!"

The chain snaps. As he barrels through, I squeeze, and the spray hits him square in the face.

"You fucking bitch!" He stumbles backward, hands covering his eyes. His massive frame crashes into my coat rack. "Shit, shit, shit!"

Red-faced and cursing, he fumbles for his phone. Tears stream down his cheeks as he struggles to see the screen.

"Boss? Yeah, she just fucking maced me. I can't see shit, let alone drive." His voice comes out raw, like he's been gargling glass. "No, I'm not kidding. My eyes are on fire."

He thrusts the phone toward me, still doubled over. "He wants to talk to you."

"Tell him I said go to hell." I keep the pepper spray aimed at him, backing toward my kitchen where I can grab a knife if needed.

"She won't take the phone," he chokes between coughs. "What do you want me to do?"

I hear Tyson's muffled voice through the speaker but can't distinguish the words. The guy nods, wincing as he wipes at his streaming eyes.

"Leave before I call the cops." I keep my pepper spray trained on the intruder, my other hand gripping my phone.

He swipes at his red, swollen eyes and lets out a dark chuckle. "You've made a big mistake, sweetheart. We'll wait."

My heart pounds against my ribs as I back further into my kitchen. The guy leans against my wall, still rubbing his face but wearing a knowing smirk that makes my skin crawl.

Ten minutes pass in tense silence. The deep rumble of a classic engine outside makes me tense up. Heavy footsteps approach my front door.

Tyson strides in like he owns the place, his jaw tight and eyes blazing. His presence fills my living room, making it feel smaller somehow. The carnival costume is gone—he's wearing dark jeans and a black T-shirt that stretches across his broad chest.

"Wait outside," he commands his guy without looking at him.

The man shuffles past, still wiping at his streaming eyes. "Boss, she—"

"I said outside." Tyson's voice carries an edge that makes me flinch.

Tyson turns those intense eyes on me when the door clicks shut behind his man. I grip my pepper spray tighter, though something tells me he won't be as easy to take down.

"What the hell, Sofia? I send a car to pick you up, and you pepper spray the driver? Are you crazy?"

I straighten, meeting his fierce gaze with as much defiance as possible. "You expect me to get in a car with some thug you send? I don't know you, yet you assume I'll come running?"

Tyson advances, stalking toward me like I'm prey. "I saved your life, and this is the thanks I get? You could've at least heard me out."

My shoulders tense, his nearness sending an unwanted shiver down my spine. "I don't owe you anything."

"No?" His eyes narrow. "That's not what I heard. Last I checked, Jimmy Moretti owed me a favor. And from the looks of it, he didn't do shit to pay me back, so maybe I'll just take payment from his daughter."

I scoff, feeling a surge of anger. "My father doesn't own me, and neither do you."

His gaze darkens as he takes another step forward, backing me against the counter. "Maybe I don't want him to owe me anymore." His voice drops to a dangerous murmur. "Maybe I want to collect what's owed from you instead."

A shiver runs through me, this man daring to threaten me in my own home. "And what, exactly, would that entail?"

His eyes flicker over me, an unspoken challenge in his expression. "I think we both know what I want from you."

I hold his intense gaze, refusing to let him see how he affects me. "Well, I'm not interested in whatever game you're playing."

His eyebrow quirks up. "You sure about that, baby girl? Your body tells a different story."

My cheeks flame at the intimate nickname. "That's none of your business."

His hand darts out, pinning my wrist against the counter. His thumb brushes the inside of my wrist, sending a wave of heat through me. "Maybe I want to make it my business."

My breath hitches at his touch, my body betraying my resolve.

"You broke into my house uninvited," I whisper, pulling against his iron grip. "Let me go."

"Only because you weren't answering my calls or texts." His thumb strokes my pulse. His hold is unyielding. "If you weren't interested, why did you respond to my messages initially?"

I refuse to answer, knowing he's right. My gaze falls to his mouth, those perfect lips I've fantasized about since our first kiss. My body betrays the fear in my heart, responding to his closeness, the pressure of his touch.

His eyes darken at my silence. "Say it, Sofia. Tell me you want me, too."

I swallow, our faces mere inches apart. "Let go of me, and I might consider it."

My wrist tingles where Tyson's grip held me moments ago. I rub it, missing his touch despite my anger.

"Fine. At least tell me where we're going for this date you've arranged without my consent."

His lips curve into that infuriating smirk. "It's a surprise."

I cross my arms, glancing down at my oversized lounge dress. "I need to change first. I'm not dressed for—"

"You're perfect exactly as you are." His eyes rake over my simple oversized lounge dress, setting my skin on fire. "Besides, you won't need those clothes for long anyway."

Heat floods my cheeks. The sheer audacity of this man! "You're unbelievable. Do you really think that cocky attitude works on women?"

"Seems to be working on you." He moves toward the door, clearly expecting me to follow. "Coming?"

I huff, grabbing my purse from the counter. "You're the most arrogant man I've ever met."

"And yet here you are, following me anyway." His deep chuckle only fuels my irritation as he leads me out of my house.

"I could still pepper spray you, you know."

"But you won't." He holds the door open. "After you, baby girl."

I slide into the passenger seat of Tyson's sleek black

Mustang, my heart hammering against my ribs. Like everything else about this dangerous man beside me, the leather seats smell so good.

What am I doing?

Every rational part of my brain screams that I should run far away from this carnival ringmaster with his piercing dark eyes and wicked smile. He's broken into my house, hacked my computer, watched me through my webcam—and yet here I am, willingly getting into his car.

My father would kill me if he knew, and Paulie would, too. I'm supposed to be the good daughter, following the path laid out for me since birth—marry into the right family, maintain the connections, keep the business strong. Instead, I'm letting this man—this absolutely infuriating, intoxicating man—lead me down a path that can only end in disaster.

The engine purrs to life, and Tyson's hand brushes my thigh as he shifts gears. Even that slight touch sends electricity through my body. God, what is wrong with me? He's everything I should avoid—unpredictable, controlling, dangerous.

But there's something in the way he looks at me like he sees past the mob princess facade to the real me underneath.

I know he's going to be my downfall. This wild attraction, this magnetic pull between us, will destroy everything I've been raised to be. But as I watch his strong hands grip the steering wheel, remember the heat of his body pressing mine against the kitchen counter, I realize I don't care. For once, I want to choose my own path, even if it leads straight to hell.

And something tells me that's exactly where the ringmaster plans to take me.

13

TYSON

When I pull up at the carnival, I glance at Sofia to see her nose wrinkling in disgust. "What's wrong? Is it not fancy enough for you?"

"Why are we here?" She crosses her arms, green eyes flashing with defiance.

"We're here because I want to show you how a real man treats your clit."

She gasps, and her cheeks flush a deep pink.

I open the door to my Mustang. "But first, dinner. Can't have you going hungry. And you'll need a lot of energy for what I have planned."

Her perfectly shaped eyebrow arches. "Dinner? Here?" She glances at the carnival entrance with disdain. "I usually dine at Michelin-starred restaurants."

"Tonight, you're getting the authentic carnival experience." I climb out of the Mustang and walk around to open her door.

She reluctantly takes my hand, and I guide her through the carnival entrance, my hand resting possessively on the small of her back. Her discomfort at being here amuses me—the mob princess is so far out of her element.

I grab her hand, pulling her toward the food stands.

"I wouldn't be caught dead eating this greasy carnival trash." She tries to dig her heels in, but I keep her moving.

"One corndog won't kill you." I order two corndogs and a couple of beers. "Here's your five-star dining experience."

"This is ridiculous." But I catch the slight quirk of her lips as she accepts the corndog, holding it delicately between two manicured fingers.

"Take a bite. Live dangerously."

She rolls her eyes but takes a small, tentative bite. Her eyes widen slightly.

"Good, right?" I take a long pull from my beer.

"It's... not terrible," she admits, taking another bite.

"High praise from someone who probably eats caviar for breakfast." I wink at her, enjoying the way her cheeks flush.

"You're impossible." But she's smiling now, really smiling, as she sips her beer.

I watch Sofia lick a spot of mustard from her finger, my cock twitching at the sight. She's loosened up after the corndog and beer, her shoulders relaxed as she leans back in her seat.

"Admit it—you're enjoying yourself." I collect our empty paper plates and bottles.

"I'll admit nothing." But her smile gives her away.

"Though I suppose there are worse ways to spend an evening than slumming it with carnival food."

"Just wait, baby girl. The night's not over." I stand up. "Stay right here. Don't move an inch."

"Where are you going?" she asks.

"To get dessert. Trust me."

"Trust you?" She laughs. "That seems unwise."

I head to Mark's stand and order two fresh funnel cakes loaded with powdered sugar. The sweet aroma fills the air as I carry them back.

Sofia's eyes widen. "What is that?" She peers at the twisted, sugar-dusted confection.

"This is a funnel cake. The crown jewel of carnival cuisine." I set one in front of her with a flourish.

"It looks like a heart attack waiting to happen." But she's already reaching for a piece, pulling apart the crispy strands.

"The best things in life usually are." I watch as she takes her first bite, powdered sugar dusting her lips.

"Oh my god." Her eyes close in pleasure. "This is incredible."

"Better than your fancy french pastries?"

"Don't push it." She breaks off another piece. "But it's good."

"The simple pleasures in life." I hand her a napkin, but she waves it away.

"No point. I'm just going to keep making a mess." She downs the last of her second beer. Gone is her stiff posture from earlier. "You know what? This is actually fun."

"Did that physically pain you to say?" I smirk as she rolls her eyes.

"Don't be smug." She tears off another piece of funnel cake.

I down the last of my beer, dragging my eyes away from the way Sofia's tongue swipes a stray bit of powdered sugar from her lip. I've been with more women than I can count, but something about this girl has gotten under my skin. I'm aching to see what's under that dress.

"Ready to go, baby girl?" I extend my hand to her, and she hesitates momentarily before placing her palm in mine. I pull her to her feet and tug her close, her body fitting perfectly against my muscles. She looks up at me, green eyes sparkling with anticipation.

"I—" She swallows, searching my gaze. "I'm ready."

I lead her away from the bright lights and noise of the carnival, back toward my trailer. The night is cool, and I wrap an arm around her shoulders, drawing her close. She doesn't pull away, instead nestling into my side. I can feel the tension radiating off her, a mix of nerves and desire.

"You know, I've thought about this moment a lot," I murmur, my lips brushing her ear. "You, coming back to my place. Letting me show you how well I can care for that body."

She shivers against me. "Oh yeah?" Her voice is breathy, and I can feel her soft breasts pressing against my chest.

"Oh, yeah." I chuckle, a deep rumble in my chest.

"I've imagined those thighs wrapped around my waist, your soft skin under my hands." I pause outside the trailer, key in hand. "And don't even get me started on that mouth."

She bites her lip, glancing up at me. "Ty—"

"You want to know what I'm going to do with that pretty little mouth of yours?" I tease, pressing even closer to her. Her breath quickens, and I can feel the pounding of her heart. I lean down, my lips ghosting over hers. "I'll let you find out soon enough."

I pull back, studying Sofia's flushed face. This girl has me completely twisted up inside. When I first spotted her, I thought she'd be just another conquest—someone to chase, catch, and eventually discard. But there's something different about her.

It could be how she challenges me, refusing to follow my usual tricks. Or how her genuine smile lights up her whole face when she lets her guard down like she did tonight over that damn funnel cake. How she fits against me feels right in a way I can't explain.

And hell, watching her enjoy simple carnival food instead of her usual fancy fare did something to my chest that I was not ready to examine too closely. I'm playing a dangerous game here—she's Jimmy Moretti's daughter, engaged to another client, and completely off-limits. But standing here with her soft curves pressed against me, the sweet scent of her perfume mixing with powdered sugar, I'm already in too deep.

This isn't just about getting her into my bed anymore. I want more. I want all of her—her sass, her smile, those moments when she drops her rich-girl act and lets herself feel. And that terrifies me more than any business deal gone wrong ever could.

14

SOFIA

My heart hammers against my ribs when I enter Tyson's trailer. The space feels smaller than I imagined, more intimate. His presence fills every corner.

"Come here, baby girl." His voice wraps around me like velvet.

I cross my arms over my chest, suddenly hyper-aware of my curves. The ones Paulie says make me look fat.

Tyson's fingers brush my chin, tilting my face up. "What's going on in that beautiful head of yours?"

"Nothing." I try to sound confident, but my voice wavers.

"Bullshit." His thumb traces my bottom lip. "You're trembling."

Heat floods my cheeks. I step back, putting space between us. "I just... I don't understand why you want me."

"Why wouldn't I?"

"Look at you." I gesture at his muscled frame, the tattoos visible beneath his rolled-up sleeves. "And I'm..." The words stick in my throat.

"You're what?" His eyes darken.

"I'm not exactly model material." I force a laugh that sounds hollow. "Paulie says—"

"Fuck what Paulie says!" He closes the distance between us, his hands settling on my hips. "That piece of shit wouldn't know beauty if it slapped him in the face."

I bite my lip, fighting the urge to pull away. "He says I need to lose weight."

"Is that what this is about?" Tyson's expression softens. His fingers trail up my sides, making me shiver. "Every curve of your body is perfect. You have no idea how crazy you make me."

I shift under his intense gaze, my skin prickling with awareness. Deep down, I know I'm not fat—I've got curves, sure, and I'm no size zero, but that's never bothered me until Paulie started his constant comments.

Tyson's fingers trail down my arm, leaving goosebumps in their wake. "You know what I'm going to do?"

I shake my head, lost in the depths of his eyes.

"I'm going to worship every fucking inch of this body." His hand slides to my hip, squeezing gently. "I will show you how gorgeous you are, baby girl. By the time I'm done, you won't have a single doubt in that pretty head that you're the most beautiful thing I've ever fucking seen."

My breath catches. The raw desire in his voice makes my knees weak. "Tyson..."

"Look at me." His fingers cup my chin. "These curves? They drive me crazy. That asshole doesn't deserve to breathe the same air as you, let alone make you doubt yourself."

The intensity of his words hits me like a physical force. No one's ever talked to me like this—like I'm something precious and desirable rather than someone who needs fixing.

"I see how you try to hide yourself," he continues, his thumb brushing my bottom lip. "The way you cross your arms over your chest, tug at your clothes. It stops now."

Tyson's thumb strokes my jaw gently as his other hand rests on the small of my back, pulling me closer. My pulse races, and desire mixes with an edge of fear as his fingers tighten around my throat. A tingle runs through me, and I tilt my head back, inviting him to apply more pressure. He knows exactly what I need.

"Look into my eyes." His voice is a low rumble, commanding my compliance.

I lift my gaze to meet his, the intensity in his eyes making my breath hitch. He stares into me, searching for any sign of hesitation or fear. I hold his gaze, silently assuring him that I want this and need it.

"Do you understand what I'm saying?" His thumb brushes my bottom lip as he speaks, his hand still wrapped around my throat. I nod, my heart hammering in my chest.

"Use your voice. Tell me you understand."

Swallowing hard, I force my voice past the tightness in my throat. "I understand."

"Good." His grip relaxes slightly, but his fingers remain at my neck. "Does it turn you on when I'm dominant?"

I can't hold back the shiver that runs through me. "Yes." My voice is barely a whisper.

"Good." The corners of his mouth lift in a half-smile. "Because I like to engage in BDSM. I'm going to tie you up, spank that gorgeous ass of yours, and make you scream my name. And you're going to fucking love it."

Tyson's words strike something deep within me, lighting a fire I never knew existed. Submitting to him and being completely at his mercy is more enticing than I imagined. And how he looks at me—like he can see straight through my walls—thrills me.

"Strip for me, baby girl." His voice is a low command.

I swallow hard, my fingers moving to the zipper of my dress. I don't need to ask why—I want to be his good girl.

Slowly, I pull down the zipper, feeling his eyes on me the entire time. With a deliberate shrug, I let the dress slide off my shoulders and pool at my feet, leaving me standing before him in nothing but my black lace bra and matching panties. The cool air of the trailer raises goosebumps on my exposed skin.

His gaze rakes over me, making me feel more naked than I already am. My nipples tighten beneath the lace, and I can't suppress a small whimper as I anticipate what's to come.

"You're beautiful." His voice is a gravelly murmur. "But you're wearing too much."

I wet my lips with the tip of my tongue. "What do you want me to do?"

He doesn't respond; he raises an eyebrow as if challenging me to disobey.

With a swift motion, I unclasp my bra, shimmying out of it and tossing it onto a nearby chair. The material of my panties is growing damp from my desire.

"Panties, too. Nice and slow." His eyes shine with lust, but he stands there, unmoving.

I grab the edge of my panties and slowly slide them down my thighs, over my knees, and finally past my ankles. I step out of them, feeling incredibly exposed but also empowered. I know he wants me, and that desire fuels my confidence.

Tyson's gaze burns a path over my body, lingering on my breasts, my hips, and then my pussy. "Get on the bed, Sofia. On your back."

I climb onto the bed, the sheets soft against my naked skin, and lie down, my heart hammering in my chest. I watch him, anticipation coursing through my veins like molten lava.

He doesn't join me immediately. Instead, he stands there, taking in the sight of me before him like a feast. "Such a beautiful sight, baby girl. Just fucking perfect."

His words thrill me. I want to be his—completely and utterly.

He reaches into a drawer and pulls out a set of handcuffs. I bite my lip, excitement fluttering in my stomach. Part of me can't believe this is happening—

that I'm willingly letting myself be handcuffed to a bed by a man I barely know. But something about Tyson makes me feel safe, even as he pushes my boundaries.

"I'm going to cuff you now. Arms above your head." His voice is soft, but an undercurrent of steel demands my obedience.

Lifting my arms above my head, Tyson snaps the cool metal around my wrists, tightening it enough so I can't move my arms. The sensation is thrilling, and I shift, testing the restraints.

"Comfortable?" His eyes glint with amusement.

"Yes," I whisper, feeling more exposed than ever.

He produces a blindfold next, and I stifle a gasp. "This is optional. Some people prefer it. I want to blindfold you, but only if you agree."

I nod, unable to speak. I've never been blindfolded during sex before, and the thought sends a jolt of anticipation through me.

"Good girl." He slides the soft fabric over my eyes, blocking my vision. Suddenly, the room feels even more intimate, and my other senses heighten. I hear the faint sound of his movement, smell his cologne, and feel the mattress dip as he settles next to me.

His fingers trail down my arm, and I shiver. "I'm going to start slow. I want to ease you into this. If it's too much at any point, your safe word is 'purple.' Can you remember that?"

"Purple," I repeat, my voice steadier than I feel.

"That's my girl." His lips brush my earlobe, sending a shiver down my spine. "Now, let's begin."

His hands explore my body, his touch light as a

feather, making me squirm. I feel the soft caress of something trace against my skin, the sensation exquisite. His strokes are gentle, sending pleasant tingles through my body. I relax into the bed, surrendering to the pleasure.

The strokes increase in intensity, and I moan, arching my back.

"Do you like the feel of my flogger, baby?" he asks, gripping my hip and holding me in place as it lands on my thighs.

I can't find the words, so, I merely nod. His lips find my neck, his tongue tracing a path that makes my breath stutter. His kisses are demanding, his teeth grazing my skin, and I can feel his stubble.

"You're doing so well." His warm breath fans the sensitive skin of my neck. "But I think you can take more."

The flogger strokes continue each landing with a satisfying smack that echoes in the small space. My skin feels alive, every nerve ending ignited. I moan as pleasure courses through me.

His fingers dip between my legs, finding my slick entrance. "You like that, don't you, baby? Feeling that sting on your skin while I touch you here."

"Yes," I manage to whisper, my chest heaving.

"Tell me what you want. Don't be shy."

"I want—" My words dissolve into a moan as his fingers push inside me. "More."

Laughter rumbles in his chest. "I can give you more."

He adds another finger, stretching me, and I rock my

hips against his hand, meeting his thrusts. My body feels electric, every touch sending jolts of pleasure through me.

Then, suddenly, his fingers are gone, leaving me wanting. I whimper, arching my back, searching for more contact.

"Shh, baby girl. I'm not done with you yet."

I squirm at the loss of his touch, my head thrumming with need. My skin buzzes with sensation—every nerve ending is alive and begging for more. The room's cool air caresses my heated skin.

"Please," I whisper, needing release.

I hear the rustle of clothing and the soft clink of metal, followed by a sharp sting of a warm hand slapping my inner thigh. I gasp, my body tensing. It's a different sensation to the flogger.

"You're so responsive. Such a beautiful sight." His voice is thick with desire. "Do you like it when I spank you?"

"Yes," I breathe.

The sting comes again, this time on the other thigh, making me moan. I anticipate the next strike, needing it like a drug.

He doesn't keep me waiting, delivering another stinging slap that has me arching off the bed. I'm lost in sensation, my body throbbing with want.

"Tell me how much you like it." His voice is a husky demand.

"I—I love it," I admit, embarrassment warring with desire. "Please, more."

The sound of his laughter surrounds me, rich and full. "As you wish, baby girl."

The next slap lands on the side of my ass cheek, making me jerk against the cuffs. A whimper escapes me, a mix of pleasure and pain. My body craves more, and he delivers, each slap leaving a burning imprint on my skin.

I lose myself in the sensation, my entire being focused on the delicious sting of each strike. The blindfold heightens my other senses, making me hyper-aware of Ty's movements, the feel of his hands on my body, and his masculine scent.

Without warning, his hand slips between my legs again, his fingers thrusting into me. I cry out, my body clenching around him.

"Fucking hell, you're so wet," he growls.

His thumb finds my clit, swirling gently as his fingers pump in and out. I moan, my body tensing as lightning zigzags through me. I'm so close to the edge—teetering on the precipice of release.

With one final thrust of his fingers, he brings me over, and I shatter, my body convulsing as I cry out. I'm only vaguely aware of his name falling from my lips—a frantic plea.

He just made me orgasm from a flogger and his fingers. No guy has ever made me orgasm before.

15

TYSON

Sofia lies before me, her creamy skin contrasting against the dark restraints. She's perfect.

I want her to know it, to see it in my eyes. With a swift motion, I rip the blindfold off. Her emerald eyes widen at seeing me, and I can't help but grin.

"Baby girl, I'm gonna taste you. And I need you to watch me devour you."

Her cheeks flush at my words, and I see the desire burning in her eyes. I know she's self-conscious about her body, but to me, she's a fucking goddess. Curves in all the right places, her thick thighs driving me wild.

I kneel between her legs, my cock twitching with anticipation. Her eyes never leave mine as I inhale her sweet scent. My tongue teases her, tasting her essence, and I groan at how good she tastes.

I feast on her, my tongue exploring every inch of her. I can't get enough. My hands grip her thighs, spreading her open wider for me.

"Fuck, Sofia. You've got no idea how good you taste."

Her breath quickens as I continue my oral assault, my pierced cock throbbing with need. I want to make her come undone, to show her just how perfect her body is and how much I worship it.

My tongue finds her clit, and I suck gently, feeling her shudder beneath me. Her hands grasp the bedsheets, her knuckles turning white as I continue.

"T-Tyson, please... I—"

I know what she needs. I press a finger inside her, feeling her wetness coat my skin. With my thumb, I rub slow circles around her clit as I add another finger, stretching her open.

"You like that? You like being touched by a real man?"

"Y-Yes..." she whimpers.

I curl my fingers, finding that sweet spot inside her, and her back arches off the bed. Her walls clench around my fingers as I continue to work her, my tongue never stopping its magic.

Sofia's breath comes in sharp gasps now, her body trembling on the edge. With a few more flicks of my tongue and swift thrusts of my fingers, she cries out, her release crashing over her. I don't stop, wanting to prolong her pleasure for as long as possible.

I savor her taste on my tongue as I pull away, admiring the sight of her flushed and satisfied. But I know she can take more.

"You're so fucking responsive, baby," I murmur, stroking her thighs gently. "I love how sensitive you are."

Her eyes shine with a mix of pleasure and embarrassment. "I can't help it," she whispers.

I chuckle, reaching for the restraints. "Don't worry, I'm not done with you yet."

I secure her wrists and ankles once more, needing to see her spread out before me, open and waiting. Her body is perfect, her thick thighs and wide hips only fueling my desire. I kiss my way up her legs, nipping at her inner thighs, and she bucks her hips toward me, seeking more contact.

Leaning over her, I speak directly into her ear, my voice a low rumble. "Do you want my cock, baby?"

"Yes," she breathes, her voice laced with need.

"Say it louder. I want to hear you ask for it."

Her cheeks flush, but her eyes sparkle with desire. "I want your cock, Ty. Please."

I chuckle, reaching down to stroke myself. "As you wish."

Teasing her, I rub the head of my cock through her wet entrance, my piercing dragging against her sensitive flesh. She bucks her hips, seeking to take me in, but I pull away, not ready to give in just yet.

"Not so fast," I taunt, circling my cock around her clit. "I want you to beg."

"Please, Tyson," she whimpers, her eyes pleading. "I need you."

I slide just the tip inside, watching her face contort in pleasure. "Fuck, you feel so good, baby. But I want to hear you beg for it."

She bites her lip, her voice hoarse as she speaks. "Please... fuck me. I want all of you."

With a growl, I thrust forward, filling her in one smooth stroke. She gasps, her back arching as she takes me in.

"That's it, baby girl. Take it all."

I move slowly at first, enjoying her tight warmth around me. Her eyes slide closed, her lips parting as she loses herself in the sensation. I lean down, my mouth close to her ear.

"Open your eyes, Sofia. Watch me fuck you."

Her eyes lock on our joining, watching as my thick cock disappears inside her again and again. The magic cross piercing on my shaft glints in the dim light, and I can't resist asking, "Do you like how my piercing feels?"

A flush creeps up her neck, but she nods eagerly. "I've never felt anything like it. It feels so... so good."

"It's all for you, baby girl. Every inch of me."

Her eyes, full of desire, burn into mine as I keep thrusting. I angle my hips, searching for that sweet spot, and her breath catches as I find it. "There it is," I mutter, thrusting again in that spot. "You feel that?"

"Oh fuck," she moans, her head tossing back. "Yes... right there."

I latch onto her full breasts, teasing her nipples with my tongue and teeth. Her hips rise to meet my thrusts, her body moving with a mind of its own. I know I won't last long with her responsiveness. She's too much, wrapping around me like a glove, her soft body cushioning mine.

She's a goddess, and I'm worshiping at her altar, praying to her with my body. I groan as the pleasure spikes, my cock throbbing deep within her. "Sofia, I'm close. Where do you want me to—"

"Inside," she gasps. "Come inside me, please."

Hearing that, my control snaps. I thrust hard into her, over and over, my grip on her thighs almost bruising. With each stroke, the head of my cock drags against that spot inside her.

She meets my rhythm, her hips slamming up to greet me. Her breasts bounce. Her full lips part, and she cries out with each thrust, her eyes squeezed shut, her back arching.

I want to watch her face as she comes, so I slow down, driving her crazy. She whimpers in protest, but I just chuckle. "Not yet, I want to see you."

Her eyes snap open, a mix of frustration and desire within them. Good. That's exactly what I want. I tease her swollen clit with my thumb, and she bucks her hips.

"Please, Ty... please. Don't stop."

"As you wish, baby."

I thrust into her again, harder this time, my thumb working her clit in circles. She's so tight, and I know she's close. I lean down, my breath hot against her skin.

"Come for me. Let me feel it."

Her body shakes, and her walls clench around me, milking my cock. It's a struggle not to just let go. This is about her pleasure. Always about her.

"That's it. Let go for me. Come all over my cock."

With a strangled cry, she explodes, her walls pulsing and rippling. I keep thrusting through her orgasm, wanting to draw it out, to make her feel everything. Her juices drip down my balls as she rides out her high.

"Fuck," I grunt, feeling my own release building. "Sofia, I'm—"

Before I can finish my sentence, her walls clamp down on me, milking my release. With a harsh groan, I spill myself into her, my eyes slipping closed as I savor my release and fill her with cum.

I open my eyes and look down at her, her body still shuddering with aftershocks. Her breathing is ragged, her skin flushed, and her hair a mess. She's fucking stunning.

"That was—incredible," she breathes, her chest rising and falling rapidly.

"I'm glad you enjoyed it, baby girl."

I unlock her restraints, needing to feel her hands on me. The moment her wrists and ankles are free, she pulls me into a passionate kiss, her arms wrapping around my neck. I kiss her deeply, pouring all my pent-up desire into this moment.

"You're something else, Sofia Moretti," I murmur against her lips. "Absolutely something else."

She smiles, looking up at me with those gorgeous green eyes. "You're not so bad yourself, ringmaster."

I chuckle, pulling her into my arms. "Get some rest, baby."

She snuggles into my chest, her body relaxing after our intense session. As I stroke her hair, my mind wanders, thinking about this mysterious woman in my arms. She's unlike anyone I've ever met, and I can't deny that I'm intrigued, maybe even a little obsessed.

But one thing's for sure. I'm not letting her go

anytime soon. It's a slight complication, considering she's engaged to marry a mobster her dad practically sold her to. Still, I'll deal with that hurdle when I come to it.

16

SOFIA

I slip my key into the front door, wincing at every tiny sound. My body aches in the most delicious ways, but the moment I saw Paulie's car in my driveway, sheer panic set in. Sure enough, he's sitting in my living room, illuminated by a single lamp.

"Where were you really?" His voice cuts through the darkness.

I clutch my purse tighter. "I told you, I was at Sasha's. We had wine and fell asleep watching movies."

"Funny." He stands, towering over me. "Because I drove by Sasha's place. Her lights were off all night."

My heart hammers against my ribs. "We were in her basement. You know how we like our movie marathons dark."

"Don't lie to me." His fist slams against the wall, making me jump. "You smell like carnival food and cheap beer."

"I went to the carnival earlier with Sasha. We got

hungry." The lies flow easier now, but my hands shake. "You're being paranoid again, Paulie."

"Paranoid?" He laughs, but there's no humor in it. "Your father arranged this marriage to unite our families. Do you understand what's at stake here?"

"Of course I do." I try to steady my voice. "I've never given you a reason to doubt me."

"Then why are you sneaking around in the middle of the night?" He steps closer, his cologne overwhelming.

I force myself to relax, knowing getting defensive will only worsen things. "You're right, I should have called. I lost track of time with Sasha. We were just having a girls' night."

"Baby, I worry." His expression softens, and I seize the opportunity.

"I know you do." I place my hand on his arm, suppressing a shudder. "But I promise, it was just movies and junk food."

Paulie's shoulders drop, the tension leaving his frame. "Next time, just let me know where you are. I don't like not knowing."

"Of course." The words taste bitter on my tongue. "I'll text you next time."

"That's my girl." He pulls me against his chest, and I force myself not to stiffen. His lips descend on mine, harsh and demanding. The kiss feels wrong—all teeth and tongue, nothing like Tyson's passionate embrace that set my body on fire. Where Ty's kisses made me melt, Paulie's made my skin crawl.

I endure it, thinking of Tyson's gentle touches, his

skilled mouth, and how he made me feel beautiful and desired. Paulie's hands grip my waist too tight, his stubble scratches my chin, and his tongue probes my mouth like he's searching for something.

When he finally pulls back, I must stop myself from wiping my mouth. "See you tomorrow?" he asks.

"Tomorrow," I agree, counting the seconds until he leaves.

The door clicks shut behind him, and I lean against it, releasing a shaky breath. My lips still tingle unpleasantly from his kiss, and I can't help but compare it to the electricity I felt with Tyson. With Ty, every touch was magic, every kiss an adventure. With Paulie, it's just... obligation.

I slide down against the door, my hands trembling from Paulie's visit, when my phone buzzes. My heart skips as Tyson's name flashes across the screen.

> Why the fuck did you sneak out? I wasn't finished with you. I had plans to wake you up in the morning with my cock.

Heat floods my cheeks, and my body responds to his words despite my exhaustion. I bite my lip, remembering how he felt inside me just hours ago. My fingers hover over the keyboard, but before I can respond, another message appears.

> You better have a good explanation. I don't like waking up to an empty bed.

I glance nervously at the door, half-expecting Paulie to burst back in.

> Paulie showed up at my house. Had to get back before he got suspicious.

I type back.

> Fuck him. Should've stayed with me where you belong.

My thighs clench at his possessive tone.

> I know. But I couldn't risk it. He was already here when I got home.

> Did he touch you?

I hesitate before answering truthfully.

> He kissed me.

Three dots appear and disappear several times before his response comes through.

> Next time you're in my bed, you're not leaving until I say so. And I'll make sure you forget all about his pathetic kiss.

I press my legs together, trying to ignore the ache between them. "Ty..." I start typing, but another message cuts me off.

> Get some sleep, baby girl. But don't think we're done here. Not even close.

I'm too wired to sleep, so I run a hot bath instead. As I sink in, my thoughts race. Steam rises around me as I trace the marks Tyson left on my skin—delicate bruises that tell stories of passion I never knew existed before him.

My engagement ring catches the bathroom light, a constant reminder of my mess. Paulie's earlier visit replays how close I came to getting caught. One slip, one wrong move, and this whole house of cards comes crashing down.

My father's voice echoes in my mind.

Family first, always.

The marriage to Paulie isn't just about me. It's about alliances, power, and peace between two volatile families. If anyone discovers I slept with Tyson...

I shudder, remembering stories of people who crossed my father or Paulie: bodies found in rivers, mysterious disappearances, families torn apart. My father may love me, but business is business. And Paulie? His toxic possessiveness already shows in the way he grips my arm too tight and how his eyes narrow when other men look my way.

Then there's Tyson himself. He's dangerous in his own right. I've seen the darkness in his eyes and felt the controlled violence in his touch. The carnival isn't just Ferris wheels and cotton candy. I know his business with my father is illegal.

I slide deeper into the water, my heart heavy. I'm playing with fire from all sides. If Paulie discovers my betrayal, his rage will be explosive. If my father finds out I'm sleeping with one of his suppliers... The thought makes me nauseous. And Tyson? He's already showing signs of possessiveness that both thrill and terrify me.

Yet despite knowing all this, my body still hums with desire when I think of him. My skin craves his touch. He makes me feel alive, wanted, and beautiful, which is addictive. But at what cost? How long before jealousy, business, or family loyalty turns this passion play into a tragedy?

17

TYSON

I stare at my phone for the hundredth time today, willing it to buzz with a message from Sofia. Five days of radio silence, or worse—one-word replies that tell me nothing. My fingers clench around the device.

"Fuck." I slam it down on my desk, making the papers scatter.

Lars pokes his head in. "Everything good, boss?"

"Get out."

He vanishes without another word. Smart man.

I pull up the security feed Phoenix installed in her bedroom. It's still offline.

My last text to her sits unanswered from this morning:

> Talk to me, baby girl.

The carnival is packed outside my trailer, with screams and laughter floating through the walls. We've got less than a week left in Dawsbury before we move on, and the thought of leaving her behind twists my gut.

I pull up our previous messages, scrolling through the heat and passion we shared just days ago. Her responses now are cold and distant: "K." "Maybe." "Busy." Each one drives the knife deeper.

I grab my jacket and head for the door. Time to pay my favorite redhead a visit.

I stalk through the carnival, ignoring the concerned glances from my crew. The smell of popcorn and cotton candy turns my stomach as I pass the food stalls. My boots crunch across the gravel lot to where my black Mustang sits waiting.

Turning the key brings the motor to life, and I zoom out onto the main road. Dawsbury's streets blur past as I push well over the speed limit, my knuckles white on the steering wheel.

Twenty minutes later, I pull onto her street, killing the headlights as I cruise past the manicured lawns and oversized houses. My heart pounds when I spot her place—and the gaudy red Lamborghini parked in her driveway.

"Son of a bitch." I recognize that car. Paulie loves showing it off around town, revving the engine.

I park a few houses down, hidden in the shadows of an oak tree. The lights are on inside her place, silhouettes moving behind the curtains. My jaw clenches as I imagine that piece of shit putting his hands on what's mine.

The leather steering wheel creaks under my grip. I could storm in there and teach him exactly what happens when someone touches my property. Although Sofia belongs to him since he's engaged to her, her heart definitely doesn't.

I sit in the dark, watching that damn car mock me with its presence. Each minute that passes feeds the rage building in my chest.

I slip out of the Mustang, tightening my black jacket around my shoulders. I flip up the hood to conceal my face as I move silently through the neighboring yards.

Voices drift through an open window on the side of her house. I crouch beneath it, pressing against the wall.

"You've been different lately." Paulie's voice drips with accusation. "Getting an attitude. Think you're too good for me now?"

"I'm not having this conversation again." Sofia's tone is tired, defeated.

"Look at you. Can't even fit in that dress properly anymore. You're getting fatter."

My fingers dig into my palms, nails biting deep enough to draw blood. The urge to burst through that window and wrap my hands around his throat burns through me.

"I'm not fat, Paulie. Stop it."

"You're a fat bitch, and you know it. Lucky I even look at you."

A sharp crack echoes—he's slammed his hand on something. Sofia's sharp intake of breath has me halfway to my feet before I force myself back down.

I could do it. One quick move, and I'd be through that window. Three seconds to cross the room. Another two to snap his worthless neck. But then Jimmy would come looking for answers, and Sofia would be caught in the crossfire.

"Maybe if you spent less time stuffing your face and more time at the gym..." His words continue to slice through the night air.

My jaw clenches so hard my teeth might crack. Every muscle screams to move, to act, to tear him apart for daring to speak to her like that. But I stay frozen, letting the rage build instead of explode.

I've killed before. Hell, I've tortured guys to death. But the things I want to do to Paulie right now? They would be more depraved. Slower. Messier. The kind of things that would have cops swarming in search of a psychopathic killer. And I doubt Sofia could look at me after she witnessed my capacity for depravity.

I listen as Sofia's voice rises, sharp with anger. "Get out, Paulie. Just get out."

"Don't you dare talk to me like that?" His footsteps thud across the floor. Something crashes—a vase, maybe.

"I said get out!"

"You ungrateful little—" His hand hitting something makes my blood boil. "Fine. But this isn't over."

The front door slams so hard that the window frame rattles. His expensive shoes click across the driveway, followed by the obnoxious roar of that ridiculous Lamborghini starting up. The engine revs several times —showing off like the insecure piece of shit he is— before the sound fades into the distance.

Sofia's sobs drift through the window, soft and broken. Each one twists the knife in my chest. I wait another thirty seconds to make sure Paulie isn't coming back, then hoist myself through the open window with practiced ease.

She's curled up on the couch, arms wrapped around her knees, tears streaming down her face. The sight of her crying over that worthless bastard makes me want to hunt him down.

"He's not worth these tears."

Her head snaps up, eyes wide. "Tyson? How did you —" She swipes at her cheeks. "Were you outside this whole time?"

"Long enough to hear what that piece of shit said to you." I cross the room and crouch in front of her. "And every word was a lie."

I gently wipe the tears from her cheeks with my thumb, my heart aching at the sight of her pain. "Come here."

Sofia hesitates for a moment before falling into my arms. I pull her close, breathing in the scent of her hair as she buries her face against my chest. Her body trembles with quiet sobs, and I stroke her back in soothing circles.

"That's it," I murmur. "Let it out. I've got you."

Her fingers clutch at my shirt as the tears gradually slow. I press my lips to the top of her head, holding her until her breathing steadies.

"Look at me," I whisper.

She tilts her face, those stunning green eyes still wet with tears. My thumb traces the curve of her cheek.

"You deserve so much better than this, Sofia. You deserve to be cherished. Treasured."

Her lips part slightly, and I can't resist any longer. I lean down and capture her mouth, pouring all my feelings into the kiss. She melts against me, her hands sliding up to my shoulders.

When we break apart, I rest my forehead against hers. "Let me show you how special you are. Let me worship every beautiful inch of you. Make you feel like the queen you are."

A small smile tugs at her lips. "Ty..."

"I mean it." I cup her face in my hands. "You're perfect exactly as you are. Those curves drive me wild. Your strength, your fire—everything about you is fucking incredible. And I want to spend hours proving it to you."

The vulnerability in her eyes makes my chest tight. No one's ever treated her the way she deserves. But I'm going to change that.

"Let me show you," I whisper against her lips. "Let me make you feel like the goddess you are."

Her breath catches as my fingers trail down her neck, loosening the buttons of her silk robe. "Yes, Ty," she breathes, emerald eyes darkened with desire.

"Say it again, baby girl," I murmur. "Tell me you want me to worship you like a goddess."

Her lips part. "I want it, Ty."

I slip the robe off her shoulders, letting it cascade to the floor. She stands before me, naked and trembling with need.

"I want to show you something," I whisper, stepping back to grab the coil of rope from my jacket pocket.

"Something that will heighten your senses and make feel better."

I show her the deep burgundy rope that contrasts with her ivory skin. Her eyes widen as I approach, curiosity warring with apprehension.

"Trust me?" I ask softly.

She licks her lips, that resolute chin of hers lifting. "I do."

I smile, tracing a finger down her cheek. "Close your eyes, then."

She obeys, allowing me to guide her to the center of the room. The rope slides through my fingers like silk as I work, watching her face for any sign of discomfort. She gasps as my hands skim over her skin, the rope slipping along her arms, her back, her tits.

This binding is an ancient art. Pressure points and strategic knots are designed to heighten her pleasure. Shibari is a delicate art that very few truly master.

"How do you feel?" I ask, my breath tickling her ear.

"Intoxicated," she admits, a flush spreading across her bound chest. "The rope, your touch... It's too much."

"Not nearly enough." My fingertips brush over her collarbone and the hollow of her throat. "I want to give you more, Sofia. Take you to places you've never been before."

Her breath hitches as I reach the rope between her legs, securing it in a way that will heighten each sensation. "I'm going to make you fly, baby girl. Surrender to me, and I promise you won't fall."

She moans, her body arching toward mine. "Please, Tyson. Take me there. I need—"

"Shh, baby." I brush my thumbs over her nipples, rolling them gently. "You've held so much back, so much tension. Let me teach you to let go."

Her eyelids flutter as I move back to appraise my handiwork. The rope accentuates her lush curves, highlighting each dip and swell. The art of Shibari transforms her into a living sculpture.

Stepping back, I admire her, my cock throbbing in my pants. I'm dying to plunge into her heat, but restraint is my game. I'm in no rush.

"Call me Master when we're fucking, Sofia," I command, letting the darkness in my voice fill the room. I want her to submit fully, to give herself over to my every desire. "Can you do that for me?"

Her chest rises and falls with each rapid breath as she submits to my authority. "Yes, Master."

That single word is my undoing. I step forward, crushing my mouth to hers, and tightly grip her hair. She whimpers, the ropes pulling taut against her skin. The sound goes straight to my cock.

With one hand, I tear open my jeans, freeing my aching erection. I stroke myself, moaning at the first touch. "You're fucking desperate for this, aren't you?"

"Let me see you, too, Master." Her voice is timid but laced with desire. "I want to see all of you."

I smirk, amusement curling in my gut. Such a simple request, but our power dynamics shift with every word acknowledging my dominance.

Slowly, teasingly, I peel off my shirt, tossing it aside. I

watch her eyes trail over my chest, taking in my muscles and ink.

I kick off my boots and strip off my pants, keeping my eyes locked on hers. A thrill runs through me as I stand before her, fully exposed. Her bound body starkly contrasts my unrestrained one, a physical representation of the power she grants me with her trust.

I hook my fingers under her bound arms and lift her from the floor. She's so beautiful, her skin flushed, breath quickening as I carry her to the couch.

Lowering her onto the soft cushions, I adjust her positioning, ensuring her arms restrained behind her back are comfortable. I gently draw the back of my hand down her cheek. "Are you doing okay, baby?"

She lets out a shaky breath, her eyes sparkling. "Yes, Master."

The title sends a heat spike through me, and I groan, tightening my grip on her hair. "Say it again."

"Yes, Master," she whispers, her body arching toward me.

The need to claim what's mine pounds through my veins like a war drum. I press her back against the couch, pinning her in place with my weight. Her curves mold against me, soft where I'm hard.

Her legs part for me instinctually, arousal clouding her emerald eyes. I feast on her, my hands drinking in her skin. My cock twitches, begging to be buried inside her wet heat.

My tongue traces the curve of her neck, tasting her pulse. "So fucking wet for me, baby."

"Please, Ty." Her voice breaks. "I need you."

My grin is wicked as I pull back to run my hand over my shaft, teasing myself almost as much as I'm teasing her. "Fuck, I need this, too. I need to feel that sweet pussy clenching down on me."

Her eyes are huge, fixed on my cock as I move into position. "But first, I want to see just how ready that pretty cunt is."

I use the tip of my cock to part her slick folds, a groan tearing from my throat at how good she feels. "You're dripping for me."

"Fuck," she gasps, her bound arms twisting as she tries to get closer. "Ty, now. Please!"

"Impatient, baby girl?" I rub the head of my cock against her clit, drawing a sharp cry from her. "Did you forget who's in charge here?"

"No, Master!" Her hips buck, searching for my cock. "Please, I'm sorry. I need you inside me."

Her pussy clenches as she begs, a sight that has me gripping tight to my control. I want to bury myself balls-deep in that hot cunt and fill her up. But I know that denying her heightens everything. Teasing her to the brink drives us both wild.

I press flat against her, capturing her lips in a searing kiss. Our tongues tangle as I grind the tip of my cock against her clit, swirling it around the swollen bud until she's almost sobbing.

"You like that, baby?" I murmur, nipping at her bottom lip. "Like the pressure?"

"Yes, Master." Her hips writhe against me, shameless in her need. "More. Please, right there."

I pull back, my eyes raking over her as I stroke my

throbbing cock. The tip glistens with pre-cum, the piercing gleaming in the low light. "Look at that pretty clit. All swollen and aching. Bet your body is desperate for my cock, isn't it?"

"Yes." Her breathless answer has my balls drawing up tight.

"Bet you'd love me to suck on those sweet tits." I drag the pierced head of my cock over her clit. "Maybe use my teeth a little. See how much I can make those tight little nipples stand up."

A broken moan tears from her throat, and she moves restlessly beneath me, the ropes keeping her securely in place. "Do it, Master. Please."

The begging has me hard as steel, the piercing rubbing deliciously over my sensitive head as I jerk myself off in front of her. I lean down and graze my teeth over her nipple, then swirl my tongue around the taut bud. She cries out, the sound going straight to my cock.

"Your body is a fucking work of art." I draw back, my eyes devouring her. "Ready to feel how hard I am for you?"

Her eyes flutter closed as her hips lift wantonly. "Yes, Master. Please, now. I need your—"

I don't give her a chance to finish the sentence. Sliding my cock between her folds, I groan as I finally sink into her heat. And the sound from her lips is the most beautiful sound I've ever heard.

18

SOFIA

At Tyson's mercy, I'm bound, helpless. I've never felt anything like this before—not even close. Every muscle in my body is clenched as he relentlessly thrusts into me, his cock piercing, hitting me in the perfect spot over and over.

I feel so full as his hips snap against mine, his hands holding my hips as he pounds into me. The rope of my bindings bites into my skin, but I barely notice as pleasure blazes through me. I'm tossed and turned by the waves of ecstasy he creates with every thrust. All I can do is surrender.

I can feel my orgasm building deep, a pressure that's about to explode when suddenly, he stops.

"No, don't stop!" I whine in protest. "Please... I need..."

The tip of his cock is still lodged inside me, but he's become frustratingly still.

"So close, baby girl," he says. "Tell me what you need."

But I can't form the words. How can I explain this desperate, overpowering need? He knows what he does to me. He knows he owns my pleasure now.

"I can feel how much you want it," he continues, his voice teasing and cruel. "Let me hear your voice telling me what you want, and I'll give it to you."

"I... I need..." I stutter, my brain cloudy with desire. "I need you to move. Please, Ty. Please!"

Instead of moving, he pulls all the way out. "You must address me properly," he says, his voice thick with command. "Say my name, and then tell me what I am to you."

I swallow, my throat dry. "Ty... You're my master."

He growls at that, the sound sending shivers down my spine. "Good girl. And you're my obedient pet."

I nod, unable to speak, my cheeks burning with embarrassment and desire. I feel exposed, but at the same time, a rush of wetness coats my core at his words.

His eyes darken as he sits next to me and lifts me from the couch using the bindings, forcing me to straddle his legs. "Now, I want to watch your beautiful body ride me. Show me how much you want it."

I feel exposed in this position, my arms still bound behind my back. This position means he can see every-thing—every curve, every roll. I try to push those insecurities aside as I lower myself onto his length, but they creep back in as I roll my hips. Even though I'm on top, I know he's still in control.

He takes charge, guiding me with his hands, his grip firm. I moan as he thrusts up into me. His eyes worship my body, admiring my curves. I try to ignore the voice that tells me I should feel self-conscious and instead focus on the pleasure that's building within.

His hard length is so deep inside me, filling me completely. It sends a jolt of pleasure through me. His hands are rough but gentle when he suddenly stills his thrusts.

"Roll your hips. Fuck yourself on my cock," he orders.

I do as he says, moving my hips in a slow, sensual rhythm. His strong thighs flex as he drives to meet each roll, and I gasp as his piercing hits a deep, sensitive spot inside me.

"You're so beautiful like this," he says, his voice appreciative. "So fucking sexy. You take my cock so perfectly, baby."

His filthy words make me want to please him even more. I want to show him I can take all of him and more. I want him to lose control because of me. I pick up the pace, rolling my hips faster despite my arms being restrained, and I feel his hands tighten on me. He meets my rhythm, his powerful hands lifting me up and down as we find a perfect harmony of movement.

His cock slides in and out of me faster now. I feel like I'm on fire, my body burning with a desperate need for release.

"Ty, please..." I whisper, my voice breathless. "Oh God, I need... I need..."

I can't finish my sentence, but he knows.

Just as I'm about to shatter into a million pieces, Tyson stops again. I whimper in frustration.

"No, baby, we're not done yet," he says. "I'm not done teasing you, feeling you clench around me."

I try to protest, to beg him to let me come, but all that escapes my lips is a needy whine. He chuckles at my reaction, that rich, deep laugh I've come to love.

"Don't worry, you will. But first, I want to edge you. When you finally let go and milk my cock with that gorgeous body of yours, it'll be the most powerful orgasm you've ever had."

He kisses me, his lips urgent and demanding and his tongue dominating mine. I can taste myself on him, and it only adds to my arousal. His kiss consumes me, stealing what little breath I have left.

He pulls away, his eyes burning with intensity as he gazes down at me. The need in his eyes mirrors mine, and he brushes a strand of hair from my face, his touch gentle.

"You've no idea how much I've dreamed of this in the last five days, Sofia," he says, his voice rough. "I've wanted to taste you, touch you, feel you squeeze tight around me again. And now that you're mine again, I won't rush."

Then his mouth is on me again, but this time, it's my body he's devouring. He kisses a path down my neck, pausing to nip at the sensitive skin before continuing downward. He teases my breasts with his mouth and hands, laving attention on each creamy swell, his touch almost painful in its delicacy.

I'm squirming, desperate for release, but he refuses to let me climax. His hands ghost over my body, avoiding the places I most want him to touch, and his mouth teases and nips at my skin, making me ache for more.

"Master, please..." I plead, my voice breathless. "I need you inside me."

I can feel how wet I am, how ready my body is for him, but he continues to deny me. His mouth hovers over my core, and I whimper as his warm breath teases me. I tilt my hips toward him, silently begging him to give me what I need, but he just smiles, a devilish grin that melts my insides.

"Soon, baby," he whispers. "But I'm going to make you wait a little longer. I want to taste every inch of you first."

With that, his mouth closes over my center, his tongue flicking and teasing me with expert precision. I cry out, my back arching as sensation after sensation washes over me. He holds me down, his hands gentle but firm, as he feasts on me, his tongue sending bolts of lightning through my body.

I'm so close, hovering on the edge of ecstasy, and yet he continues to hold me back, drawing out my pleasure. "Tyson!" I cry, my voice hoarse. "Oh God, please let me come!"

"Not yet, baby," he murmurs. "It's not time yet." I whimper at the denial, my core aching for release, my body throbbing with need. Ty uses the ropes to lift me, and then I'm straddling his strong thighs, his cock beneath me, hard and insistent, demanding my attention. Every fiber of my being is focused on that thick length, and with a silent plea for forgiveness, I lower myself onto him.

My body welcomes him like a key to a lock, and as he fills me, I can't help but moan. I feel whole again, complete in a way I never knew I could.

19

TYSON

Sofia moves like warm honey, rolling her hips against me as she rides me hard. I sense her orgasm building, and it spurs me on, but I'm not done playing yet—not even close.

I bite my lip, forcing myself to pull out of her and shift her off my lap. Both of us standing, I position her over the arm of the sofa with her feet firmly planted on the floor, her back arched and ass high in the air, inviting me to take what's mine.

I kneel behind her, my eyes locked on her dripping core. With slow, deliberate movements, I tease her swollen clit with my tongue again.

I want to taste all of her. I grip her hips, pulling her closer and spreading her ass cheeks with my thumbs. Then, I dive in, my tongue teasing her asshole.

She tenses before me, unsure of this new sensation. I keep licking, wanting to hear her moan as she gives in to the pleasure. My thumbs press into the soft flesh of her ass, holding her open for me as I feast.

"Relax," I murmur, pushing my tongue into her tight hole. "I'm gonna lick that sweet ass every time I fuck you. Get you nice and ready for when I finally bury my cock deep inside it."

She gasps at my filthy words, her hesitation melting away. I smile against her, knowing that one day, I'll take her here. I'll stretch her out and make her scream as she takes my cock. But for now, her pussy is what I crave.

She's so fucking responsive, it's beautiful to watch. Her skin flushes, her body trembles, and her breath quickens with each kiss and lick. She's putty in my hands.

Standing behind her, I tease my pierced cock against her swollen pussy lips, dragging the tip up and down her slit. She squirms, needing more, but I'm taking my sweet time. Her soft whimpers and pleas only encourage me to keep teasing.

I lean forward. "You like that? You like my cock teasing that sweet little pussy?"

"Please," she breathes. "Please, Master. I need your cock. I'm begging for it."

Hearing her call me Master sends a surge of power through me, and my cock twitches. I love how she yields to me, how she craves me.

I slide my cock between her slippery folds, using my pre-cum as lubrication as I trace slow circles around her clit. "I want you to beg for it, Sofia. Tell me how much you want my cock inside you."

Her voice shakes as she speaks. "I want it so bad, Master. Please fuck me. I need your cock to fill me up."

"You want my thick cock to stretch that tight little

pussy?" I tease, giving her a few shallow thrusts, only sinking the head inside.

"Yes, Master! Please, all of it. I need you so badly."

I grip her hips and pull her onto me, burying my length inside her in one smooth stroke.

I move, my hands gripping her hips as I set a steady, relentless pace.

She's on the edge. Her body is trembling, her breaths are coming in short gasps, and her pussy is clenching around me like a vise. But I'm not done pushing her yet. I want to hear her beg for release.

With each thrust, I spank her ass, leaving a red handprint on her creamy skin.

She throws her head back, her moans filling the room. "Oh, fuck, I'm so close!"

I slow down my thrusts, driving her wild with anticipation. "Not yet, baby girl. I didn't say you could come."

"Please, Master," she whimpers. "I need to come. Please let me."

I smirk, loving how desperate she is. I pull out, letting my cock slip free from her pussy with a lewd sound. She whines at the loss, her eyes wide as she looks back at me over her shoulder.

I give her a predatory smile and grab the ropes to position her on her knees on the floor. She gazes up at me with her lips parted and her chest heaving.

"You want my cock?" I ask.

"Yes, Master," she replies. "Please, let me taste you."

I step closer, my cock heavy and aching. I grip the base, aiming it at her mouth. "Be my good girl and suck it. Show me how much you love my cock."

Her pink tongue darts out, swirling around the head before taking me deep into her warm mouth. She moans around me, her eyes fluttering closed as she bobs her head, taking me in and out. Her lips are soft, her suction perfect, and her enthusiasm fucking beautiful.

I thread my hands into her hair, holding her still as I begin to thrust slowly, fucking her throat. She gags a little, but she takes it like a pro, relaxing her throat and letting me slide down. I pull out, slick with her saliva, and offer, "You're doing so good, baby girl. But I want it deeper. Can you do that?"

Her eyes burn with determination as she nods, licking her lips. She takes a deep breath and goes down on me again, relaxing her throat as she takes me deeper than before. I groan at the sensation of her tight throat squeezing my cock, and I can't help but thrust a little harder, my hips moving in a steady rhythm.

I lift her up in my arms, and she gasps, her eyes widening as I show off my strength. She's not a small woman, and I know her size has made her feel insecure in the past. I want to prove to her just how perfect her body is and how much I crave every inch of it.

I press her back against the wall, loving how she yields to me, her arms restrained behind her back. With a powerful thrust, I slam into her, her wetness welcoming me home.

"You feel so good," I growl, eyes locked on hers.

I pull out slowly, then slam back into her, loving how her eyes roll back in her head at the force of my thrusts. She's so responsive, her body clenching around me, her moans filling the room.

"You like that, Sofia?" I ask, my voice hoarse with desire. "You like being manhandled and fucked hard?"

"Yes, Master," she breathes. "I love it. Please don't stop. Fuck me harder."

I smirk, loving her enthusiasm. I pull her away from the wall, still buried deep inside her, and spin her around. Before she can process what's happening, I bend her over, pressing her upper body against the wall with my hand on her back. Her arms are trapped between our bodies, leaving her completely at my mercy.

I start to move again, my hands gripping her thick hips as I slam into her with force. "You're so wet and tight. This perfect pussy was made to be fucked by me."

She moans, her head falling forward as she takes my cock deep. "Yes, Master. It's yours. All yours."

Her filthy words spur me on, and I begin to move faster, my hips slapping against her ass with each powerful thrust.

"That's it, take it all," I encourage, my hands gripping her hair. "Take my cock, Sofia. Come all over me."

I know she's close, and I'm right there with her. But I want to push her over the edge, so I reach between our bodies, my thumb finding her swollen clit.

As I start to rub circles, she cries out, her body shaking. "Master, I'm gonna come. I can't hold it."

"Come for me," I command. "Let me feel that pussy shatter all over my cock."

At my command, she comes apart, her pussy clenching and squirting around my cock. The feeling is incredible, and I'm so close to the edge, too. Her pussy grips my cock like a vise.

"That's it, baby girl, milk my cock," I growl, my own orgasm building at the amazing sensation of her tightness. "You're gonna make me breed that tight cunt."

Hearing those words pushes her over the edge again. She cries out, her body shaking as she experiences another powerful orgasm. I'm so close now; her pussy is gripping and massaging my cock in the most incredible way.

"Fuck, I'm gonna breed you," I warn, my voice hoarse. "Gonna fill that tight cunt with my cum."

With a few more powerful thrusts, I lose it. "Fuck, yes!" I grunt, my cock twitching as I release deep inside her. "Take it, baby, take all my cum. That's it, let your master breed you."

Sofia shudders and moans. "Yes, Master," she manages to gasp out. "I—I love it. Fill me, breed me. I'm yours, completely."

I shudder at her words, my cock still twitching inside her as I release the last of my cum. Hearing her call me Master, knowing she's mine, sends me a rush of power and satisfaction.

I pull out slowly. As I do, my cum starts to drip out of her, a visual reminder of my claim. I grin, knowing I've marked her, and she won't forget this night anytime soon.

I pull her close, her back against my chest, and wrap my arms around her. "That was incredible," I whisper, nuzzling her hair. "You take my cock so well. Your body was made for me."

She turns her head, her eyes shining as she looks at me over her shoulder. "You're incredible, Master. I—I've never felt pleasure like that before."

I smile, feeling a surge of possessiveness. "You're mine now, Sofia. And I plan to remind you of that every chance I get."

Hearing myself say those words, the reality of my growing obsession hits me. But instead of scaring me off, it only makes me want her more.

I'm drawn to her like a moth to a flame, and I'm starting to realize that I might be willing to risk everything for this woman.

20

SOFIA

I stir awake to the harsh buzz of my phone, wrapped in Tyson's strong arms. After he comforted me and gave me the best orgasm I've ever had in the wake of Paulie being a jackass, I spent three nights in his bed here at the carnival.

The warm cocoon of his body makes me want to ignore the intrusion, but Paulie's name flashes on the screen. My stomach drops. We haven't spoken since the argument.

"Where the fuck are you?" Paulie's voice cuts through the peaceful morning.

I ease out of Tyson's embrace, careful not to wake him. "I stayed at Sasha's last night." The lie rolls off my tongue with practiced ease. "Just heading home now."

"Sasha's?" His tone drips with suspicion. "She'll back that up if I ask?"

A smile tugs at my lips. Sasha's been covering for me since we were teenagers sneaking out to parties. She'd lie to the devil himself if it meant protecting me.

"Of course, she will. You can call her right now if you want."

"And what about what we discussed. I told you to tell me when you stay somewhere other than your home."

I grind my teeth. "Considering the last time we spoke, we had a fucking row, I didn't think to notify you."

"Whatever," he grunts and hangs up.

I let out a breath I didn't realize I was holding.

"Everything okay, baby girl?" Tyson's sleep-rough voice sends shivers down my spine.

I turn to find him watching me through heavy-lidded eyes, his chest bare and inviting. Seeing him makes me want to crawl back into bed and forget about the rest of the world.

I sink back onto the bed beside him, his warmth drawing me in. My fingers trace the hard planes of his chest, remembering how his muscles flexed beneath my touch last night.

"Just Paulie being Paulie," I mutter, but the name tastes bitter on my tongue now.

Tyson pulls me closer, and I breathe in his scent—a mix of leather and something uniquely him. "You deserve better than that snake."

He's right. Last night, Tyson worshipped every curve, every soft edge of my body. His hands claimed me with reverence, not criticism.

"The way you look at me..." I trace one of his tattoos. "No one's ever made me feel so beautiful."

"Because you are beautiful." His fingers thread through my hair. "Every gorgeous inch of you."

I think about Paulie's cold touches and his mechanical kisses. There's no fire like Tyson ignites in me. Where Paulie demands I change, Tyson celebrates who I am. The arranged marriage my father set up feels more suffocating than ever.

"You make me feel alive," I whisper against his skin. "Like I can be myself without apologizing."

His arms tighten around me. "That's exactly who I want you to be. No pretending. No hiding."

The truth of his words settles deep in my chest. With Tyson, I don't have to be Jimmy Moretti's perfect daughter or Paulie's proper wife-to-be. I can just be Sofia, curves and all, and that's exactly what I want.

I pull away from Tyson's warmth, reality crashing back like a bucket of ice water. "We can't keep doing this."

"Why not, baby girl?"

"Because you'll end up dead." I sit up, wrapping the sheet around myself. "If my father found out, he'd have you killed. And if not him, then Paulie would do it himself. They don't share what they consider theirs."

Tyson's laugh surprises me. Deep and rich, completely unfazed by my warning. "You underestimate me, Sofia. I've been in this game longer than you think. I'm not that easy to kill."

"What do you mean?"

"I'm thirty-eight. Been running things since before you were legal."

I whip around to face him. "Thirty-eight? But I thought..." My eyes trace over his face, searching for signs I missed. Sure, there are subtle lines around his eyes when he smiles, but nothing that tells me he's in his late thirties.

"Thought I was closer to your age?" His fingers brush my cheek. "Does it bother you?"

"I'm twenty-six," I say, still processing. "And no, it doesn't bother me. I just... you don't look thirty-eight."

"Good genes." His cocky grin returns. "But more importantly, I've survived this long because I know how to handle myself. Your father and Paulie aren't the only ones with connections."

I trace my fingers over the sheet, lost in thought. "Every night with you is better than the last. And I love that you don't monitor what I eat, but this can't continue. We're kidding ourselves."

Tyson's hand slides over mine. "I'd never monitor what you eat. I want you to be real with me. No pretending, no counting calories."

My chest tightens with the admission. "With you, everything feels so free and unrestrained."

But freedom comes with a price. I've seen what happens to people who cross my father. The memory of my father's former associate's "disappearance" sends a chill down my spine.

"I can't let anything happen to you." The words catch in my throat. "My father... The things he's capable of..."

"And what about what you're capable of?" Tyson questions. "You're stronger than you think, baby girl. The real you, not the perfect daughter act."

He's right. With him, I feel alive for the first time in years. No judgment, no expectations. Just me, being exactly who I wanted to be. The carnival I'd initially turned my nose up at became a haven of freedom. Even now, the memory of walking with Tyson through the twinkling lights makes my heart race.

"I want to choose my own life," I whisper, more to myself than him. "I'm tired of being told who to be, what to eat, how to act. But wanting something and having the courage to take it are two different things."

His fingers trace my jaw, tilting my face to meet his gaze. "You're not some delicate flower that needs protecting. I've seen your fire, your strength. The way you stood up to me when we first met? That's who you really are."

My heart stutters at his words. No one's ever spoken to me like this before. Even Sasha, bless her heart, treats me like I need saving from my family, Tyson, and myself.

"But my best friend said—"

"What? That I'm dangerous?" His thumb brushes across my bottom lip. "I won't deny I pursued you hard. But that's because I saw past the mask you wear for everyone else. I saw you."

Tears prick at my eyes. He's right. From that first confrontation in the carnival, he's been the only one to challenge me, to push back against my walls instead of trying to shelter me behind them.

"You think I'm strong?" My voice comes out smaller than I intended.

"I know you are. The question is, do you believe it?"

I think about how everyone in my life treats me—Dad's overprotective control, Paulie's constant criticism, even Sasha's well-meaning concern. They all see me as something to be managed, fixed, or saved.

But Tyson? He sees me as an equal. Yes, he's intense. Yes, his pursuit of me bordered on obsessive. But he's never once tried to change me or cage me. He wants me exactly as I am—curves and attitude.

"Maybe I am strong enough," I whisper, leaning into his touch. "I've never had anyone believe in me like this before."

His eyes darken with something fierce and protective but not suffocating like Dad's protection. This feels like having someone at my back, supporting me, not trying to direct my path.

"Then believe in yourself like I believe in you. You're not just Jimmy Moretti's daughter or Paulie's fiancée. You're Sofia. And that's more than enough."

I stand up from the bed, letting the sheet fall away as I gather my clothes. My hands are steady as I slip my dress back on, no longer feeling the shame or uncertainty from before.

"I'm done living by everyone else's rules," I say, turning to face Tyson. "Done letting Dad control my life, done letting Paulie tear me down. I'm taking back control."

Tyson watches me from the bed, a mix of pride and desire in his eyes. "That's my girl."

"I mean it." I smooth my dress, checking my reflection in his small trailer mirror. "I'm going to tell Dad I won't marry Paulie. I don't care about the business alliance or his other reasons. It's my life."

"Come here." Tyson beckons me over. When I reach

him, he pulls me down for a kiss that makes my toes curl. His lips are firm against mine, possessive but not controlling. When we break apart, he rests his forehead against mine. "Show them who you really are, baby girl."

I grab my purse and phone, squaring my shoulders. "I will. No more perfect daughter act. No more letting them decide my future."

Tyson's kiss still burns on my lips as I head for the trailer door. My heart pounds, but not from fear—from excitement. For the first time in my life, I feel truly powerful, truly in control.

21

TYSON

Lars bursts through the door without knocking while I'm hunched over paperwork in my trailer. My head snaps up, ready to tear into him for the interruption, but the look on his face stops me cold.

"Boss, we got trouble. Paulie's here, causing a scene by the main tent."

My blood runs ice-cold. Sofia left this morning with fire in her eyes, talking about taking control of her life. Did she go straight to that piece of shit and tell him about us?

"What kind of scene?" I rise from my chair, already reaching for my jacket.

"He's throwing shit around, demanding to see you." Lars blocks the doorway. "You want me to handle it?"

"No." My jaw clenches. "I'll deal with this myself."

My mind races through the possibilities. If Sofia told him everything, this could blow up our whole operation. Jimmy Moretti finding out I've fucked his daughter—his engaged daughter—could destroy everything we've built. And yet, I don't care. All I care about is Sofia taking back control of her own fucking life.

"Get Nash and Colt to clear the area," I order Lars as I check my phone and find Sofia still hasn't replied to my earlier message. "Keep the civilians away. The last thing we need is witnesses if this goes south."

Lars nods and disappears. I take a deep breath, steadying myself. The memory of Sofia in my bed this morning, her red hair spread across my pillow, her curves pressed against me—I push it aside. I need a clear head for whatever's coming.

I step out of my trailer into the sun, heading toward the sound of breaking glass and shouting. Whatever Paulie knows or doesn't know, I'm not letting him destroy what Sofia and I have started. She's mine now, whether he likes it or not.

I stalk toward the main tent, my hands already curling into fists. The familiar weight of my knife presses against my ankle, and for once, I don't try to push down the darkness rising inside me.

Sofia is worth any price. Worth burning everything to the ground. Worth killing her piece of shit fiancé, worth taking down Jimmy himself if that's what it takes. The thought should scare me—Jimmy Moretti isn't someone you cross lightly. But all I feel is cold certainty.

I'll risk my empire, my freedom, and my life because the alternative is letting her go, and that's not happening —not now, not ever.

Movement catches my eye. Paulie spots me through the gathering crowd, his face twisted with rage. He shoves past a couple of carnival workers, sending popcorn flying. His expensive suit is wrinkled, tie askew—he looks unhinged.

"You motherfucker!" He charges toward me like a bull, face red with fury.

Turning, I walk into the big top, needing to keep this private. Paulie follows me, and once inside, I turn to face him, letting a slow smile spread across my face. This is it, then. Whatever he knows, whatever Sofia told him—One way or another, Paulie won't be a problem after today.

My fingers twitch to grab my gun at my waist, but I force them still. Not yet. Let him make the first move. Let him give me the excuse I need to end him.

"What seems to be the problem?" I keep my voice level, watching him with cold amusement. Nash and Colt linger near the entryway, leaving just me, Lars, and Paulie in the main tent.

Paulie's face contorts as he gets in mine. His breath reeks of expensive scotch. "You fucked my girl, you piece of shit carnie trash. You're a dead man."

I arch an eyebrow, maintaining my calm despite the rage building inside me at hearing him refer to Sofia as 'his girl.' She's not his anything. Not anymore.

"That's quite an accusation." I keep my hands loose at my sides, ready. "Got any proof?"

"Don't play dumb with me." Spittle flies from his mouth. "I know all about your little late-night meetings. Did you think I wouldn't find out? In my town?"

I notice Lars shifting closer, hand inside his jacket. I give him a subtle shake of my head. This is my fight.

"Your town?" I laugh, the sound sharp and hollow. "Funny. Last I checked, this was Jimmy Moretti's town. You're just the errand boy he's trying to marry his daughter off to."

Paulie's face goes purple. "You're fucking dead." His hand moves toward his waistband. "I'm going to put you in the ground myself."

I don't hesitate, grabbing my gun and firing before he can reach his. The shot echoes through the tent as Paulie crumples, a look of shock frozen on his face.

"Fuck," Lars swears beside me. "This is really bad, boss."

Movement catches my eye as two of Paulie's men burst through the tent flap, weapons already drawn. But we're ready. Lars, Nash, and Colt have their guns trained on them before they can get off a shot.

"Drop them," I order, my voice ice cold as I keep my gun steady. "Unless you want to join your boss."

The goons exchange glances, clearly weighing their options. Four guns against two isn't great odds.

"Now," I bark, taking a step forward. "On your knees, hands behind your heads."

They comply slowly, weapons clattering to the ground. Nash moves in swiftly to kick their guns away while Colt covers him.

"Don't even think about moving," Lars warns them as he secures their weapons. "Your next breath depends on how still you can stay."

I look down at Paulie's body, my mind already racing through the implications. Jimmy Moretti's future son-in-law lying dead in my carnival tent. This is going to require some careful handling.

I keep my gun trained on Paulie's men while checking his pulse. Dead. No going back now.

"Get their phones," I order Lars, who pats them down efficiently. "And their wallets. I want to know exactly who we're dealing with."

Nash and Colt move in perfect sync, zip-tying the men's hands behind their backs. One starts to protest, but Colt's fist connects with his jaw before he can get a word out.

"That empty trailer behind the Ferris wheel," I tell them, holstering my weapon. "Make sure they're secured and unconscious. We might need them later when Jimmy comes looking for answers."

Lars hands me their phones and wallets. "What about him?" He nods toward Paulie's body.

"We'll deal with that next. First, get these two somewhere they won't be found." I flip through one of the wallets, memorizing the details. "Check them for tracking devices or anything that could give away their location."

Nash and Colt haul the men to their feet. One tries to resist, but Nash twists his arm until he whimpers.

"Move," Colt growls, shoving them forward.

I watch them disappear through the tent flap, then turn to Lars. "Get Phoenix. We need to start damage control now."

"You think Jimmy will believe Paulie shot first?"

"He better." I glance at the body cooling on my

carnival floor. "Because if he doesn't, we'll need every bargaining chip we can get."

Lars nods and pulls out his phone while I plan our next move. Having Paulie's men as leverage might make the difference between survival and all-out war with the Moretti family. The family of the woman I'm obsessed with.

22

SOFIA

I smooth my dress and take a deep breath before entering Dad's study. The familiar scent of leather and cigars fills my nose as I find him behind his massive mahogany desk.

"Daddy, I need to talk to you about the wedding."

He looks up from his paperwork, steel gray eyes fixing on mine. "What about it?"

"I can't marry Paulie." My voice cracks. "I'm not happy with him. He's cruel and controlling, and I deserve better."

Dad's jaw tightens. "This isn't about happiness, Sofia. It's about family, about business. The wedding goes ahead as planned."

Tears spill down my cheeks. "But I don't love him! I... I have feelings for someone else."

"What did you just say?" His voice drops dangerously low.

I wrap my arms around myself, shoulders shaking. "There's someone else."

"Who?" When I hesitate, he slams his palm on the desk. "Tell me who!"

"Tyson," I whisper. "The carnival ringmaster."

Dad's face turns purple with rage. He stands so fast that his chair crashes against the wall. "A carnival worker? Have you lost your mind? You're a Moretti! You're better than some piece of carnie trash!"

"He's not trash! He's kind and makes me feel—"

"Enough!" Dad roars. "No daughter of mine will throw away everything for some circus freak. You will marry Paulie, and that's final." He stands and moves toward me, eyes ablaze with fury.

I stumble back from Dad's desk, my vision blurred by tears. All these years, I thought he actually cared about my happiness. Every time he bought me presents, every moment he seemed proud of my achievements—was it all just because I was his perfect little puppet?

My throat tightens as memories flash through my mind of him teaching me to ride a bike. Holding my hand at Mom's funeral. Cheering the loudest at my dance recitals. How could that same man now look at me with such cold, calculating eyes?

"I'm your daughter," I choke out. "Doesn't that mean anything?"

"It means everything." His voice cuts like ice. "Which is exactly why you'll do as you're told. The Moretti name comes with responsibilities."

The weight of his words crushes my chest. I wrap my arms around myself, trying to hold the pieces together as my world crumbles. All those times I defended him to others, insisted he was different from other mob bosses because he loved his family first—I was just fooling myself.

"I thought..." My voice breaks. "I thought you wanted me to be happy."

"Happiness?" He scoffs. "You think your mother was happy when we first married? She learned to be content, just like you will."

That strikes deep. Mom always told me to follow my heart and never settle. Now I wonder if those private conversations were her way of trying to save me from her own fate.

Tears blur my vision as Dad's words about Mom cut deep. The familiar ache in my chest returns—the same hollow feeling I've carried since that rainy Tuesday morning when I found her fourteen years ago.

Mom had always struggled with depression, but none of us saw the signs getting worse. She hid her pain behind perfect makeup and designer clothes, just like Dad wanted. The perfect mob wife on the outside. But inside, she was drowning.

I was twelve when I discovered her in the master bathroom, empty pill bottles scattered across the marble counter. Her final note read: "I'm sorry I wasn't strong enough. Be braver than me, my sweet girl."

Dad never spoke about it. He packed away her photos and donated her clothes and expected me to bounce back just as quickly. He'd send the housekeeper to check on me when I cried myself to sleep at night instead of coming himself. His solution was to shower me with expensive gifts—as if diamonds could fill the void Mom left behind.

"Your mother understood duty," Dad continues now, his words reopening old wounds. "She knew what it meant to be a Moretti."

My hands clench into fists. "Mom killed herself because of that 'duty.' Because you forced her to be someone she wasn't, just like you're doing to me."

The truth I've never dared speak hangs heavy between us. Mom's death shaped everything—my relationship with Dad, my fears about marriage, my desperate need for genuine connection. She taught me through her absence that living a lie slowly kills your soul.

I touch the delicate gold locket around my neck—the last birthday gift she gave me. Inside is a tiny photo of us laughing together at the beach, back when her smile still reached her eyes before Dad's world of control and appearances consumed her entirely.

"I won't end up like Mom," I whisper, more to myself than to him. "I won't let this life destroy me, too."

Something flickers in his eyes for a moment—pain, regret maybe—but it's gone so fast I might have imagined it. The mask of the mob boss slides back into place, and my daddy disappears completely.

He grabs my arm forcefully. "This foolishness ends here."

"I won't marry him!" I try to wrench my arm away from Dad's grip. "You can't force me!"

"The hell I can't." Dad grabs me again, his fingers

digging into my flesh. "I've given you everything. This is how you repay me?"

"By being honest?" I try to pull away again. "By telling you what I want?"

"What you want?" He laughs humorlessly. "You're my daughter. Everything you are belongs to me."

"No!" I slam my fist against his chest. "I'm not your property!"

Dad drags me across the study, my heels scraping against the hardwood floor. I fight him every step down the hallway to my childhood bedroom, but his grip is iron. Once we reach the door, he grabs my cell phone from my jeans pocket and pushes me inside.

"You'll stay here until you remember who you are. Until you come to your senses."

I rush for the door, but he slams it shut. The lock clicks.

"Daddy, please!" I pound my fists against the wood. "Don't do this!"

He ignores my pleas. Through my tears, I hear him pull out his phone and dial.

"Paulie? Yeah, we've got a problem." Dad's voice carries through the door. "That carnival trash has been sniffing around my daughter and your fiancée... Yeah, the ringmaster... Tyson."

"No!" I slam harder against the door. "Daddy, stop!"

"Handle it," Dad continues. "Make him disappear. Permanently."

I slide down the door, my sobs wracking my body. "Please don't hurt him! Please!"

"Keep it clean," Dad says into the phone. "No traces."

My screams echo through the room as I hear Dad's footsteps fade away down the hall, leaving me locked in my gilded prison. At the same time, he orders the death of the only man who's ever made me feel truly alive.

23

TYSON

The stench of blood still clings to my nostrils, even after changing. My phone sits silent on the desk, mocking me with its blank screen. No messages from Sofia.

"Fuck!" I slam my fist into the wall. The pain grounds me, but barely.

How did Paulie find out? The question circles my mind like a vulture. Sofia wouldn't have told him. Would she? No. She hates that abusive piece of shit as much as I do.

I grab my phone again and type another message:

> Baby girl, please. Just let me know you're safe.

Nothing.

I'm hunched over my desk, staring at spreadsheets that might as well be written in Sanskrit, when Phoenix raps on my door.

"Come in."

He slips inside, laptop tucked under his arm. Dark circles shadow his eyes, suggesting he's been up all night working.

"Got some intel about Sofia's place," Phoenix says, setting up his equipment. "Finally cracked back into her iMac."

My head snaps up. "And?"

"She had it wiped clean. Took me hours to get back in." He runs a hand through his messy hair. "But that's not all. The computer's facing the wall now."

My jaw clenches. She must have moved it after I told her about watching her. Admitting that was a stupid mistake.

"Any activity?" I grip the edge of my desk.

Phoenix shakes his head. "No login attempts, no keyboard clicks. I've also been monitoring the house through the mic—complete silence."

Ice floods my veins. "How long?"

"Two days now."

"Fuck." I push away from my desk, pacing the small space. Two days of silence. Two days since Jimmy found out about us. Two days since Paulie's men left here in body bags.

My fingers itch to call her again, but I know her phone will ring endlessly into the void. Jimmy must have her locked away somewhere. I can feel it in my gut.

I run my hand over my jaw, stubble scratching my palm. "What about other devices? Her iMac must be linked to something else."

Phoenix sits at my desk, his fingers dancing across his tablet screen. "She's got quite the digital footprint:

three iPhones, two iPads, a MacBook Pro, even an older iMac." He squints at the screen. "The problem is I can't tell which ones are still active. Some might be sitting in a drawer somewhere."

"Try them all." I lean over his shoulder, scanning the list of devices. "Every single one. I need to know she's okay."

"I'm already on it." Phoenix's typing speeds up. "But breaking Apple's encryption isn't exactly quick. It will likely take hours."

"I don't care how long it takes." My voice comes out rougher than intended. "Just find her."

Phoenix nods, not looking up from his screen. "I'll start with her most recently active devices first. The iPhone's probably our best bet, assuming Jimmy hasn't confiscated it."

"And if he has?"

"Then we move down the list until something hits." He pulls up another window filled with code. "Even old devices might give us a breadcrumb trail. Social media logins, cloud backups, location history—anything that could point us to where Jimmy's keeping her."

I grip the back of the chair, watching strings of numbers and letters flash across the screen. Each second feels like an eternity, knowing Sofia could be anywhere, trapped and alone.

I pace behind Phoenix like a caged animal, my breath hot on his neck as I watch him work. Every keystroke seems to take an eternity.

"Boss, if you don't back off, I'm taking this back to my trailer," Phoenix mutters, his fingers flying across the screen. "Can't concentrate with you breathing down my neck."

"Just work faster." I grip the back of his chair, knuckles white.

A smirk plays at the corner of his mouth. "Never seen you this worked up over a girl before. The mighty Tyson, brought low by a redhead."

"Shut your fucking mouth." Heat rises in my chest. "This isn't funny."

"Reminds me of when I first spotted Tilly." Phoenix's typing slows, his voice taking on a distant quality. "Couldn't eat, couldn't sleep. Just had to know everything about her. Had to have her."

"I said shut up." I slam my hand on the desk, making him jump. "This isn't the same thing."

"No?" Phoenix raises an eyebrow, finally looking up at me. "You're stalking her through cameras, obsessing over her every move, ready to tear apart anyone who gets between you. Sound familiar?"

The truth in his words stings. "Focus on finding her."

"Just saying, I recognize that look in your eyes." Phoenix turns back to his screen. "It's the same one I see in the mirror every morning."

I slam my palms against my desk, rage boiling through my veins at Phoenix's words. His smugness about keeping Tilly locked away in his trailer sets my teeth on edge. This obsession with Sofia—it's different. It has to be.

"And I've had Tilly for over a month now. Nothing can tame it." Phoenix's voice drips with satisfaction.

"Even when she's yours, you'll still be driven mad by it."

"I need some fucking air," I growl, pushing away from the desk. The metal legs screech against the floor as I storm toward the door.

Phoenix's amused chuckles follow me out of the trailer, making my hands clench into fists. The sound echoes in my ears as I march across the carnival grounds, past the silent rides and empty food stalls.

I slump against the side of my trailer, lighting a cigarette with trembling hands despite quitting two years ago. I'm too stressed right now, but the nicotine does nothing to calm my racing thoughts.

What the fuck is wrong with me? I've never lost control like this over a woman. I've had my share of conquests—carnival groupies and local girls looking for a thrill. One night, maybe two, if they were particularly skilled. But never this... this constant ache.

Sofia's got under my skin in ways I can't explain. Her curves, her sass, the way she challenges me instead of just falling at my feet like the others. Even now, I can feel the phantom touch of her soft skin against mine, taste the sweetness of her lips.

"Fuck." I take another long drag, watching the smoke curl into the night air.

The smart move would be to let her go. Cut ties and focus on business. Jimmy Moretti's wrath isn't something to take lightly, and I've got the whole carnival operation to consider. My crew depends on me to keep things running smoothly.

But the thought of never seeing her again, never

holding her, tears at something deep in my chest—something I didn't even know existed until she walked into my life.

Phoenix is right. I'm acting just like him with Tilly. Obsessed. Unhinged. The kind of man I swore I'd never become. Love makes you weak, makes you vulnerable. I learned that lesson watching my old man destroy himself over my mother.

I take another drag of my cigarette, memories of my old man flooding back. That pathetic shell of a man drowning himself in whiskey after my mother left. I was twelve when she packed her bags, leaving nothing but her wedding ring on the kitchen counter.

"She'll come back," he'd slur, night after night. "Your mother loves us. She's just... confused."

Bullshit. Mom wasn't confused. She was tired of his weakness, his desperate need for her. I watched him waste away, calling her number until it was disconnected, driving past her sister's house, hoping to catch a glimpse of her.

He put his fist through the wall the day we got the news she'd remarried. I still remember the blood dripping from his knuckles as he sobbed on the kitchen floor. That was the moment I swore I'd never let a woman have that kind of power over me.

"Love is a fucking poison, son," he told me that night, his eyes glazed from the bourbon. "It gets in your blood, makes you forget who you are. Makes you weak."

He was right about one thing—it is a poison. I can feel it coursing through my veins whenever I think about Sofia. But he was wrong about the weakness part. This thing with Sofia... it's not making me weak. It's making me dangerous. Making me willing to burn everything down just to keep her.

My old man died alone in that house, still wearing his wedding ring, still keeping her picture on his nightstand. The doctors called it liver failure, but I know what really killed him. He let love destroy him, let it eat away at his soul until there was nothing left.

Yet here I am, ready to risk everything, my business, my freedom, maybe even my life—just to keep Sofia safe. To make her mine.

I crush the cigarette under my boot, disgust rising in my throat. When did I become this pathetic? This desperate?

The night offers no answers, just the distant sound of carnival music and my tortured thoughts.

24

SOFIA

I jolt awake, my heart racing. Tyson's deep voice echoes in my ears, but that's impossible. Dad's locked me in my childhood bedroom like some fairytale princess. I rub my eyes, trying to shake off the lingering dream.

A faint blue glow catches my attention. My old iMac sits on the desk, its screen illuminating the darkness. My breath catches when I see Tyson's face filling the screen.

"Baby girl," his voice comes through clear as day.

I leap out of bed, not caring that I only wear a black lace bra and matching panties. The wooden floor is cold under my bare feet as I rush to the desk.

"Tyson? How did you—"

"Phoenix hacked your old computer. Are you okay? Has your father hurt you?"

His concern warms my chest. I lean closer to the screen, drinking in the sight of him. Even through the pixelated video, his presence makes my skin tingle with awareness.

"I'm fine. Just locked up until I 'come to my senses' about marrying Paulie." I wrap my arms around myself, suddenly aware of how naked I am. "Dad's men are everywhere. There's no way out."

My heart skips a beat. "What do you mean?"

"Let's just say Paulie won't be body-shaming anyone else ever again, baby girl. He's not breathing anymore." Tyson's voice carries a dangerous edge that should terrify me.

But it doesn't.

A shiver runs through me—not of fear, but of something darker, more primal. Heat pools in my belly as I process his words. The man who made me feel worthless, who constantly criticized my curves and told me I needed to lose weight... he's gone.

I should be horrified. Instead, my skin flushes with arousal. My nipples tighten against the lace of my bra.

"You killed him?" The words come out breathy, almost like a moan.

"He threatened what's mine." Tyson's eyes darken through the screen. "Nobody gets to make you feel less than perfect, Sofia. Nobody gets to hurt what belongs to me."

My thighs clench together at his possessive tone. This dangerous man eliminated someone who hurt me and made me doubt myself. The thought should repulse me, but instead, it makes me want to climb through the screen and straddle him.

"You're not scared, are you?" His voice drops lower, knowing exactly what effect he has on me.

"No," I whisper, trailing my fingers down my stomach. "I should be, but... God help me, Tyson, it's turning me on."

I watch Tyson's expression change through the screen, his eyes darkening with desire. My fingers hover at the waistband of my panties, teasing.

"Fuck, baby girl. Nothing would make me harder than watching you touch yourself right now." His groan sends shivers down my spine. "But we can't risk your dad walking in and taking away our only way to talk."

I shake my head, leaning closer to the screen. "I haven't seen him in over two days, not since I told him about us. The maids bring my meals and leave them outside the door. He won't even look at me."

My heart aches at the admission. Dad's always been controlling, but this silent treatment cuts deeper than any of his threats or angry outbursts. The last time I saw him, his face had turned purple with rage when I confessed my feelings for Tyson.

"His goons patrol outside my bedroom window, ensuring I stay put."

"Then give me a fucking show, Sofia. Show me what you do when you're alone and thinking of me." His voice deepens, taking on that commanding tone that makes my knees weak.

My breath quickens. I know what he's asking. I shift on the chair, biting my lip as I reposition myself so the camera has a perfect view of my bare core. My skin feels hot, the ache between my legs growing with each passing second.

"Are you ready for your show, Ty?" I ask, my voice husky.

"Always, baby girl."

I watch his broad shoulders shift as he adjusts in the chair, his movements deliberate and full of promise. He wheels his chair back, stopping only when I have a clear view of his cock—the one I've fantasized about since our first time. I bite my lip, my eyes widening at his thickness and the magic cross piercing.

"Touch yourself, Ty."

He wraps his hand around his length, giving a slow stroke as he moans.

I can't help but reach down, my fingers sliding between my folds as I mimic his movements. The sensation sends sparks through me, igniting the fire that's been burning since the moment I saw him.

"Ah, fuck, Sofia. Feels so good, baby. Stroke your pretty cunt for me." His demand rips a moan from my throat, and I do as he says, the muscles in my stomach tightening with each touch.

"Good girl," he rasps. "Keep going. Faster now, baby girl."

His words push me further, and I comply, my breath coming in short gasps as my fingers work faster. I lean back, throwing my head to the side, exposing my neck as my hips rock instinctively to meet my rhythm.

"That's it, Sofia. Let go for me. I want you to come, baby girl."

His husky words and the sight of his hard, straining cock push me over the edge. My head falls back, my hand moving frantically as I call out his name.

My eyes fly open as I climax, my body tightening with waves of pleasure. Through the screen, I see

Tyson's hand moving faster, his face twisted in ecstasy as he chases his own release.

"Come with me, Ty," I whisper, my body still trembling.

With a final groan, he spills himself over his bare stomach, his face a mask of pleasure.

"Fuck, baby girl. That was fucking beautiful." His breath comes in heavy gasps, his eyes never leaving the screen or me.

I smile, feeling a rush of power at seeing this powerful man undone by me. "That's what you do to me, Ty."

For a moment, we stay connected through the screen, our chests heaving as we revel in the aftermath of our shared pleasure.

I wipe the sweat from my forehead, still catching my breath from our intense video call. Tyson's eyes burn with determination through the screen.

"Now, let's talk about how I'm getting you the fuck out of there so I can bury my cock in you for real, where it belongs."

I shake my head, reality crashing back down. "It's impossible, Ty. Dad's men are everywhere. The house is like a fortress – armed guards at every exit and cameras on every corner. I can't even open my window without someone spotting me."

"Nothing is impossible," Tyson growls, his jaw clenching. "I'll tear the fucking city to the ground if that's what it takes to get you back in my arms."

My heart skips at his words. The intensity in his eyes tells me he means every word, which should terrify me.

Instead, it fills me with a warmth I've never known to be worth fighting for.

I glance at my bedroom door, thinking of the guards posted outside. Of my father's iron grip on this city. Of all the walls and obstacles between Tyson and me.

But when I look back at his face on my screen, I see something that makes all those barriers seem paper-thin: pure, unstoppable determination.

25

TYSON

My jaw clenches tight as I look at my most trusted crew. Lars leans against the wall, arms crossed. Nash and Colt stand shoulder to shoulder, synchronized energy crackling with tension. Phoenix sits at my desk, fingers flying over my keyboard, while Gage looms in the darkest corner, that skull mask revealing nothing.

"We're storming Jimmy Moretti's mansion tonight," I announce, planting my hands on the desk. "I'm getting Sofia out of there."

"You've lost your fucking mind." Lars pushes off the wall. "That's suicide, Ty. Jimmy's got an army."

"He's right." Colt steps forward. "We're good, but we're not that good. Jimmy's got eyes everywhere."

Nash shakes his head. "The carnival's our cover. If we blow this, everything we've built. Years of work, gone."

"You think I don't know that?" I slam my fist on the

desk. "She's trapped in there because of me. Because I couldn't stay away."

"Then maybe you should've thought about that before getting involved with a mob boss's daughter," Lars snaps.

I lock eyes with each of them. "I'm not asking for permission. I'm telling you what's happening. You're either with me or against me."

Phoenix's typing never falters, but his silence speaks volumes. He knows every security system and every camera angle. We'll need him.

Gage hasn't moved an inch, that mask hiding whatever thoughts churn behind it. But I know he'll come. He lives for chaos like this.

"Jimmy trusts us," Nash tries one last time. "We've built that relationship for years."

"And now I'm going to destroy it." I straighten up. "Because he locked away his daughter like she's property. Because he'd rather see her miserable than with me."

Lars runs a hand through his hair. "This is going to start a war."

I let their concerns wash over me as a plan crystallizes. "Phoenix, pull up the blueprints for Jimmy's security system."

The screen flickers to life, showing detailed schematics. I trace the outline with my finger. "There's something Jimmy values more than his daughter or his pride—his reputation."

Lars raises an eyebrow. "What are you thinking?"

"We've got evidence of every deal he's made with us.

Every dirty transaction, everybody we've buried." I tap my fingers on the desk. "Phoenix has been documenting it all."

"Blackmail?" Nash's lips curve into an appreciative smile.

"Better. Insurance." I straighten up. "We leak just enough to make him nervous. Then I walk in alone, unarmed. Show him I'm not there for war."

"He could just kill you," Lars points out.

"He won't. Because the moment anything happens to me, everything goes public. His empire crumbles." I turn to Phoenix. "Set it up so if I don't check in every hour, it drops automatically."

"Consider it done." Phoenix's fingers dance across the keyboard.

"Jimmy's smart. He'll see reason." I roll my shoulders. "He loses his daughter but keeps his empire. Or he loses everything trying to keep her caged."

"And our business with him?" Colt asks.

"We've got other clients in Dawsbury. And all over the fucking state and neighboring states. Jimmy may be big here, but we've got the Blackwood brothers, who are still our biggest clients." I meet their gazes one by one. "This isn't about business. It's about Sofia."

Lars nods. "No bloodshed. No war. Just leverage."

"Exactly. Jimmy's a businessman first. He'll make the smart play." I check my watch. "Phoenix, start the countdown. If I don't make contact, I want those files ready to drop in two hours."

"At least let us wait outside," Nash says, his usual

grace replaced with tension. "You shouldn't go in completely alone."

I shake my head. "The whole point is to show Jimmy I'm not there for war."

Colt steps closer, his muscled frame blocking my path. "Having backup doesn't mean starting a war. It means making sure you walk out alive."

"He's right," Nash adds. "We can stay in the shadows. Jimmy won't even know we're there unless things go south."

I run a hand through my hair, knowing they have a point. The thought of Sofia keeps me focused, but they're not wrong about needing a safety net. "Fine. But you stay completely out of sight."

Phoenix's chair scrapes against the floor as he stands, reaching into a drawer. "Here." He pulls out several small earpieces. "Latest tech. Clear sound, encrypted channel. You'll be able to hear everything happening inside, and Ty can signal if he needs help."

I take one of the devices, studying the sleek design. "These are new."

"Been working on them." Phoenix hands the others to Nash and Colt. "Range is good for about half a mile."

I slip the earpiece in, and the fit is perfect. "Testing."

"Crystal clear," Nash's voice comes through the earpiece.

"Let's move." I grab my keys. "Time's ticking on those files. And Lars, you step in for me tonight for the show, got it?"

Lars nods in reply. He's the only one with the charm

to pull it off. And he's already filled in for me countless times.

We head out to my Mustang, the muscle car gleaming under the carnival lights. Nash and Colt slide into the back while I take the wheel. I can't help but think how different this drive might be from the return journey.

I guide my Mustang through the quiet streets of Dawsbury, the engine's purr matching my heartbeat. The further we get from the carnival's neon glow, the more residential mansions appear. Jimmy's neighborhood reeks of old money and power.

"There it is," I murmur, spotting the wrought iron gates of Jimmy's estate. I ease the car to a stop behind a row of trees about two hundred yards from the entrance.

Nash leans forward between the seats. "Those cameras sweep the perimeter every thirty seconds."

"Guards change rotation every two hours," Colt adds. "Phoenix sent the schedule to our phones."

I kill the engine and turn to face them. "Stay in the car. I mean it."

"Let us at least check the grounds." Colt's jaw sets stubbornly. "Find the weak spots in case you need backup."

Nash nods. "We can stay invisible, map out entry points and blind spots in their security. Could make the difference if things go wrong in there."

I drum my fingers on the steering wheel, weighing the risks. Having a solid escape plan wouldn't hurt.

"Fine. But stay out of sight. If anyone spots you, this whole thing falls apart."

"We know how to move without being seen." Nash's voice carries that quiet confidence I've come to rely on.

"Like ghosts," Colt adds with a dangerous smile.

"One hour," I remind them, tapping my earpiece. "After that, Phoenix drops everything."

They slip out of the car, immediately melting into the shadows of the tree line. I watch them disappear, knowing they'll find every weakness in Jimmy's fortress while I walk through the front door.

I check my phone one last time. My jaw clenches as I imagine Sofia locked away in that house.

I approach Jimmy's gates with my hands raised, ensuring the guards can see I'm not holding anything. The security cameras swivel toward me, their red lights blinking in the darkness.

"I need to see Jimmy. It's about business," I call out, keeping my voice steady and professional.

Two guards emerge from the gatehouse, hands on their weapons. I recognize Marco, Jimmy's head of security, his weathered face creased with suspicion.

"You got some balls showing up here, Tyson," Marco growls, nodding to his partner to pat me down.

I stay still as rough hands check my jacket, pockets, and pants' waistband. The guard's fingers brush past my ankle, missing the thin blade strapped there. Amateur.

"I'm clean," I say calmly. "Just want to talk business with Jimmy."

Marco studies me for a long moment, then speaks into his radio. The gates creak open slowly.

"One wrong move," Marco warns, grabbing my arm roughly, "and you won't make it out of here breathing."

They lead me up the winding driveway, gravel crunching under our feet. The mansion looms ahead, its windows dark except for Jimmy's study on the second floor. My earpiece crackles as Colt and Nash confirm they can see me entering. But I keep my eyes forward, focused on the task ahead.

26

TYSON

Marco leads me into Jimmy's study. The mob boss stands by his window, silhouette dark against the city lights below. His shoulders are tense, hands clasped behind his back.

"You've got some fucking nerve coming here." Jimmy's voice cuts through the silence.

"We need to talk about what happened."

He whirls around, his face contorted with rage. "Talk? You killed my future son-in-law, you piece of shit! Made a grave mistake there."

"It was self-defense." I keep my voice steady. "Paulie came at me with a gun, threatening to kill me."

"Because I sent him!" Jimmy slams his fist on his desk. "You touched my daughter. Nobody touches her."

"Speaking of your daughter..." I take a calculated step forward. "Remember who saved her life? You owe me for that."

"I don't owe you shit." Jimmy's lip curls. "You think

that gives you the right to fuck my daughter? She's not for some lowlife carnie."

"Paulie's dead. Things have changed."

"Nothing's changed." Jimmy's eyes narrow dangerously. "Get your carnival out of my town. Tonight. Before I expose every dirty operation you're running and leave you with nothing."

"Jimmy—"

"I mean it, Tyson. You're done here. And you're done with my daughter."

I maintain my composure, though my blood boils at his dismissal. "Let's talk business then. There must be a way we can work this out."

"Business?" Jimmy scoffs, pouring himself a whiskey. "You've got nothing I want."

"I can pay for her hand." I watch his reaction carefully. "The carnival's just a front. You know that. My operation brings in millions each month."

Jimmy takes a long sip, studying me over the rim of his glass. "You think I give a fuck about money? I've got more than enough."

"Then name your price. Whatever it takes."

"You don't get it, do you?" He sets down his glass with a sharp crack. "This isn't about money or business. It's about legacy. The Moretti name means something in this city. Has for generations."

"And what exactly is wrong with my name?"

"Your name?" He barks out a laugh. "What name? You're a fucking carnie who sells drugs. No history, family connections, or respect in the circles that matter."

"The same circles that buy their drugs from me?"

"That's business." Jimmy's face hardens. "This is family. My daughter deserves better than some upstart criminal hiding behind a circus tent."

"I love her."

"Love?" He spits the word like poison. "Love doesn't mean shit in our world. Status, power, connections—that's what builds empires. That's what protects families. What can you offer besides dirty money and a traveling freak show?"

My jaw clenches. Everything I've built, everything I've accomplished, is meaningless to him. But I won't let him dismiss what Sofia and I have. "She chose me."

"She doesn't know what she wants. And even if she did, it doesn't matter. In our world, daughters don't choose. Fathers do."

I pull out my phone and check the time. "Is that your final answer, Jimmy? Because in exactly thirty minutes, my man will release everything we have on you to every news outlet in the country."

"Bullshit." But there's a flicker of uncertainty in his eyes.

"You think I came here unprepared?" I scroll through my phone, turning it to show him. "These documents detail every transaction, every dirty deal, every murder you've ordered. Bank records, witness statements, photographs—everything."

Jimmy's face drains of color as he swipes through the evidence. His hand trembles slightly.

"I wanted to do this the right way." I take my phone back. "Ask for her hand like a gentleman. But you wouldn't listen to reason."

"You're bluffing." His voice lacks conviction.

"Twenty-eight minutes now." I pull up a live feed of Phoenix at his computer, finger hovering over the enter key. "One text from me, and he hits send. Your empire crumbles and your reputation is destroyed. The Moretti name becomes synonymous with scandal."

Jimmy slumps into his chair, sweat beading on his forehead. "You wouldn't dare."

"Try me." I lean forward, placing both hands on his desk. "All I want is Sofia. Let me walk out of here with her unharmed, and these files disappear forever. Your choice."

His eyes dart between my phone and face, searching for any sign of deception. Finding none, he loosens his tie with shaking fingers.

"You ruthless bastard."

"I learned from the best." I check my watch again. "Twenty-five minutes, Jimmy. What's it going to be?"

Jimmy's shoulders sag in defeat. He reaches for the intercom on his desk and presses the button with trembling fingers.

"Marco, get my daughter. Bring her here."

The minutes drag as we wait in tense silence. Instead, Jimmy won't look at me, fixating on his half-empty whiskey glass. The door opens, and Sofia steps in, Marco hovering behind her. Her eyes widen when she sees me.

"Sofia." Jimmy's voice is cold. "This... man wants to take you away from here. Is that what you want?"

She glances between us, confusion evident on her

face before understanding dawns. "Yes," she says without hesitation. "Yes, I want to go with Tyson."

Jimmy's face twists with disgust. "Then get out. You're no daughter of mine. Don't ever show your face here again, you ungrateful little—"

"Watch how you speak to my girl." I cut him off, my voice sharp enough to make Marco's hand twitch toward his gun. "She deserves your respect, even if you're too blind to see it."

Sofia moves to my side, her hand finding mine. The warmth of her touch steadies me, keeping me from doing something I might regret.

"Let's go, baby girl," I murmur, squeezing her hand. As we turn to leave, Jimmy's bitter voice follows us.

"You're making a mistake, Sofia. Running off with this circus trash. Don't come crying when he shows you what he is."

I guide Sofia down the winding driveway, my arm wrapped protectively around her waist. The night air feels electric with victory, and her warmth against my side makes everything worth it. As we approach my black Mustang, I spot Nash and Colt's familiar silhouettes lounging against either side of the car.

"You're safe now." I kiss her temple as we reach the car. "No one's going to hurt you again."

Nash's signature smirk plays across his face while Colt crosses his arms. Both are pleased with how smoothly the operation went.

"Sofia, meet Nash and Colt. They're two of my most trusted guys." I gesture to each of them. "They helped make tonight possible."

"Hi." Nash gives her a slight nod.

"Welcome to the family," Colt adds with a wink.

I fish my keys from my pocket. "You two mind grabbing an Uber back to the carnival? I got to take my girl to get her things from her place."

"No problem, boss." Nash pushes off the car, already pulling out his phone.

"Take care, as Jimmy may have submitted for now, but he'll be out for blood," Colt says as he straightens up.

"Don't I know it," I mutter, opening the passenger door for Sofia and helping her slide into the leather seat before rounding to the driver's side. I watch Nash and Colt heading down the street through the windshield, already deep in conversation.

As I slide into the driver's seat, Sofia turns to me, her green eyes sparkling with curiosity.

"How did you convince my dad to let me go? He never backs down."

I start the engine, the Mustang's powerful rumble filling the silence. "Let's just say Phoenix has some impressive skills with computers."

"What do you mean?"

"He dug deep into your father's private files." I pull away from the mansion, watching the imposing gates shrink in my rearview mirror. "Found enough dirt to bury Jimmy ten times over. Bank records, proof of murders, every dirty deal he's ever made—all documented."

"You blackmailed him?" Her voice holds a mix of shock and admiration.

"Had to play dirty to win. I threatened to release everything to the media if he didn't let you go." I reach over and take her hand, threading our fingers together. "And it was worth it to get you out of there."

Sofia grabs my hand and squeezes. "Thank you, Ty. For coming for me and not giving up."

I lift her hand to my lips, pressing a soft kiss against her knuckles. "I'll always come for you, baby girl. No matter what."

Her breath catches, and the air between us crackles with electricity. Her green eyes pierce straight through my defenses, making my heart race like some lovesick teenager.

"You risked everything for me." She shifts in her seat to face me. "Your business, the carnival, maybe even your life."

"And I'd do it again." The words come out raw and honest. "You're worth more than all of it."

I never planned on falling this hard, this fast. Not far off turning forty, I thought I was beyond this all-consuming need for another person. But Sofia... she's different. Everything about her calls to something deep inside me—her fierce spirit, that brilliant mind, and how she challenges me while still trusting me completely.

"I've never felt like this before," I admit, keeping my eyes on the road because looking at her right now might break what little control I have left. "You've gotten under my skin. Made me want things I never thought I wanted or deserved."

Her fingers tighten around mine. "What things?"

"Everything. A real life. A future." I swallow hard. "Love."

The word hangs between us, heavy with meaning. I've spent years building walls, protecting myself from this vulnerability. But Sofia walked right through them like they were nothing.

My grip tightens on the steering wheel. Jimmy's surrender came too easy. A man like him doesn't just roll over and accept defeat, especially not when it comes to his only daughter. He'll be plotting his revenge right now, probably already making calls to his connections across the state.

The carnival gives us mobility since we can pack up and move within hours. But it also makes us visible because it's hard to hide a whole damn circus. I'll need to get Phoenix to strengthen our digital security and maybe set up some false trails. Lars and the boys will have to increase security, and we'll need extra muscle for the shows. Can't risk Jimmy's men slipping in among the crowds.

He might try to hurt Sofia to get to me or target my operation to cripple our income. Hell, he might even try to expose our drug running to the feds just to watch everything burn. Fifteen years of building this empire, and now it's all balanced on a knife's edge because I couldn't stay away from his daughter.

But looking at her now, I know I'd risk it all again. We'll need to be ready, though. Every exit route needs to be planned and every contingency covered. Jimmy Moretti didn't become the most powerful man in Dawsbury by letting people walk all over him. When he strikes back—and he will strike back—it'll be with everything he's got.

27

SOFIA

I fold another sweater, one of my favorites, and add it to the small pile of clothes. The rest—countless designer dresses and gowns worth more than some people's yearly salary—hang pristine in my walk-in closet. I won't need them anymore.

"You sure about leaving all this behind?" Ty leans against my bedroom doorframe, arms crossed over his chest.

"These weren't me." I run my fingers over a beaded Valentino gown. "They symbolize what Dad wanted me to be—the perfect mob princess."

My hands shake as I pack my grandmother's silver locket and a few cherished photos. The rest of the jewelry can stay—blood money transformed into diamonds and gold.

"Besides," I gesture at the massive closet, "your trailer would burst if I tried bringing all this."

Ty's eyes follow me as I move around the room,

selecting only what matters. Each item I choose feels like breaking another chain that kept me bound to this life. No more charity galas where I'm paraded around like a prized horse. No more stuffy dinners with Dad's associates eyeing me like merchandise.

"Just need the essentials." I toss my favorite jeans and t-shirts into the duffle bag. "And you."

My heart feels lighter with each piece I leave behind. The designer bags, the stilettos that pinched my feet, the shapewear that made me feel like I was suffocating—they can all stay here with the rest of my old life.

"You're different than the others, you know that?" Ty pushes off the doorframe and walks over to me. "Most women would be crying about leaving all this luxury behind."

I zip up my bag of belongings. "This was never a luxury to me. It was a cage."

"Though you sure acted prissy about our food on our first date." Ty's lips quirk up in that knowing smirk. "What was it you said? 'I wouldn't be caught dead eating that greasy carnival trash?'"

Heat floods my cheeks as I remember my snobbish behavior. "God, I was awful, wasn't I?"

"You looked at that corndog like it might bite you first."

"Old habits." I shake my head, remembering how I'd held that corndog between two fingers like it was radioactive. "Dad drilled it into me since I could walk. Only the finest restaurants, only the most expensive meals. Heaven forbid anyone see Jimmy Moretti's daughter eating street food."

"And now?" he probes.

"That corndog was better than half the overpriced meals I've had." I zip up another section of my bag. "Do you know how many fancy dinner parties I sat through, pushing around thousand-dollar plates of food that tasted like nothing? All because Dad said those were the 'right' places to be seen."

"Sounds miserable."

"It was. Every bite came with rules. Elbows off the table, small portions, never show too much enthusiasm. God forbid I enjoy my food—it might make me look uncouth." I mimic my father's stern tone on the last word. "Even Paulie got in on it. Always watching what I ate, making comments about my weight."

Tyson's jaw clenches, eyes flashing with rage, but he keeps listening to me.

"But that first bite of carnival food?" I smile at the memory. "It felt like freedom. Even if my knee-jerk reaction was to turn my nose up at it."

Ty pulls me against his chest, his strong arms wrapping around my waist. The familiar scent of leather and musk surrounds me, and I melt into his embrace.

"You're free now. Free to be whoever you want to be." His voice rumbles through his chest. "Though maybe you've just traded one cage for another. I'm never letting you go."

I press closer to him. "This isn't a cage, Ty. Or if it is, it's the one I want. I'd choose it a thousand times over."

His grip tightens, and I feel his lips brush against my hair. The warmth of his body seeps into mine, grounding me. This is what safety feels like. This is what love feels like—not the suffocating rules and expectations of my father's world, but this raw, honest connection.

"With you," I whisper against his chest, "I can breathe, laugh, and eat a corndog without worrying about what people will think." My fingers curl into his shirt. "That's not a cage. That's freedom."

His lips capture mine, and he backs me up against the wall. The bookshelf rattles behind me, the sound of tumbling books forgotten as his tongue tangles with mine. I'm devouring him just as he's devouring me, our desperation growing with each touch.

With a yank, he rips my shirt over my head, the buttons popping off and scattering across the floor. His mouth finds my breasts, his lips and tongue working magic on my already sensitive flesh. I moan, my fingers tightening in his hair as he sucks and nips, sending jolts of pleasure down my spine.

"I'll never get enough of your tits, Sofia." His deep voice rumbles against my skin, sending shivers through me. "So fucking perfect."

His mouth trails lower, his tongue dipping into my belly button before he hooks his fingers in the band of my skirt and yanks it down, leaving me in nothing but my panties. I leave the ruined fabric, longing for his touch on my bare skin.

"Fucking glorious." His hungry eyes devour me as he pushes me back against the wall, his palms sliding up my thighs. "All these curves are mine."

I bite my lip, watching as he slides his fingers beneath my panties, teasing me with a featherlight touch.

"Don't hold back, baby girl." He smiles that wicked smile. "You know how much I love the sound of your pleasure."

My inhibitions melt as his fingers dance closer to where I need them most. His thumb finds my clit, circling gently at first and then with more insistence as he watches my reactions. I'm putty in his hands, squirming against the wall as waves of pleasure pulse through my body.

"Ty," I pant, my head resting against the wall. I can feel the heat building, coiling tighter and tighter within me.

He presses closer, his hard body trapping me against the wall as his fingers work their magic, knowing exactly what I need. A few more strokes, and I'm arching off the wall, crying out his name as my orgasm rips through me. I feel his mouth on my neck, sucking gently as I ride out the waves of my release.

I'm still trembling when he lifts me, wrapping my legs around his waist. His mouth captures mine while he carries me toward the bed. With one hand, he rips off his shirt, and I gasp at the sight of all that sculpted flesh covered in intricate tattoos. I can't get enough, dragging my fingers over his shoulders and chest. So much strength, so much raw power.

He lays me down, kissing a trail down my body as he pushes my panties down my thighs and tears them away from me. I spread my legs eagerly, wanting all of him. Needing to feel him inside me.

He kneels between my thighs, his lips finding my sensitive flesh. With each flick of his tongue, each lap at my wetness, he claims me as his own.

"This cunt is mine," he growls, sending vibrations through my core. "I missed the taste of you. I was going fucking insane not knowing where you were."

I moan as he sucks my clit into his mouth, swirling his tongue around the bundle of nerves. I'm completely at his mercy, my hands twisting in the sheets as his fingers join in, thrusting inside me.

"God, you're soaked." His gaze is fixed on my soaking pussy. "Know what that means?"

I shake my head, unable to form words, as he teases me with featherlight touches, sending pleasure sparking through me. I'm a live wire, crackling with electricity.

"Means you missed me, too." He smirks. "Bet that pretty little pussy of yours was aching for this tongue the past few days."

"Yes." My admission comes out strangled, the word torn from me by his relentless touches. "God, Ty, I've missed you."

He chuckles, the vibrations dancing along my nerve endings. "Thought so, you'd never forget about me, would you?"

"Never." I arch my back as he sucks my clit gently, his fingers pumping faster inside me. "I'll always want you."

His eyes are dark and intense as he watches my face. "Tell me what this pussy needs."

I can barely think straight. "I need you. God, Ty, please. Don't tease me."

"I'm not teasing, baby girl." He smirks wickedly. "Just making sure you're ready for me."

"I'm ready." I nod fervently, my head feeling too heavy for my neck. "Please give it to me now."

"Impatient." He chuckles but obliges, thrusting his tongue deep inside me.

I cry out as my body clenches around him, pleasure shooting through me like lightning. His tongue dances and flicks, knowing exactly what my body craves.

"Don't hold back." He pulls back, stroking my clit with his thumb as he speaks. "I want to hear that beautiful voice of yours. Scream for me." And then he returns his tongue, flicking at my clit in a way that sends me over the edge again.

"Ty!" I cry out again as my orgasm crashes over me, my back arching off the bed. "Oh, God, don't stop."

But he does stop, at least for a moment. He pulls away, his eyes consuming the image of me, stretched out in front of him, completely exposed.

"Look at you, all sprawled out for me." His fingers trace lazy patterns on my inner thighs. "I want to taste every inch of this beautiful body."

I'm unable to respond, panting and quivering from the intensity of my release. I feel boneless, like my limbs might just melt into the bed.

"I've been dreaming about this every damn night since your dad locked you away." He bends to kiss my inner thigh, his lips brushing the sensitive skin. "I already can't get enough of eating your pussy, but there's so much more to explore."

His lips leave a trail of fire as he kisses his way up my body, pausing to tease my breasts before his mouth finds mine. I can taste myself on his lips, and I moan, pulling him closer and devouring him.

"So fucking beautiful." His hand cups my cheek, his thumb brushing over my lower lip.

Our eyes lock, and I see the inferno burning in his gaze. This man would burn the world down for me.

His thumb strokes my swollen lower lip. "You're floating on cloud nine, aren't you, baby girl?"

I nod, my whole body humming with pleasure. "Mmm, you know how to make a girl feel good."

"I'm just getting started." His lips crash down on mine, devouring me once more.

He steps out of his jeans and boxers, and I'm left breathless at seeing him. Hard muscle, powerful thighs, and a throbbing cock that promises delicious pleasure.

My eyes are drawn to his piercing—that damn magic cross that turns me into a puddle every time I see it. I can already feel it—that perfect mix of pleasure and pain.

"Ready for this?" His voice is low and husky, sending shivers down my spine.

I nod, unable to form words, as I watch him take himself in hand, stroking his length slowly, the metal of his piercing glinting in the light.

"Fuck, I love how you look at me." He inches closer, his cock twitching as he strokes himself. "Like I'm the only man on the planet for you."

It's true. I'm transfixed by him, every muscle, every movement, every ripple of his flesh as he moves closer. Even after everything, after all the danger and my father's threats, all I want is him. This man standing before me, hard and hungry, is the only thing in the world I need.

"Now, I'll make you feel so good." He climbs back onto the bed and teases my swollen clit with the tip of his cock.

The metal of his piercing brushes against me, sending sparks through my core. It's so damn sensitive.

"Please, Ty." I'm begging already. "Stop teasing."

"But I'm enjoying myself." He drags his cock against my clit again, a slow, excruciatingly delicious drag that makes me cry out. "I don't want to rush this."

"You know exactly what you're doing to me." I squirm under his touch, my body thrumming with need. "A little more, and I'm going to explode."

"Mmm, I like it when you get demanding." He chuckles, his warm breath tickling my sensitive skin. "Tell me exactly what you need."

"I need you inside me." My voice is strained, raw with desire. "Now, Ty, please."

He chuckles again and lines himself up with my entrance. "You sure about that? This cock is gonna stretch you wide."

"Yes," I breathe, trying to push back against him, but he holds me still. "I want all of you."

With a firm grip on his thick cock, he pushes inside me and fills me inch by inch. I'm so wet, but he still has to go slowly. It's a tight fit, and he knows it. He enjoys torturing me with it. But soon, he's buried to the hilt.

"Fuck, you feel amazing." His groan reverberates through me, his hands squeezing my hips. "So damn tight around my cock."

He starts to move, pulling back almost all the way and then thrusting deep once more, setting a relentless pace. He knows how much I love the feel of his cock stretching me, taking me, branding me as his. There's an edge of desperation to his movements, like he's been waiting for this moment just as much as I have, even though we've had each other before. Our few days apart felt like an eternity.

His metal piercing drags against my G-spot as he thrusts, sending sparks of pleasure through me. I can feel every vein, every ridge, every inch of him pumping inside me.

"Ty," I gasp, my head falling back. My core clenches around him, drawing him in deeper.

"That's it." His voice is thick with desire. "Take it all."

He knows how to move his hips just right, angling his cock to hit every sweet spot. Each thrust is pure bliss. Each drag of his piercing against my sensitive walls is like lightning. I feel the tension building, tightening my body like a coiled spring.

"Don't hold back." His voice is rough against my ear as he bites down on my earlobe. "Let me hear you."

He pulls out almost all the way and then slams back into me, his piercing scraping deliciously against my walls. I cry out his name as he keeps thrusting, drawing out my release, driving me higher.

"Fuck." He groans, his teeth gritted as he grinds his hips, his cock pulsing inside me. "I'm not gonna last much longer with you milking me like that."

"Me neither," I whisper, my body throbbing around him.

"Please, Ty, I'm so close again." I claw at his back, needing that final push.

He groans, his thrusts becoming more frenzied. "You're into it when I breed your tight little cunt, aren't you, baby girl?"

His dirty words push me over the edge. My body convulses around him, my release exploding through me as I cry out his name. At the same time, I feel him swell inside me, his cock twitching as he spills himself, breeding me like he promised. His thrusts slow, and he pulls me closer, whispering against my ear.

"That's it, baby girl. Come all over my cock."

The tightening in my core intensifies, and I feel my release gushing out around him. It's too much, too good, and I'm left boneless and quivering, my breath coming in ragged gasps.

Ty's body shudders as he comes down from his high, his cock still buried inside me. We're both sweating, our hearts pounding in time.

"God, that was—" I can't even find the words to describe what happened between us. I've never experienced anything like it, a connection so intense it's frightening.

He chuckles, his hands tracing patterns on my skin.

"I told you I was gonna make you feel good." He lays beside me, pulling me close so I'm nestled against his chest, my head tucked under his chin.

At this moment, it's just the two of us. No mob, no danger, no secrets. Just two lovers intertwined, our hearts beating in harmony.

But I know it can't last. The weight of the reality I'm running from settles on my chest. I fear that our love story can only end in tragedy.

28

TYSON

My most trusted men are gathered in the office trailer, the familiar smell of carnival popcorn drifting through the window. Gage looms in the corner, his skull mask reflecting the dim light, while Lars and Nash flank either side of my desk. Colt paces near the door, his restless energy filling the small space.

"Listen up. Sofia's here now, which means we must be on high alert. Jimmy Moretti isn't going to take this lying down." I lean forward, studying my men. "Phoenix, what's our digital security looking like?"

Phoenix glances up from his laptop. "I've got eyes on every camera in a mile radius. No one approaches without us knowing."

"Good. Remy, double the security rounds, especially after dark." I turn to Lars. "We need to move our supply routes. Jimmy knows too much about our operation."

Lars nods, already pulling out his phone to make arrangements. "I'll have it sorted by morning."

"Colt and Nash, I want you two to coordinate with the regular carnival staff. Keep everything running smooth, business as usual. We can't afford to draw attention."

"What about Moretti's men?" Colt stops pacing. "They'll come sniffing around."

"That's where Gage comes in." I glance at the silent giant. "Anyone gets past our perimeter. They deal with you."

Gage's nod is all the confirmation I need. His presence alone will deter most.

"And the cocaine shipments?" Nash raises an eyebrow.

"We continue as planned but through different channels. Jimmy's not our only client. We must maintain our reputation." I stand, signaling the end of the meeting. "Keep your eyes open. Protect Sofia at all costs. She's family now."

The men file out, leaving me alone with my thoughts. Through the window, I watch Sofia talking with some female carnival workers, her red hair catching the afternoon sun. She belongs here now, and I'll burn down anyone who tries to take her away.

I stare at the papers scattered across my desk, numbers, and routes that need immediate attention. But my mind keeps drifting to the flash of red hair outside my window. Sofia's laugh carries through the thin walls, and my cock twitches.

"Fuck it." I shove away from my desk, the chair scraping against the floor.

The afternoon sun hits my face as I step out of my

trailer. Sofia stands with Aurora and Lily near the cotton candy stand, her curves highlighted by her tight black dress. My mouth goes dry at the sight.

"Sofia!" I call out, watching her shoulders tense. "I need you for a minute."

Aurora and Lily exchange knowing looks as I approach. Sofia's cheeks flush pink.

"Ladies, if you'll excuse us." I place my hand on the small of Sofia's back. "Business to discuss."

"Of course," Lily says, tugging Aurora's arm. They disappear, leaving me alone with her.

"What kind of business?" Sofia turns those green eyes on me, and my resolve crumbles.

"The kind that involves getting you alone." I guide her toward the back of the trailers, away from prying eyes. "You're distracting me."

"I'm talking with the girls."

"You're existing. That's enough to drive me crazy." I pull her closer, inhaling her sweet perfume. "How am I supposed to work when all I can think about is bending you over my desk?"

I push her against the wall of the trailer. Her eyes spark with surprise and desire.

"I want your mouth on me." I reach for the button of my jeans. "Right here. Right now."

Sofia's breath hitches as I free my cock from its confines, but she doesn't hesitate. Her movements are graceful and confident as she drops to her knees.

Her tongue teases the tip, flicking against the metal. I grit my teeth, my fingers tangling in her hair. "Fuck, your mouth..."

I want to thrust into the warmth of her throat, but I force myself to hold back, enjoying the torture of her tongue swirling and dancing along my length. She explores every inch, her hands resting lightly on my thighs.

But I need more. I tug on her hair, pulling her away. "Hands by your sides."

Her breath comes in short gasps as I gather a fistful of her fiery locks, guiding her back to my cock. This time, I take control, fucking her throat as she relaxes and opens for me. Her hands remain by her sides, her back arching slightly as I thrust.

Her lips stretch around me, the slight sting of her teeth adding to the pleasure. I can feel her swallowing, taking me deeper. My grip tightens in her hair as I lose myself in the sensations.

I relish the way she takes my orders, my cock disappearing between her lips again. She's greedy for it, those big green eyes looking up at me as she sucks and tongues my cock. Her palms rest on my thighs.

"Look at you, taking my cock so fucking well." I tug her hair, guiding her back and forth, the pace increasing. "You're a natural-born cock sucker, baby girl."

I thrust into her mouth, holding her head still, my eyes fixed on hers. She whimpers, the vibrations teasing my sensitive tip. "You love this, don't you? Being on your knees, taking what I give you."

She moans in response, her eyes fluttering shut. I know she's falling into that subspace where my commands rule her, and her body responds instinctually.

Her throat relaxes around me as I piston my hips,

and I take advantage, fucking her mouth harder. My balls rest against her chin, slapping lightly with each thrust. She groans, the vibrations sending shocks of pleasure up my spine.

"Such a good girl." I praise her, my tone laced with dominance. "You exist to pleasure me, don't you, baby girl?"

She swallows around me, and I can feel the wetness of her mouth, her throat working to accommodate me. My grip tightens, pulling her hair to the point of discomfort, and she moans, her eyes screwing shut, her cheeks hollowing as she takes me deep.

My hips stutter as I struggle to hold back. "Fuck, you're gonna make me—"

I control myself, pulling out before I shoot my load. She's so fucking good at that, but I need to be in her cunt.

I step back, and she stares at me with confusion and desire warring in her eyes. "On all fours for me."

Her emerald eyes flash as she maneuvers herself onto all fours between the trailers. Her chest rises and falls with anticipation.

I kneel behind her, my fingers curling around her hips. With one smooth motion, I slide deep inside her, thrusting into her with purpose.

Her nails dig into the dirt while I grip her hips tighter, the slap of skin reverberating through the air.

"You like it rough, don't you?" I ask. "You like it when I take what I want."

She whimpers, her head hanging low as I piston my hips. My clothed chest covers her back as I lean forward and reach around to squeeze her breasts, rolling her tight nipple through her blouse between my fingers. "Tell me you want more."

"Please," she gasps, her voice hitching. "More, Ty. Harder."

Her words send a rush of heat through my veins, and I tighten my grip on her hips, pounding into her with abandon. The trailers shake with the force of my thrusts, the sound of skin slapping against skin filling the air.

I groan, my eyes squeezing tightly as I lose myself in the sensations. Her pussy clenches around me, milking my cock, and I know I won't last much longer.

"You like it when I breed that tight pussy, don't you?" I growl, pulling her hair back to whisper in her ear. "Making you mine."

I revel in the wicked sound of her flesh meeting mine. My cock glides smoothly in and out of her slick heat, the friction sending sparks of pleasure through my body.

I pull her hair back harder, tilting her head to the side to expose her neck. I nip at the sensitive skin with my teeth, marking her as mine. Her moans become sharper, louder, each signaling that I'm doing something right.

"Louder, baby girl," I encourage. "Let everyone hear how much you love my cock."

But my focus is interrupted by a flicker of movement from the corner of my eye. Remy stands frozen in his tracks with wide eyes. My first instinct is to tell him to fuck off, but something holds me back. I've always been an exhibitionist, enjoying the thrill of sex clubs and voyeurism.

I grind my teeth, my cock buried deep inside Sofia as I consider the possibilities. Remy shifts his weight, his eyes glued to Sofia's body.

"We have an audience," I murmur in Sofia's ear. "It's up to you if he stays or goes."

"What?" She twists her head, her eyes widening as she notices Remy. Her body tenses, all the blood rushing to her cheeks. "Oh..."

I tighten my grip on her hips. "It's your call. You want to give him a show?"

She hesitates, her body stilling momentarily before she surprises me by relaxing. "Let him stay," she breathes.

A smile spreads across my face. "As you wish."

I rock my hips, pulling almost all the way out before slamming back into her, drawing a cry from her that echoes through the space between the trailers. I watch Remy's eyes, taking pleasure in the way he studies Sofia's body, his pupils dilated with desire.

I lean forward again. "You've got his full attention, baby girl. He's loving the show."

Her breath hitches, and I know she wants to be watched at that moment. The thought excites me, and I thrust harder, my balls slapping against her clit.

She whimpers, her hands reaching back to grip my thighs. Together, we move in perfect sync.

Remy shifts his weight, his hand rubbing his crotch as he watches. I smirk. He's enjoying the show, getting off on our raw, animalistic fucking.

But it's not enough. The devil on my shoulder whispers, and I listen. With a quick movement, I flip Sofia onto her back, her legs wrapping around my waist as I tower over her.

"What a sight you are." I trail my fingers down her body, from her throat to the swell of her breasts. "Exhibiting yourself so beautifully."

I hear Remy clear his throat and glance over. His hand hovers at his zipper, eyes questioning. The bastard wants to jerk off watching us.

"Baby girl," I murmur, slowing my thrusts. "Remy wants to stroke his cock while he watches me fuck you. What do you think about that?"

Sofia's eyes dart to Remy, her chest heaving. She bites her lip, considering, before nodding. "Yes... let him."

A deep groan escapes me at her words. Remy echoes the sound as he pulls out his cock, wrapping his hand around it.

I slam into Sofia harder, spurred on by Remy's heavy breathing and the rhythmic sound of his hand working his length. My possessive side should be furious; I should want to tear him apart for looking at what's mine. But something is intoxicating about being watched, about showing everyone that Sofia belongs to me.

"Fuck," Remy grunts, his hand moving faster.

I trust him—that's what makes this okay. He knows his place, knows this is just watching. My grip tightens on Sofia's hips as I pound into her.

I smirk, watching her reactions. I do this best—orchestrating a show, commanding attention, and drawing out reactions. Only now, instead of the center ring, I'm between the trailers with my cock buried deep in Sofia's pussy.

Sofia's pupils are blown wide as her eyes dart between me and Remy, lingering on his hand and stroking his length.

"You like seeing what you do to him, baby girl?" I thrust deeper, making her gasp. "How hard your perfect fucking body gets him?"

She bites her lip, those green eyes locking with mine. "Yes... God, yes. It's so hot being watched like this." Her hands grip my shoulders tighter. "Showing him that I'm yours."

Something snaps inside me at her words. Mine. I crash my lips against hers, claiming her mouth as I pound into her relentlessly.

Her pussy clenches around me, her body convulsing with pleasure. I feel her nails dig into my shoulders as she rides out her climax, her juices flooding my cock. That sensation, combined with the sight of her green eyes rolling back in ecstasy, pushes me over the edge.

With a deep groan, I thrust one last time, burying myself as deeply as possible within her. My cum spills deep inside her.

Remy grunts as he reaches his own climax.

Despite already coming, I give her one last deep thrust, feeling the aftershocks of her climax squeeze my cock. I hold still, my eyes closing as I savor the euphoric sensation.

"Fuck, baby girl." I pull out, my legs feeling like jelly,

as I tuck myself back into my pants. "You're something else."

Sofia straightens her blouse and skirt, her chest heaving as she looks up at me through her lashes. "You, too."

I take a moment to catch my breath, my heart rate slowly returning to normal. I glance over at Remy, who has tucked himself back into his jeans.

I stand and stride over to him, feeling a sudden surge of possessiveness. This is my territory, my carnival, and Sofia—she's mine.

"Listen," I say. "She gave you a show, and I gave you permission. But if you ever touch her..." I pause, letting my gaze speak for me. "...there will be hell to pay."

Remy's eyes widen, and he holds up his hands. "No way, Tyson. I know the rules. I know she's yours."

I study him for a moment, seeing the sincerity in his eyes. Good. Remy's loyal, and he knows better than to cross me.

"Appreciate it." I clap him on the shoulder. "Now, I suggest you get back to work. We've got a carnival to run."

He nods and hurries off, likely embarrassed now that the arousal has worn off. Can't say I blame him.

But me? I'm feeling pretty fucking satisfied. This is what I live for—the thrill of voyeurism and the rush of power that comes with possessing someone as perfect as Sofia.

I glance back at Sofia. Her cheeks are flushed, her eyes sparkling with a combination of arousal and something more.

"You okay?" I approach her, unable to resist her magnetic pull on me.

She nods, her chest rising and falling rapidly. "Yeah... just a lot to process." A playful smile dances on her lips. "I've never done anything like that before."

I chuckle, reaching out to tuck a stray strand of hair behind her ear. "Well, we make quite the team, don't we?"

She ducks her head. "Guess so."

The sight of her, all flushed and disheveled, does something to me. I want to keep her like this forever, always wanting and needing me. I shake my head, clearing my thoughts.

"Come on, I'll walk you back." I offer her my arm, and she loops hers through mine. "We have work to do."

Sofia smiles at me, and it hits me right in the chest. This is it, I realize, with a start. This is the rush I've been seeking.

As we walk through the carnival, I feel like I'm soaring a hundred feet above the ground, untouchable and immortal. Sofia's presence by my side, her soft laughter, and the scent of her vanilla perfume muddle my thoughts and leave me craving more.

Being near her makes me feel alive for the first time in years.

29

SOFIA

My hands are sticky from cotton candy and caramel apples as I wipe the sweat from my brow. The late evening crowd has thinned to a trickle, leaving me a moment to catch my breath. Who knew standing for hours could make your feet hurt this much?

"You're doing great," Aurora says, flashing me an encouraging smile as she restocks the napkin dispenser. "Most people don't last half the time you have their first time."

I laugh, flexing my fingers. "I never thought I'd say this, but I like it. It's... real, you know?"

The carnival lights paint everything in soft blues and pinks, creating a magical atmosphere that feels worlds away from my father's sterile mansion. A cool breeze carries the mingled scents of popcorn and funnel cake.

"Trust me, I get it." Aurora hands me a water bottle. "The first time I worked here, I was terrified I'd mess everything up. But there's something special about being part of a family like this."

I take a grateful sip, nodding. "My whole life, everything has been handed to me. Designer clothes, fancy cars... but this?" I gesture at my simple carnival uniform, with a small grease stain. "This feels more honest."

"That's the carnival life for you." Aurora wipes down the counter. "Everyone pulls their weight, from the owner to the newest addition. Even Ty works the stands sometimes when necessary."

The mention of Ty makes me smile. He was so supportive when I insisted on working, even though I could tell he wanted to give me a pass from earning my way.

"Speaking of weight," I say, lifting a heavy box of supplies, "I think my arms are getting stronger already."

Aurora chuckles. "Just wait until you've been here a month. You'll be carrying boxes like a pro."

I survey our nearly empty stand with pride. Despite my aching feet and tired muscles, I feel more accomplished than I ever did attending my father's fancy galas.

I'm wiping down the last section of the counter when I spot Ty approaching. My heart skips as his powerful frame cuts through the carnival's dancing lights. Even after all this time, seeing him still makes my skin tingle.

"Time to wrap it up," he demands, with that powerful tone that weakens my knees. "We're closing down for the night."

I nod, trying to focus on helping Aurora count the register rather than the heat of Ty's gaze. His presence fills the small stand, making it hard to concentrate on simple tasks.

"Just need to finish the count and take out the trash," Aurora says, but I barely hear her. Ty's leaning against the counter, his eyes following my every movement as I gather empty boxes.

I bend to pick up a fallen napkin, and I swear I hear his breath catch. When I straighten, his eyes are darker and hungrier. He's not even trying to hide how he's watching me, like a predator waiting for the perfect moment to pounce.

"The register's done," Aurora announces, breaking through the tension. I grab the trash bag, but Ty's voice stops me.

"Leave that. Aurora can handle it." His tone brooks no argument. "You've done enough for your first night."

I hesitate, not wanting to burden Aurora, but she waves me off with a knowing smile. "Go on. You've earned your rest."

Ty's patience is clearly wearing thin as I finish. His intensity makes my hands shake as I untie my apron. I can feel the promise in his gaze, and I'm about to find out exactly what it means.

I follow him through the darkened carnival grounds, our footsteps crunching on scattered popcorn and paper wrappers. The main tent looms ahead, its canvas walls rippling in the night breeze.

"Where are we going?" I ask, but Ty just squeezes my hand and leads me inside.

The tent feels different without the crowds and performers—empty but somehow more intimate. Our footsteps echo across the sawdust floor, and moonlight filters through gaps in the canvas.

Ty releases my hand and moves to a trunk near the center ring. He pulls something out—a black leather half-face mask for the upper half of his face. My breath catches as he slides it on. The mask accentuates his sharp jawline, making him look dangerous and incredibly sexy.

"What's that for?" I ask, mesmerized by how the mask transforms him into something almost mythical.

"It's part of the game." He steps toward me, his eyes burning through the mask. "Tonight, I'm your masked master. And you, baby girl, are my submissive slut."

A thrill runs through me at his words. "Oh?" I try to keep my tone light, but my voice comes out breathless. "Why would I be your slut?"

He smirks. "Because I'll own you. I'll control your pleasure, and by the time I'm done, you'll be begging me for more."

The authority in his voice sends a shiver down my spine. His words ignite the deepest desires I've kept hidden for so long. It's as if he's speaking directly to the secret cravings that have driven me to the carnival, to him.

I wet my lips, trembling with anticipation. "And what if I don't want to be owned?"

"I know you do." He closes the distance between us, his voice dropping to a husky murmur. "Your body betrays you, my little slut. Your pulse and your breathing quicken just from the thought."

His hand cups my throat, his thumb gently stroking

along the sensitive skin. I gasp as a thousand sensations race through me—excitement, fear, longing.

"It's all right." His thumb continues to stroke. "You'll learn to crave my commands. You'll feel more alive than you ever have before."

"And if I don't?" I whisper, my voice almost lost in the heavy silence of the tent.

His grip tightens, and his eyes flash dangerously. "Then I'll enjoy teaching you to submit."

My heart is pounding. His mask-covered face adds to the fun. The urge to lean into him, to surrender, wars with my instinct to run.

"You're trembling." He leans closer. "Are you afraid, baby girl?"

I nod, unable to speak, my confession trapped in my throat.

"Good." He smirks. "That fear will make the pleasure much sweeter. It will make you appreciate every touch and sensation."

Ty caresses my lower lip with his thumb, his eyes never leaving mine. "Do you want your first lesson in submission?"

My pulse thunders in my ears. I'm afraid, but not of Ty. I'm afraid of the power he holds over me and the parts of myself I can no longer ignore.

"Yes," I whisper.

"Get on your knees. Show me how much you want this."

I sink to my knees, watching him appraise me with his piercing gaze. Apprehension drives me wild as I wait for his command and the rush that will come when he finally touches me.

He moves back toward the trunk and grabs it, carrying it back to me so I can see the contents.

His fingers trail along the variety of toys laid out before him—whips, paddles, vibrators, and clamps—before finally selecting a small, slender dildo. Seeing it makes me bite my lip, and a mix of excitement and apprehension floods me.

"Have you ever had anything in your ass?" he asks.

I shake my head, unable to meet his eyes. "N-no."

His eyes darken. "A virgin ass. That makes this even better."

He steps closer, his presence overwhelming. His scent of leather and musk surrounds me, clouding my thoughts. "Kneel on the hay bales, baby girl. Show me that beautiful ass."

I obey, climbing onto the soft hay bales and kneeling, my chest pressed against the rough strands. His fingers dance along my spine, sending tingles through me. "This might sting a little, but I'll make it feel so good."

I whimper as he coats my untouched hole in lube and then presses the cool tip of the dildo against my ass. Slowly, he eases it inside, adding more lube when necessary. I gasp at the burn that spreads through me.

"It's okay. Play with your clit, baby girl. It will make you relax." His voice is like a caress. "Take it for me. Feel that stretch."

I groan and reach beneath me to rub my clit with one hand, while the other digs into the hay. I can sense him watching me, his eyes devouring my every reaction.

My cheeks are hot, but a dark thrill courses through me.

"Good girl." His hands slide around my hips. "Fuck, that's beautiful." His voice is strained. "Now, I want you to relax while I move it in and out."

I obey, moaning as I try to relax. He slowly moves the dildo in and out, and I can feel the heat pooling between my legs.

"That's it. Soon, you'll take my cock here. Imagine it—my thick cock stretching you open, pounding into you while I pull your hair."

His words send a lightning bolt to my core. The image floods my mind—being taken by him in the ass. My clit throbs as I rub it in tight circles.

"Now, baby girl. Come for me like a good slut."

My breath hitches as his words strike a chord deep within me. The build-up, the forbidden nature of my desire, the rough hay against my chest... it's all too much. I cry out, my body shaking as pleasure floods me. I'm overwhelmed, consumed by the intensity of my release.

"Good girl." Ty's thumb brushes my lower back. "I knew you'd be a natural submissive."

I whimper, still lost in the aftershocks of my orgasm. My body feels like it's made of jelly, boneless against the hay. But his praise sends a thrill of satisfaction through me.

"But we're not done yet." His voice drops an octave. "Not even close."

I gasp for breath, my body still trembling from the intensity of my orgasm. The hay pricks against my skin, but I barely notice it through the haze of pleasure coursing through my veins. God, how does he do this to me? Turn me into this wanton creature who begs and moans at his command?

I've never felt so exposed, so vulnerable or free. I've been trapped in a gilded cage of expectations—be the perfect daughter, fiancée, mob princess. But here, on my knees before him, I'm just his baby girl. His slut. And somehow, that feels more real, more honest than any role I've ever played.

My breath finally steadies, but the aftershocks still ripple through me. I can feel his eyes on me, assessing and appreciating. And despite my exhaustion, despite the ache spreading through my muscles, I want more—whatever he's willing to give me.

Because in this tent, under his control, I'm finally living instead of just existing.

30

TYSON

The sight of Sofia on her hands and knees, presenting her perfect ass to me, stirs something primal within. I feel the familiar heat in my veins, a rush of desire that demands action. Her skin glows and she moans, anticipating more, and I know she's ready for the next step.

I take in the alluring sight of her body—the graceful curve of her spine, the way her red hair spills over her shoulders, and the roundness of her ass, offered up like a gift. I select a larger dildo and coat it generously with lube. I want to test her limits, take her to that delicious edge between pleasure and pain.

Slowly, I ease the larger dildo into Sofia's ass, watching as her body opens up to accept it. Her muscles tense at first, resisting the intrusion, but I keep my movements slow and deliberate. A whimper escapes her lips.

"Breathe, baby girl," I murmur, my free hand stroking her lower back. "Let it in."

She exhales shakily, and I feel her relax. The dildo slides deeper, stretching her tight ring of muscle.

"That's it," I praise, watching the toy disappear inch by inch. "You're taking it so well."

Sofia pushes back, silently asking for more. I oblige, pressing the dildo further while monitoring her reactions. Her breath catches when I hit a particularly sensitive spot.

The dildo is fully seated inside her, and I pause to let her adjust to the fullness. Her ass grips the toy tightly, and I can't help but imagine how she'll feel around my cock. But for now, this is about preparing her, stretching her slowly and carefully.

"You like that?" I ask, my voice rough with desire. "You like the way that big dildo stretches you open?"

Sofia's response is a soft whimper as I rotate the toy inside her. She takes a sharp breath, her body tensing while I work it in and out. Slowly, I tease her with the length.

"That's it, take it all," I urge. "Relax and let it fuck you. And keep playing with your clit."

Her body adjusts to the girth, embracing it, and I know she's loving the feeling of being so deliciously filled. I move it in and out, slow and steady, but soon, she's rocking back against me, craving more. I quicken the pace, relishing the sounds of pleasure she's making.

"Does my girl like her ass played with?" I tease. "You love the feeling of being stretched, don't you?"

"Yes," she breathes. "I love it. More, please, Ty."

I smirk, proud that I've reduced her to such a state that she's begging. I begin to pump the dildo in and out with purpose. With each thrust, her body trembles, and I know I'm pushing her closer to the edge again. She clenches around the toy, her ass tightening.

"Come for me, Sofia," I instruct. "Let go. I want to watch you fall apart."

She does as I command, crying out as she shatters for me. I pull the dildo out slowly, enjoying the sight of her ass clenching in response.

Running my fingers over the sensitive skin of her ass, I lean down, my mouth close to her ear, and whisper. "That was just the beginning. I plan to fill you so fucking full you won't be able to think straight."

Watching Sofia on her hands and knees before me fills me with a primal hunger. I want to brand her as mine, mark her skin with my touch, and hear her moans of pleasure.

I reach for the butt plug, knowing it will stretch her a little more. With deliberate movements, I work the plug into her ass, taking my time to ensure she adjusts to the size. Her breath quickens as I push it deeper, her body tensing and relaxing with each thrust. Finally, it pops inside, and I admire the sight of her ass stuffed.

My cock twitches with anticipation, and I tease the tip through her slick folds, making her whimper. I want to bury myself deep inside her, but I hold back, enjoying the power I have over her at this moment.

"You want my cock?" I ask. "Tell me how much you want it."

She hesitates, her eyes sparking with defiance, but the desire in her voice is clear. "I want it, Ty. Please, fuck me. I need you."

I smirk, loving the way she begs. But I'm not done teasing her yet. "Not yet, baby girl. There's one more hole that needs filling."

Sofia watches me over her shoulder, and her eyes widen as I produce a cock gag from my trunk—a short, veiny dildo attached to a leather strap that will go around her head, keeping the dildo in her mouth. I position her on all fours in the middle of the tent, her body exposed and vulnerable. Her breathing has quickened, her chest rising and falling with anticipation.

"Now, let's get that pretty mouth of yours stuffed," I purr, securing the gag behind her head. "There, that's better. All nice and full."

She tries to adjust to the gag, saliva already dripping down her chin. The sight sends a jolt of desire straight to my cock. "Can you breathe freely?" I demand, ensuring her airways aren't entirely blocked.

She nods in reply.

"If you need me to stop at any point, snap your fingers for me," I demand.

Sofia attempts it, leaning on one arm and snapping her fingers with the other hand.

"Good girl," I praise, positioning myself at her entrance, my cock aching to plunge into her.

"Are you ready for this?" I ask, my voice a rough whisper. "My cock in your pussy, the plug in your ass, and a penis gag in your mouth. That's a lot for a good girl like you to handle."

She looks at me over her shoulder and nods, her eyes fixed on me. I thrust forward, sheathing myself in her. Her breath catches, and she arches her back, moaning around the gag as I begin to move. I set a relentless pace, my cock sliding easily in and out of her slick passage. The sounds of our passion fill the tent—the slap of skin, her muffled whimpers.

My eyes drift shut struggling to keep it together with her tightness. I lose myself in the feel of her body.

"You like being stuffed in every hole and fucked hard, don't you?" I ask.

Her body is a playground I'm desperate to explore. Her muffled cries of pleasure drive me insane. This is what I want—to be surrounded by the sound of her desire always. I reach for a small vibrator from my trunk, something to push her over the edge.

Withdrawing my cock from her pussy, I line up the toy with her clit, pressing it against that bundle of nerves but without turning it on. Her hips buck greedily, seeking more pressure, but I hold the vibrator still, enjoying the power I have.

She whimpers, the gag muffling the sound. Slowly, I drag the vibrator in circles around her clit, teasing her mercilessly. Watching me over her shoulder, silently begging for more. I smirk, loving her responsiveness, and turn on the vibrator, starting at the lowest setting.

She moans around the gag as the vibrations dance over her sensitive flesh.

Slowly, I work the setting to medium and continue to circle her clit. She's so wet as I tease her entrance with my cock, groaning when I slide back inside her. I begin to thrust in time with the vibrations, pushing her closer to the edge.

I know she's on the brink. Her body is tense, her

breaths coming in short gasps, and her ass clenching rhythmically around the plug. So, I stop and ease the plug out of her ass before I grab the dildo that I'd used on her cunt earlier. It's still slick with her arousal, and I slide it back into her pussy.

Coating my cock generously with lube, my cock twitches with anticipation. I crave the moment when I'll finally be buried deep inside her asshole.

I take a moment to appreciate the sight before me—Sofia, wanton and flushed, waiting to be taken. Then, I guide my cock to her ass, teasing the pierced tip at her entrance. With a slow, deliberate thrust, I enter her, relishing the feel of her tight heat yielding to me.

Sofia makes a keening moan while I sink into her slowly, feeling every twitch of her muscles until I'm fully seated inside her ass. I pause, giving her a chance to adjust to the intense sensation. Her body clenches around me, and I know she's savoring the stretch.

"You like that?" I whisper, my cock throbbing with the effort of remaining still. "You like my thick cock in your tight little ass?"

She whimpers, the sounds vibrating around the penis gag in her mouth. It's a beautiful symphony of desire, and I want to hear her make more music.

Drawing out slowly, I thrust back in. With each thrust, I feel her relax, her body welcoming my invasion. Her ass is so tight, massaging my cock as I slide in and out. I feel the dildo between her thin walls, increasing the friction.

"Fuck, you're so fucking tight," I groan. "I love your ass."

I quicken the pace, pounding into her with purpose, my balls slapping against the dildo in her pussy. The combination of the two is driving me wild, and I know it's driving her crazy, too.

"That's it, baby girl, take it all," I encourage. "You're doing so good. Feel me stretch that ass wide open."

She moans, her ass clenching and releasing as I thrust, and I know she's loving it. I rub her clit in time with my thrusts. Her whole body jerks, and she glances over her shoulder at me, flushing deep red.

"That's my good girl," I praise, staring at her through the mask holes. "I bet this is exactly what you needed. All your holes stuffed, a good stretch and fill."

I'm close to the edge, but I want to hold on to give Sofia the release she deserves. With one hand, I rub her clit in tight, quick circles, feeling her buck beneath me in response. My other hand reaches around to squeeze her breast and pinch her nipple, with my chest covering her back.

"Come for me," I growl. "Show me how much you love having all your holes stuffed full. You're my perfect princess, taking everything I give you."

She whimpers, her body tightening around me, and I feel the telling flutter. Her ass clenches rhythmically around my cock, milking me.

"That's it, Sofia, let go," I encourage. "I want to feel you fall apart around my cock."

Her body obeys, shuddering uncontrollably as her orgasm washes over her. I fuck her through her release, extending her pleasure for as long as I can. Her juices squirt around the dildo in her pussy, making a mess—a beautiful fucking mess.

I feel her asshole tighten like a vise around my cock as her second orgasm ripples through her body. That's my girl—taking everything I give and loving it. I pound into her relentlessly, feeling my climax build like a tidal wave about to crash.

"Fuck, I'm gonna breed that tight ass," I growl. "You're gonna take my cum."

I grab her hips and thrust forward with all my might as I bury myself to the hilt inside her. With a powerful surge, I release, shooting my hot cum deep into her ass.

"Feel me fill you up, marking you as mine," I groan, my voice strained with pleasure.

My cock twitches as I empty myself inside her. Her orgasm is still spiking through her, the muscles of her ass rippling around my still-hard shaft, milking every last drop from me.

"You're incredible, Sofia," I whisper, my mask brushing against her ear. "I want to fuck you forever."

With a gentle, loving kiss against the back of her head, I unfasten the gag, freeing her mouth. Once free, she glances at me over her shoulder, and the sight is fucking beautiful. Her lips are swollen and red, and she looks utterly wrecked.

Our eyes lock, and my heart thrums at the depth of emotion I see within her green gaze. Her eyes shine with passion, desire, and something more—something that makes my own heart stutter in recognition.

"You're so fucking beautiful," I whisper.

I lean over her back, still buried deep inside her ass,

and kiss her tenderly. Our lips mold together in a messy kiss, and in that moment, all the words that have gone unspoken pass between us. I don't need to say "I love you" because she can feel it in this kiss.

Reluctantly, I withdraw my cock from her ass and the dildo from her pussy, leaving her body empty. I want her to know how much she means to me, how she's become my whole world.

I shift so I sit on the hay bale, and she's sitting in my lap. "You're my world, Sofia," I confess, cupping her cheek. "I've never felt this way about anyone. You've completely consumed me."

I search her eyes, needing her to understand the depth of my feelings, the way she's affected me like no one else ever has. I'm a man of few words, but I want to express everything swirling inside me now.

"I don't do relationships, but with you, I want something different," I continue, my voice rough. "I know this is crazy, but I can't let you go. Not now, not ever."

She bites her lip, her eyes sparkling with unshed tears, proving that she feels it, too. This isn't just lust or desire; it's something deeper, something that scares the hell out of me because it's unpredictable and uncontrollable.

"Say you feel it, too," I urge. "Tell me this isn't me losing my damn mind."

She nods. "I do. I feel it. You've consumed me, too, Ty. I'm terrified because I've never felt this way, but I don't want it to stop."

Relief washes over me, and I kiss her knuckles.

"We're in this together. Whatever this is, whatever it becomes—we're in it together."

I lean forward, kissing her tenderly, wanting to forever mark this moment in my memory. In her eyes, I see the reflection of my own emotions—love, desire, and a hint of fear. But it's a fear we can face together.

For now, we're caught in this perfect, passionate moment, our bodies still buzzing with the aftermath of pleasure. And tomorrow? Well, we'll face the complexities of our situation then. But for tonight, we're simply Tyson and Sofia, two people deeply in love, and that's all that matters.

31

TYSON

I pace Phoenix's trailer, scanning his latest security report. The mounting pressure from Jimmy shows in every line. Three more suppliers canceled contracts this morning alone.

"He's getting creative," Phoenix mutters from behind his wall of screens. "Had to fight off another breach attempt last night. These hackers he hired are good."

I rub my temples. "How's our digital fortress holding up?"

Tilly clears her throat. "So far, we're secure, but they're probing constantly. One slip from me and Phoenix, and they could get in."

A crash outside draws my attention. I see one of our newly installed lighting rigs lying in pieces through the window—the fourth "accident" this week.

"Another coincidence, I'm sure," I growl.

Lars bursts in, waving a stack of citations. "Health

inspector's back. Says our food storage temperatures are off by half a degree. Threatening to shut us down."

"Jimmy's flexing," I say. "Want to show us he can make life difficult without breaking our agreement."

"The suppliers are killing us, though," Lars continues. "Can't feed crowds without food vendors. He's trying to strangle us slowly."

I nod. "Keep working alternate supply chains. And Phoenix—double the security protocols. No chances."

"Sure thing. But boss, this is getting expensive. All these workarounds, new security, repairs..."

"I know." I stare at the shattered light fixture. Jimmy's playing a smart game. Death by a thousand cuts rather than open warfare. But I won't let him win. Not when Sofia's finally free.

A message flashes on Phoenix's screen—another attempted breach. "Tilly, they're trying again. Help me fight it." His fingers fly across the keyboard, reinforcing our digital walls. While Tilly helps him. Without Tilly, I'm not sure Phoenix could have held up the cyber security alone.

The carnival has survived worse. We'll weather this storm, too, no matter what Jimmy throws at us. I just have to stay one step ahead.

I lean against my desk, the weight of Jimmy's constant attacks bearing down on me.

"We can't keep playing defense," Lars says, pacing the trailer. "Every time we patch one hole, he finds another. We need to hit back, show him we're not just going to roll over."

I'm about to respond when Phoenix clears his

throat, his eyes fixed on one of his monitors. "We've got a problem." He swivels his chair to face us. "I've been monitoring Jimmy's communications. He's told the cops about our operation. There's a drug bust planned for tonight."

"Fuck." I slam my fist on the desk. All these little attacks were a distraction, keeping us scrambling while he set up the real blow.

Lars waves his hand. "So they know. Big deal. We'll clear everything out before they arrive."

"Yes, move the product to the backup location."

"Already messaging the crew," Phoenix says, fingers dancing across his keyboard. "Nash and Colt can handle the transfer. We'll be clean by midday."

I nod, but something doesn't sit right. Jimmy wouldn't play this card unless he was certain it would work. He's too smart for a simple drug bust that we could dodge.

"Have someone sweep every inch of storage," I tell Lars. "Check for planted evidence. Jimmy might try to leave us a surprise."

Lars pulls out his phone and starts texting. "I'll get Gage on it. We'll make sure there's nothing for the cops to find."

I snatch my jacket, making my way to the door. "I'll help Gage sweep storage. Four eyes are better than two."

Lars raises an eyebrow. "You sure? Usually, you delegate the grunt work."

"We can't risk missing anything. There's too much at stake."

I stride across the carnival grounds, nodding at Duke

as he tinkers with the Ferris wheel controls. The old-timer's been with the carnival before me, and he still thinks we're just a traveling show bringing joy to small towns. It's better that way.

Performers practice their routines nearby—jugglers tossing pins in perfect arcs. They're all good people, honest workers who'd be horrified to learn what really keeps this carnival running. Only Colt and Nash know the truth among the performers.

I spot Gage's hulking form by the storage containers, his skull mask reflecting the morning sun. He acknowledges me with a slight nod as I approach.

"Start with the main unit," I tell him, pulling out my keys. "Check every crate, every hidden panel. If Jimmy planted something, it'll be well-hidden."

Gage moves silently. His massive hands are surprisingly delicate as they probe for false bottoms or hollow spaces. I take the opposite end, checking behind the legitimate carnival supplies—cotton candy machines, spare parts, maintenance equipment—all the mundane items that make our cover so effective.

"Found something," Gage's deep voice breaks the silence. He holds up two bricks of cocaine, which he found behind an air vent.

"Motherfucker," I mutter, taking them. "Keep searching. There's probably more."

Jimmy's trying to make sure we can't clear everything in time. Plant enough evidence in enough places, and even a thorough sweep might miss something. One missed brick is all it would take to give the cops evidence we sell and fucking destroy us.

I wipe sweat from my forehead as Gage continues our methodical search. The morning sun turns the storage container into an oven. Another brick appears wedged behind electrical cables—Jimmy's men got creative with hiding spots.

"That's number twelve," I say, adding it to our growing pile.

I wave them over when Colt and Nash return from moving our main supply. "I need your help. Jimmy's boys planted the product everywhere. Check anything that looks suspicious."

Nash nods, his graceful movements belying his deadly nature. "Got it, boss."

I spot Remy near the carnival gates. "Remy! Get over here. Need all hands on deck."

Remy enters the unit when Cade's voice cuts through the morning air. "What the fuck are you all doing?"

I turn to see him striding toward us, his face twisted in confusion as he takes in the scene—me, Gage, Nash, Colt, and Remy all huddled around an open storage container with bricks of cocaine in our hands.

"Shit," I mutter.

No point lying now.

Cade's eyes lock onto the drugs. "Since when do we move product?"

"Since always," I admit, running a hand through my hair. "The carnival's been a front for distribution."

"And you didn't think to tell me?" His fists clench at his sides. "I thought we were friends, Ty. Brothers even.

But you've been running this operation right under my nose?"

"It was need-to-know," I say, but the excuse sounds weak.

"Need to know?" Cade laughs, but there's no humor in it. "I've had your back since day one. Kept every secret you've ever told me. And now I find out you've been running drugs this whole time?"

"He's right," Nash interjects. "Cade's proven himself loyal."

I let out a heavy sigh, meeting Cade's furious gaze. "You're right. I should have told you sooner. But this work requires a delicate touch, careful planning—"

"Delicate?" Cade barks out a laugh, stepping right into my face. His breath hits my cheek as he jabs a finger into my chest. "This kind of fucking work is the kind that needs unhinged, for fuck's sake. You need someone willing to get their hands dirty, someone who won't hesitate when shit goes sideways."

"That's exactly why I kept you out of it," I counter, holding my ground. "You're a loaded gun, Cade. One wrong move in this business gets everyone killed."

"Oh, and Mr. Careful over there isn't dangerous?" He jerks his thumb toward Gage, who stands silently watching our confrontation. "The guy who wears a skull mask twenty-four-seven?"

"Gage follows orders," I say firmly. "He thinks before he acts."

"And I don't?" Cade's voice rises. "I've proven myself time and time again. I've cleaned up messes, kept secrets, done whatever needed doing."

I run a hand through my hair. "Look, you're right. I should have allowed you to prove yourself with this, too."

"Damn straight you should have," he growls.

"Let me make it up to you," I offer, placing a hand on his shoulder. "We need all hands for this sweep; there's plenty of work after that. You're in if you want it."

Cade studies my face for a long moment before his shoulders relax. "Fine. But no more secrets, yeah?"

"No more secrets," I agree, relieved to have defused the situation. "Now help us find what Jimmy's men planted before the cops show up."

Cade's anger shifts focus. "That bastard's trying to take us down?" He rolls up his sleeves. "Where do you need me to look?"

I point toward the far side of the container. "Start with the maintenance supplies—they planted some behind the air vents. Check every panel, every loose screw. These fuckers got creative."

Cade nods and gets to work, his earlier anger channeling into focused determination. Nash takes the food storage area while Colt checks the props and costumes.

"Found two more!" Colt calls out, pulling bricks from inside a hollow juggling pin.

"Three here," Nash adds, emerging from behind stacked boxes of cotton candy mix.

I wipe sweat from my forehead as the pile grows. The morning sun beats down mercilessly, turning the metal containers into ovens. But we can't stop. One missed brick could destroy everything.

"Got another," Cade announces, fishing one from behind an electrical panel. "Clever bastards wired it in place."

The search continues, everyone working in tense silence. Every few minutes, someone finds another brick—behind the popcorn machine, inside a spare tire, wedged between support beams.

"Jesus," I mutter as Remy adds two more to the collection. "They must have had hours to plant all these."

Gage's quiet voice breaks through the heat. "Found more." He holds up three bricks tucked inside a fake bottom of a tool chest.

The pile keeps growing as we work through every nook and cranny. Jimmy's men left no stone unturned, no potential hiding spot unused. By the time we finish checking the first section, we've uncovered over thirty bricks.

"Keep going," I order, moving to the next container. "We've got five more units to search."

"How the fuck did they even get in here?" Lars voices what we're all thinking. "Security's tight as a drum. Phoenix has cameras on every inch."

I wipe sweat from my brow, studying the growing pile of planted cocaine. "Already got Phoenix reviewing the feeds. But Jimmy's crew is smart—they wouldn't walk past our cameras."

"Inside job?" Nash suggests, his eyes scanning our group.

The tension thickens. Trust is everything in our business, and the thought of a rat among us sets everyone on edge.

"Phoenix will find them," I say firmly. "He's checking every feed, every timestamp. If someone helped Jimmy's men get in, we'll know."

"Could be one of the regular carnival workers," Colt offers. "They don't know about our operation, but they could've been paid to let someone in."

Cade snorts. "Or it could be someone in this circle. Someone who knows all our security measures."

"Watch it," Lars warns.

Cade just shrugs. "What? We're all thinking it. How else would they know exactly where to hide this shit?"

My phone buzzes—a message from Phoenix.

> Found something. Come to the office.

"Keep searching," I order the group. "And remember, we're family here. A rat threatens all of us. Nobody in this circle would risk that."

But as I stride toward Phoenix's trailer, doubt gnaws at my gut. Someone got Jimmy's men past our security. Someone who knows our operation inside and out. The question is, who would dare betray us?

32

TYSON

I burst into the office trailer, my jaw clenching as I spot Duke's weathered face on the security feed. He moves purposefully through our storage area at 2 a.m., leading Jimmy's men straight to our most vulnerable spots.

"Fucking hell." My fists curl at my sides. "He knows every inch of this place."

Phoenix nods, rewinding the footage. "Three hours they were here. Duke showed them all the hiding spots and helped them plant the evidence in the main storage unit. They didn't put anything in the other units, so you don't need to continue. They cleared out before anyone stirred."

The betrayal burns in my chest. Duke's been with the carnival more than anyone. But I'd seen the resentment in his eyes when Gary handed me the reins instead of him. The sideways glances, the subtle challenges to my authority.

"Pull up his movements for the past two weeks," I

order, leaning over Phoenix's shoulder. "I want to know every contact he's had with Jimmy's people."

More footage rolls across the screens—Duke in conversations by the Ferris wheel, accepting thick envelopes, pointing out our security cameras. The old bastard's been plotting this.

"He's in his usual spot," Phoenix says, switching to a live feed. "Working on the Ferris wheel controls."

My blood boils as Duke tinkers with the machinery, probably planning his next betrayal. After everything Gary taught us about loyalty about family—Duke threw it all away because his ego couldn't handle being passed over.

"Get Lars," I growl. "Tell him to bring Duke here. Quietly."

Phoenix's fingers fly across his keyboard. "What about the cops? They'll be here in six hours."

"First things first." I straighten up, cold rage settling in my bones. "Duke needs to learn what happens to rats in this family."

I stand behind my desk as Lars shoves Duke into my trailer, Phoenix trailing behind them. Duke's weathered face shows confusion, but a flicker of fear in his eyes tells me he knows exactly why he's here. Lars's murderous glare confirms my suspicions—he's figured it out, too.

"Have a seat, Duke." I gesture to the chair in front of my desk, keeping my voice steady and calm. "We need to discuss something important."

Duke settles into the chair, his hands gripping the armrests. "What's this about, Tyson?"

Phoenix pulls up a video on his monitor and turns it

to face him. "Why don't you tell me what I'm looking at here?" The footage shows him leading Jimmy's men through our storage area, pointing out hiding spots.

His face drains of color as he watches himself betray us. The confident facade cracks, replaced by naked fear.

"Interesting viewing, isn't it?" I lean forward, placing my hands on the desk. "Twenty-seven years with this carnival, Duke. Twenty-seven years of trust, of family. And you threw it all away because Gary chose me instead of you ten fucking years ago."

Duke's mouth opens and closes, but no words come out. Sweat beads on his forehead.

"You want to know what we found this morning?" I continue. "Thirty-eight bricks of cocaine, planted exactly where you showed Jimmy's men to put them. The cops are coming in a few hours, thanks to your new friend Jimmy."

Lars steps closer, his presence looming over Duke's shoulder. The old man shrinks in his chair.

"So here's what's going to happen," I say. "You're going to tell me everything. Every conversation with Jimmy, every detail you shared, every penny he paid you. And maybe I'll make it quick when we're done with you."

Duke's face crumples. "Please, Tyson. I can explain—"

The sharp crack of Lars's palm against Duke's cheek cuts through his pleading.

"Pull it together," Lars snarls. "Traitors don't get mercy."

I watch Duke's shoulders shake as tears stream down

his face. After all our years together, the sight should move me and stir some emotion, but I feel nothing except cold purpose.

"Stand up," I order, my voice steady.

Duke stumbles to his feet. "I'll do anything. Please, I—"

"You had your chance to be loyal," I cut him off. "Now you pay the price."

I grab his arm and guide him toward the door, maintaining a firm but measured grip.

"Where are you taking me?" Duke's voice breaks.

"Somewhere more appropriate." I lead him across the grounds toward my Mustang. "Can't have the office getting messy, can we?"

I shove Duke into my Mustang, his body folding into the leather seat like a broken puppet. Turning to Lars, I keep my voice low and controlled.

"Get the guys. Meet me at the storage unit where we moved the stash. Ensure they scan the bricks for any tracking devices or bugs. If they're clean, bring them to the unit. If not, dump them in the river on the way. I want everyone to see what happens to rats in this family."

Lars nods. Duke didn't know about our drug business until Jimmy approached him, but that doesn't excuse his betrayal.

"On it, boss." Lars strides away.

Phoenix slides into the back seat of my Mustang, laptop balanced on his knees. His fingers fly across the keys as I start the engine.

"Message Tilly," I tell him. "Have her monitor our

cyber security while you're out. Can't risk any more surprises today."

Duke stares straight ahead as I pull away from the carnival grounds. We can't deal with him here—not with the cops due within hours. But the storage unit will serve our purpose just fine. And there's no way Duke could have told Jimmy about it, as he has no idea we have a storage unit nearby. We have units in every major town and city where we sell, just in case.

Phoenix's typing provides a steady backdrop to Duke's ragged breathing. The old man hasn't said a word since I shoved him in the car, probably realizing that begging won't save him now.

I grip the steering wheel tighter, focusing on the road ahead. The storage unit isn't far—just enough distance to ensure no connection to the carnival when the cops arrive.

Pulling up at the unit, I put on gloves and throw a pair to Phoenix. Then, I drag Duke into the dimly lit storage unit, his feet stumbling as he tries to resist. With practiced efficiency, I loop some rope through the rafters and secure his arms above his head, leaving him dangling with his toes barely scraping the concrete floor.

"Please, Tyson. I made a mistake. I wasn't thinking straight—" Duke's voice cracks.

"Wasn't thinking straight?" I tighten the knots. "You led Jimmy's men right to us. Showed them every hiding spot and set us up to take the fall."

"He promised me—"

"What? The carnival?" I circle him slowly. "That

was your price? Getting me out of the way so you could finally run things?"

Tears stream down Duke's weathered face. "You don't understand. After all those years working alongside Gary, teaching me everything he knew... he just handed it all to you."

I lean against a support beam, studying Duke's tear-streaked face. "You want to know why Gary chose me? Because you didn't have what it takes. Not for the show, and definitely not for the side business."

"I ran this carnival while Gary was sick!" Duke struggles against his bonds.

"You maintained it. There's a difference." I push off from the beam. "Gary needed someone young, someone who could handle both sides of this operation. Someone with the darkness it takes to do what needs to be done."

Duke's face twists. "Darkness? Do you mean running drugs behind everyone's backs? Taking huge paydays while keeping us in the dark?"

"That's what this is really about, isn't it?" I step closer. "Jimmy told you about the side hustle and the money I was making, and you got angry."

"Damn right, I got angry!" Spittle flies from Duke's mouth. "Twenty-seven years of loyalty, and you're making millions while I fix rides for not much more than minimum wage?"

"And instead of coming to me, you went straight to Jimmy." I shake my head. "Why didn't you ask me about it, Duke? Why betray your family to an outsider?"

"Would you have told me the truth?" His voice cracks. "Would you have let me in?"

"We'll never know now, will we?" I study his broken expression. "Because you chose Jimmy over family."

Duke hangs his head, shoulders shaking. "I was angry. Felt like you'd betrayed me first."

"The difference is, my secrets kept you safe. Your betrayal put us all at risk."

The storage unit door creaks open, and my men file in individually. All of them are wearing gloves, too, as Lars knows the drill by now. Their faces are grim, and they understand the gravity of the situation. Lars shoulders a heavy bag, and so do Colt and Nash. "The bricks were clean?" I confirm.

Lars nods. "Yep, swept them all."

Cade's eyes lock onto Duke, and his body tenses like a coiled spring. Before I can react, he lunges forward with a snarl.

Lars catches him by the shoulder, yanking him back. "Cool it," he growls in Cade's ear. "This isn't your show. Ty calls the shots here."

"But that fucking rat—" Cade struggles against Lars's grip.

"I said cool it." Lars's voice drops lower. "We follow the boss's lead. That's how this works."

Cade's jaw clenches, but he stops fighting. His chest heaves with controlled breaths as he steps back in line with the others. Nash and Colt flank him.

Gage leans against the doorframe, silent as always, while Remy unloads the planted bricks from a duffel bag. The evidence of Duke's betrayal piles up on the concrete floor.

I meet each of their eyes, seeing anger and determination. They're ready to follow my lead, to deal with this threat to our family. Even Cade has settled, though his fingers still twitch at his sides.

Duke hangs between us, his sobs the only sound breaking the tense silence. I grab him by the shirt, wrenching him forward until our faces are inches apart.

"You're gonna tell me everything you told Jimmy." My voice is barely a whisper. "Names, dates, locations. And then you're gonna beg for mercy, so I let you die quick."

His eyes dart wildly. "Just let me go. I didn't tell him anything else, I swear—"

"Cut the bullshit." Lars shoves him. "We know you played us. Now it's time to pay."

The fear in Duke's eyes shifts to resignation as he realizes his pleas won't save him.

I stand in front of him, meeting his gaze with cold steadiness. "You wanted to run things, Duke? Be careful what you wish for."

I signal my men to follow and move to the far end of the storage unit. Behind me, Duke's whimpers grow more desperate. He knows what's coming.

"Lars, Cade, secure him to that pillar." I nod to the steel pillar at the unit's center. "Remy, bring me the box of tools from my trunk."

They spring into action while Duke thrashes against his bindings. I consider the impending violence and how a sculptor might select just the right tools for his masterpiece.

"Here, boss." Remy holds out a metal toolbox.

I take it with a nod, careful not to break eye contact

with him. It is a silent reminder that our family is strong, and betrayals only strengthen us.

"Ty." Duke's voice quavers. "Don't do this. Please."

His legs squirm, trying to keep his feet on the ground, but Cade and Lars tighten their hold on the rope around his torso, lifting him up until he dangles a foot off the concrete.

"I don't like getting my tools dirty," I explain. "Now, let's see what you gave Jimmy besides access to our operation."

I pluck a pair of needle-nose pliers from the toolbox and maneuver them so Duke can see them gleaming in the fluorescent light.

Duke's whimpers turn to screams as I wrench the first nail from his index finger. Blood wells up from the exposed nail bed, dripping onto the concrete floor.

Cade bounces on his heels, eyes bright with excitement. His grin stretches wide as Duke's screams echo through the storage unit. The unhinged bastard always did enjoy violence.

Behind his skull mask, Gage remains motionless, watching with his usual eerie silence. His massive frame casts long shadows in the dim light.

Lars stands at my right shoulder, face impassive as I move to the next fingernail. He's seen enough of my torture to stay cool, methodically noting Duke's reactions for signs of breaking.

Phoenix keeps typing on his laptop, occasionally glancing at the traitor. We've done this dance before—he knows the routine.

"Please, stop—" Duke's plea cuts off in another shriek as the second nail tears free.

"Ready to start talking?" I ask Duke, positioning the pliers around his third nail.

His head thrashes. "I'll tell you everything! Just please—no more!"

I pause, keeping the pliers in place. "Start with the first meeting. When did Jimmy approach you?"

Blood continues dripping from his mangled fingers as Duke starts spilling his guts. Three nails was all it took to break him. Amateur.

"Three days ago," Duke gasps, his fingers twitching. "Jimmy came to my trailer after hours. Said he knew about the drugs, knew you were making millions while keeping me in the dark."

I twist the pliers, drawing another whimper. "And?"

"He offered me a cut. If I helped frame you, he'd let me take over the carnival." Duke's words tumble out between ragged breaths. "Wanted me to show his men the best places to plant evidence."

Lars steps forward. "What exactly did you tell them about our route?"

"Everything." Duke's head hangs low. "Where we're headed next—Burlington, then Cedar Rapids. Showed them the maintenance schedules, when security would be lightest."

"The bricks?" I press.

"Jimmy's men brought them last night, as you saw on the feeds. I showed them the best places to hide them in the main storage unit." His voice cracks. "They said the cops would find them during inspection tonight."

Cade snarls from behind me. "You fucking piece of—"

"Quiet," I snap, keeping my eyes on Duke. "What else?"

"That's all, I swear." Blood drips steadily from his exposed nail beds. "Just the routes and helping plant the drugs. Jimmy said that would be enough to take you down."

I share a look with Lars. We've already seen the security footage confirming Duke's story of him leading Jimmy's men through our grounds and accepting an envelope that could only be payment last night.

"Please," Duke whispers. "That's everything I know. I told you everything."

I set down the pliers. His confession matches what Phoenix caught on camera. There's no point in dragging this out further. We have what we need, and it won't be long until the cops return to the carnival.

The men stand silently.

"Who wants the privilege of ending him?" I ask, meeting each of their eyes in turn.

Cade shifts forward, a sinister grin on his face. "I do."

I smirk, unsurprised. Cade's always been the most unhinged among us—a primal force yearning for release.

"Go on, then. Make it quick." I reach into my toolbox and pull out a hunting knife, handing it to Cade by the blade. "Do it right."

Cade's eyes light up as he takes the knife, his fingers wrapping around the handle. Without hesitation, he steps forward and slashes Duke's throat in a swift, brutal move that sends blood spurting across the floor.

Duke's body jerks, his eyes wide. A gurgling sound escapes his throat as his life spills into a red geyser. He twitches once, twice, then goes still.

As his life slips away, silence descends on the storage unit. The only sound is the soft patter of blood dripping from the body onto the concrete floor. I eye each of my men, judging their reactions.

Cade's eyes glint with sadistic satisfaction.

Lars is unreadable, his face a carefully neutral mask. He's seen enough death to know the importance of staying steady.

Gage remains silent, his features hidden behind his skull mask. Only his eyes are visible, icy pools that give nothing away.

Remy's breath quickens. Nash's jaw is set with determination as he watches the light fade from Duke's eyes with a dark glint in his own.

Colt shifts, his fingers curling into fists, but he holds his ground. He knows the price of weakness, of showing hesitation.

I nod with satisfaction. "Well done." I turn to Lars. "Clean this up, boys, and get rid of the body. I'll take care of the carnival."

Lars nods, already reaching for the duffel bag. We've dealt with enough bodies that the process is routine now.

Cade sheaths the knife, wiping his hands on his pants. Blood stains his shirt. "That was fun."

I grab a rag, wiping down the toolbox to remove any traces of blood. "You did good, Cade. He deserved it."

His chest puffs out with pride. "He did, didn't he? I'm just glad I was the one who got to do it."

"But, you'll have to burn those clothes," Lars says, returning with a heavy-duty black garbage bag, efficiently wrapping up Duke's body.

"Where should we dump him?" Remy asks.

"Bury him out in the woods," I say.

"Woods it is, boss." Lars gets to work trying to shift Duke into a bag.

"We'll handle everything," Nash adds, already gathering cleaning supplies.

"Like it never happened," Colt agrees.

"We'll make it deep," Cade chimes in with that manic grin. "Wouldn't want any animals digging him up."

Gage nods, his massive frame moving to help Lars with the body.

"On it, boss," Remy confirms, grabbing shovels from the corner.

I motion to Phoenix, who's already closing his laptop. "Let's roll."

We leave the storage unit, the sounds of my men's cleanup fading behind us. The cool air hits my face as we stride toward my waiting Mustang. Turning the key brings the engine roaring to life, and I pull away from the carnival grounds, leaving my crew to their grim task.

Phoenix types away on his phone beside me. The streetlights flash across his face as we speed toward the carnival, neither of us speaking. Some things don't need words.

33

SOFIA

I'm adjusting one of the carnival banners when I notice Ty pull up in his Mustang with a thunderous look on his face. Phoenix is in the passenger's seat.

I didn't even know he'd left. "Hey, where did you go?" I ask, approaching him. "You seem on edge."

Ty's jaw tightens, and he pulls me aside. "Your father's latest move. He tipped off the cops about our operation."

My stomach drops. "What? How?"

"Planted evidence. His men hid thirty-eight bricks of cocaine throughout our storage with the help of Duke, our longest-standing member of the carnival. If we hadn't found them…" He runs a hand through his hair. "The cops will be here tonight, expecting to bust us."

"Shit. So you were moving everything before they arrived?"

"Yeah. We've cleared it all out now, but it was close. And dealt with the rat."

The way he says that makes me shudder. "And the cops won't find a thing?"

Ty shakes his head. "No chance. We're all good now. And still have a few hours to spare until the raid."

I feel sick thinking about how much planning must have gone into this. My own father trying to destroy the man I love. "I'm so sorry, Ty. I never thought he'd—"

"Hey." He cups my face. "This isn't on you. We caught it in time. The cops won't find anything when they show up."

"But he'll try something else. You know he will."

"Let him try." Tyson's eyes harden. "I've dealt with worse than Jimmy Moretti. We'll handle whatever he throws at us."

I lean into his touch, but I can't shake the knot of worry in my gut. My father's resources are vast, and his determination to separate us is absolute.

"It's fine, baby girl. We've got everything under control." Tyson wraps me in a strong embrace, and I lean into him, soaking in his reassurance. "My guys are on it. We'll be ready for whatever your father throws our way."

I nod, but it's hard to shake the fear that grips me. "We should be double-checking. Making sure we didn't miss anything."

His thumbs stroke soothing patterns on my lower back. "We're certain we got it all. There's no need to worry."

Sensing my lingering tension, he takes my hand and leads me toward his trailer. Inside the trailer, Ty shuts the door behind us. Before I can say another word, he pulls me roughly against him, his lips crushing mine in a fierce kiss.

Without breaking our lip-lock, he maneuvers us toward the bed. His hands move roughly over my body, tearing at my silk blouse.

I whimper into his mouth as his teeth nip at my lower lip. Part of me wants to ask him to slow down, but another part hungers for the release only he can give me. The fear and tension of the day melt away under the heat of his touch.

Tyson pushes me onto the bed, his hands already working to free himself from his pants. "Time to take out some of this frustration on that perfect body of yours."

I sit up, tugging at his shirt. "Wait—I want you to wear the mask again." My cheeks get hot, and I lower my eyes. "Please?"

He freezes momentarily, and then a slow smile spreads across his face. "Hell, yes."

In a fluid movement, he shrugs off his shirt and reaches for the mask, settling it over his face. It transforms him into a figure of pure domination.

"Does it turn you on?" His voice is deep and gravelly. "Imagining I'm a stranger, taking what I want from that gorgeous body?"

My breath quickens as a rush of desire hits me. "Yes. Pretend to be an intruder. Force yourself on me, take me against my will."

"Is that what you want?" His deep voice sends shivers down my spine.

I nod, feeling my heart pounding in my chest.

He tilts his head, considering me for a moment. "Say it."

"I want you to force yourself on me." My cheeks grow even warmer, but I hold his intense gaze.

A growl rumbles in his throat, and he steps forward, crowding me on the bed. "Say it again."

"I want you to force yourself on me," I repeat.

He wraps a hand around my neck, pulling me closer. Our lips are mere inches apart. "You'll have to fight me then, baby girl."

"I will." My breath comes in short gasps as his lips brush mine, his fingers digging into my skin.

"Good." His whisper is laced with desire. "But remember, this is make-believe."

"Yes."

"Safe word?"

"Purple," I recall from before.

"Good girl," he murmurs. "Not that you'll need it."

Before I can respond, he releases me and steps away. I watch as he opens the trailer door and slips out, leaving it ajar.

I sit up, my heart pounding.

What am I doing?

This is crazy. A thrill runs through me at the thought of what will happen.

The trailer door swings open with a creak. I jump, then relax as the masked figure steps in, his eyes locking onto me.

"Hey, beautiful." He grins, his voice slightly different as he speaks. "Didn't expect to find such a pretty lady home alone."

My breath catches as I notice the change in his demeanor. He's playing the part perfectly. A surge of dampness pools between my legs as he strides toward the bed.

"Get away from me!" I scramble backward on the bed, my heart hammering. "Leave now, or I'll scream!"

His eyes darken. "Scream all you want. No one's coming to save you."

"Stop!" I yelp as he looms over me, grabbing my wrists and pinning them above my head with one hand. "What do you want?"

"Oh, I think you know," he growls.

His grip tightens on my wrists as I struggle against him. "You're gonna be real fun, aren't you?"

I try to wriggle out of his grasp, but his hold is relentless. "Let me go!" A rush of adrenaline and desire flood me as his body hovers over mine.

"No chance." His voice is like velvet, dangerous and smooth. He pulls my wrists above my head with one hand while the other slides down my body roughly. "I'm going to make you scream for me."

"No—stop!" My protests sound weak even to my own ears. I can feel his hard cock pressing against my thigh.

In one swift motion, he tears my blouse, exposing my lace bra. His fingers reach for the clasp, and it pops open, setting my breasts free.

"So beautiful," he growls. "But I think we need to teach you a lesson in manners."

His hand snakes out to grab a fistful of my hair,

wrenching my head back. Pain shoots through my scalp, but it only heightens my desire.

I whimper as he tugs. "Please..." My voice catches, betraying my conflicting emotions.

"Please, what?" His mask grazes my neck, sending tingles down my spine.

"Please, don't."

"Oh, I will," he promises. His hand releases my hair, only to land a stinging slap on my inner thigh. The pain is brief, like a spark of electricity. I cry out, my body arching off the bed.

Without warning, he hooks his fingers into the waistband of my panties and rips them off. I lay bare before him, completely vulnerable.

"What a pretty sight." He rubs himself through his pants, his eyes never leaving my body.

Panic rises in my chest. "What—what are you doing?"

He frees his thick, pierced cock, stroking it slowly as he eyes my nakedness. "I'm going to fuck you whether you like it or not."

"No—you can't!" My struggles intensify, but it's useless. He's too strong, and I don't want him to stop. He knows that because unless I say purple, he isn't stopping.

He chuckles, low and dangerous. "Safe word, remember? That's the only way I stop."

The thrill silences me. "I—I don't want the safe word."

His eyes glitter with victory. "Good girl."

With that, he pulls me to the edge of the bed, my

legs dangling off the side. I feel vulnerable, entirely at his mercy.

His hands grip my thighs, and he thrusts into me in one fluid motion, his cock stretching me deliciously.

He stares down at me, his eyes hooded with desire. "See? You're gonna like this after all."

His words spark defiance within me. "No, I won't!"

A cruel light flashes in his eyes through the mask's holes. "Won't you?"

His hips move, slow and deep, each thrust taking him even further inside me. I want to keep up my resistance, but my body responds to his invasion with hunger.

"You're a feisty one." He quickens his pace, his cock plunging ruthlessly into my core. "Let's see how long you can hold out without shattering on my cock like a dirty slut."

My moans fill the trailer, mingling with the rhythmic slapping of our bodies. "No—please..."

"Please, what?" His thrusts are relentless, driving me to the brink of release.

"Please, don't stop." The words escape my lips before I can stop them.

He grunts, his grasp on my thighs tightening. "That's what I thought."

His pace increases, pounding into me with force. The friction of our bodies sends sparks of pleasure throughout my nerve endings. I'm overcome by a tidal wave of sensation, my body becoming a slave to his command.

"Come for me." His demand sends me over the

edge. My body convulses around him, waves of pleasure rippling through me.

His thrusts become erratic as my walls clench around him. With a final, powerful thrust, he spills inside me, his grunt of satisfaction filling the room.

Our bodies remain joined as our breathing slows. He reaches up to remove the mask. And I fucking love him even more. The way he played that was goddamn intoxicating, and I can't wait to do it again.

He strokes my cheek. "Baby, are you okay?"

I nod, unable to speak.

"You're sure?" His thumb brushes away a stray tear. "I pushed you, but I would've stopped if—"

I silence him with a kiss, my hands clutching his shoulders. "Don't ever stop," I whisper against his lips. "It's what I wanted."

He pulls me closer, his lips finding mine in a passionate embrace. "You've got me, baby girl. Whatever you want, all you have to do is ask."

And I know without a doubt that despite the danger involved, I'm exactly where I'm meant to be, in the arms of my master.

34

TYSON

$\mathcal{A}$ few days after Jimmy's botched attempt to bring us down, I lean over Phoenix's shoulder, watching lines of code scroll across his multiple screens. "You sure that'll work? Jimmy's hackers need to think they've struck gold."

The cops came that night and left empty handed, as expected. Luckily, Phoenix is the best at what he does. If he hadn't caught wind of the raid, I don't want to think about what would have happened... All of us would be staring at fucking bars for years.

"Already planted the breadcrumbs." Phoenix's fingers tap rhythmically on his keyboard. "Made it look like they broke through our first layer of security. When they dig deeper, they'll find exactly what we want them to see."

I pace behind him, my boots scuffing against the trailer floor. "And they won't trace it back to us?"

"Please." Phoenix shoots me an offended look. "I've got Tilly working on reinforcing our security in my trailer. She's the best at what she does—nobody's getting near our real data."

"How's she holding up? Still nervous about being involved?"

Phoenix's typing pauses for a moment. "She's good. Actually enjoying herself, said something about it being like the ultimate video game challenge."

I nod, relief washing over me. Having Tilly on our side has doubled our digital defense capabilities. "Ensure the shipping manifests look legitimate enough to pass the initial inspection. Jimmy must think this is the motherload he's been waiting for."

"Already done. The documentation shows three times our usual volume through the back channels. His hackers will think they've hit the jackpot when they 'discover' it."

I grip the back of his chair, watching the screens flicker with activity. "How long until they bite?"

"Given their pattern of attacks?" Phoenix pulls up a timeline. "I'd say they'll find it within the next few hours. They're getting desperate, making mistakes. Perfect time to feed them what we want them to see."

With a creak, the door opens, and Lars walks in, Nash trailing right after him.

"You wanted to see us, boss?" Lars asks.

"Yeah, come in." I wave them closer, moving away from Phoenix's screens. "Got a special job for you two. Time to play the disgruntled employees card."

Nash's eyebrows lift. "You want us to flip on you?"

"Exactly." I pull out a manila envelope from my desk drawer. Inside are shipping manifests, bank statements, and route information—all carefully crafted to match what Phoenix planted for their hackers to find. "Take these to Jimmy, tell him you're tired of my leadership, that I've lost my mind over his daughter."

Lars takes the envelope, thumbing through its contents. "How much of this matches their digital finds?"

"Every detail." I lean against my desk. "The numbers, dates, locations—it all lines up perfectly. When Jimmy's people cross-reference what you bring them with what their hackers 'discovered,' everything will check out."

"And our story?" Nash asks.

"Keep it simple. Say, I've been cutting your percentages, taking bigger risks, and making you nervous. Hell, throw in that I've been unstable since taking Sofia—that'll appeal to Jimmy's ego."

Lars nods. "He'll eat that shit up. Anything that paints you as the villain in his daughter's story."

"Make it convincing," I stress. "Jimmy's paranoid, but he's not stupid. He needs to believe you're genuinely turning on me."

"Don't worry," Nash says, a cold smile on his lips. "We know how to play our parts."

I clap Nash on the shoulder. "Thanks. Get it done."

Leaving him to work, I stride out of the trailer into the early morning air. The carnival is just starting to wake up, workers setting up for another day of cover operations. The scent of cotton candy and popcorn already drifts through the grounds.

I find Colt and Remy by the Ferris wheel, clipboard in hand, as they inspect the machinery.

I approach them. "How's it looking?"

Colt looks up from his checklist. "Every ride's got fresh inspection certificates. Maintenance logs are detailed down to the smallest bolt change."

"Safety permits are all current," Remy adds. "Even got the food vendor licenses renewed early. Health department won't find a single violation to nail us on."

"Good." I examine the documentation they've gathered. "We need everything above board. One slip in the legitimate business could give the cops the excuse to shut us down."

"Already handled the employee paperwork, too," Colt says. "Work visas, tax forms, social security—it's all clean and organized."

"Insurance policies are paid up," Remy chimes in. "Got extra coverage on everything, just in case Jimmy tries to arrange any more serious 'accidents.'"

I nod, satisfied with their thoroughness. "Keep at it. If anyone official shows up, we give them nothing to work with."

They return to their tasks as I head in search of Gage. Near the haunted house attraction, I spot the tall figure of Gage, his skull mask in place as always as I approach.

"Need a word, Gage." I gesture for him to meet me to one side, leading him to a quieter corner where we won't be overheard.

His gaze pierces right through me. He waits, silent and expectant.

I study Gage's masked face, knowing the perfect watchdog stands before me. "I need your eyes on everything. Every stranger lingering too long, every worker acting suspicious, every shadow that seems out of place."

Gage tilts his head.

"You see anything—and I mean anything—that feels wrong, you sound the alarm. I know you notice things others miss." I lower my voice. "Jimmy's going to try something. The question is when and where."

A single nod from Gage.

"Good. Keep to the shadows; do what you do best." I turn away, knowing he'll disappear into the darkness like always. And then, I head toward my trailer, where I find Sofia curled up on the leather couch, her phone clutched in her hands.

"Baby girl, it's time." I sit beside her. "We need to make that call to the feds."

She bites her lip, conflict clear in her eyes. "I know what he is, what he's done. But he's still my father."

"And he'll keep trying to tear us apart unless we stop him." I brush a strand of red hair from her face. "You're stronger than you think."

Sofia takes a deep breath and unlocks her phone. Her fingers shake as she dials the number we got from Phoenix.

"Federal Bureau of Investigation," a voice answers.

"I... I need to report organized crime activities." Sofia's voice steadies as she continues, "My name is Sofia Moretti. I have information about Jimmy Moretti's criminal enterprise in Dawsbury."

I squeeze her hand as she details years of her father's illegal operations, providing dates, names, and locations that will give the feds everything they need for tomorrow's raid. And then she tells them about tomorrow's meeting. The feds arrange a meeting for the morning beforehand to get more evidence in person.

When she hangs up, tears streak her cheeks. I pull her into my arms, letting her cry against my chest.

I hold Sofia, feeling her tears soak through my shirt. Her body trembles with each sob, the weight of betraying her father hitting her full force. I stroke her hair, letting her process the gravity of what she's just done.

After a few minutes, her crying subsides. She pulls back just enough to look up at me, her green eyes rimmed red.

"We could never be together with him out there," she whispers, her fingers clutching my shirt. "He'd never stop hunting us or trying to tear us apart."

"I know, baby girl." I cup her face, wiping away a stray tear with my thumb.

She leans into my touch. "Everything I've ever wanted was right here, but he'd destroy it all just to keep me in that gilded cage."

I lean down, pressing my lips to hers. She responds with a softness that contrasts sharply with our usual passionate encounters. This kiss holds something deeper.

She breaks the kiss, resting her forehead against my chest. We stay like that, wrapped in each other's arms, as the distant sounds of the carnival drift through the trailer walls.

35

SOFIA

After calling the feds, I sit in the front row, watching Tyson command the circus ring with his usual charisma. My heart pounds as I observe his every move, knowing this is one of the last shows in Dawsbury before we move on.

Tomorrow everything changes—my life, family, everything I've ever known.

Tension radiates from his shoulders as he guides the performers through their acts. Even beneath his showman's smile, I can see the worry in his eyes when they meet mine. He's been protective today, keeping me close or having Nash or Colt nearby whenever he can't be with me.

The crowd gasps and cheers at Nash's and Colt's death-defying feats as they perform on the trapeze, but my focus remains on Ty. His voice booms through the tent, directing attention to each spectacular moment. I marvel at how he maintains such control despite everything weighing on his mind.

As the final act concludes and the audience exits into the cool night air, I remain seated. The emptying tent feels vast and quiet, with only the soft creak of ropes and canvas above. Cleanup crews move efficiently around the edges but fade into the background.

Ty approaches, his ringmaster's coat catching the gleams of the spotlight. His expression softens as he reaches for my hand. Standing before me in the dimming tent, authority still radiating from his presence, he says, "Step right up, baby girl, into the arms of your master."

I do as he says and stand, stepping into his arms and inhaling his masculine scent. The familiar mix of leather, musk, and something distinctly Tyson fills my senses. His strong arms envelop me, and I press my face against his chest, feeling the steady thump of his heart beneath his ringmaster's coat.

"You were amazing out there," I murmur, tightening my grip around his waist. Despite what happens tomorrow looming over us, this moment feels safe.

His hand slides up my back, fingers tangling in my red hair as he tilts my face to meet his gaze. Those dark eyes that first caught my attention at the carnival entrance now look at me with such intensity it steals my breath.

"My beautiful girl," he breathes, thumb brushing my cheek. The calluses on his hands graze my skin. "So perfect in my arms."

I rise on my tiptoes, pressing closer. His coat buttons dig into my chest through my thin dress, but I don't care. All that matters is being held by him, breathing him in.

His fingers trace patterns on my back as we stand in the dimming tent. The silence stretches between us, comfortable yet weighted with unspoken thoughts.

"Tell me about your mother," Tyson says against my hair. "You never mention her."

My body tenses. The memories I try so hard to keep locked away come rushing back. "She couldn't handle this life," I whisper, my voice catching. "The constant pressure, the expectations..."

"What happened?"

"She was like me—young, swept into this world by her father's position. And the deeper she got, the more trapped she felt." I pull back, meeting his gaze. "The arranged marriage, the rules, the constant surveillance broke her. She left a note, and I found her on the master bath floor. Pill bottles scattered across the marble countertops."

Ty's arms tighten around me. "How old were you?"

"Twelve. I watched her spiral for years before that. She'd cry in her room when she thought no one could hear her. Sometimes, she'd look at me with such sadness, like she knew I'd end up like her." My fingers grip his coat harder.

"Baby girl..." Ty cups my face in his hands. "You're stronger than that. You fought back."

"Because of you." I lean into his touch. "You showed me there was another way. Mom never had that chance."

His lips capture mine in a tender kiss, cradling my face with his hands. The gentle pressure speaks volumes, so different from his usual domineering touch. When we part, I rest my forehead against his chest, listening to his steady heartbeat.

"What about your family?" I ask. "You know everything about my family, but you never talk about yours."

His fingers pause their gentle strokes through my hair. "Not much to tell. Dad was a con man who dragged us from town to town, always one step ahead of the law."

"And your mother?" I press.

"Left when I was eleven. Dad's schemes broke her." His voice carries a bitter edge. "The last thing I remember is her kneeling down, promising to return for me. She never did."

I squeeze him tighter. "That must have been awful."

"Dad raised me the only way he knew—teaching me every trick in the book. How to read people, how to gain their trust, how to spot an easy mark." Ty's laugh holds no humor. "By twelve, I could run a better con than most adults."

"What happened to him?"

"Love killed him." Tyson's words come out harsh. "After Mom left, Dad fell apart," he says, his voice rough with old pain. "Started drinking heavily. He could barely function most days, so I had to step up and run the cons myself."

My heart aches to imagine a young Ty, eleven years old, shouldering such responsibility. "That's too much for a child to handle."

"Someone had to keep us afloat." His fingers absently stroke my hair. "I got pretty good at it, too.

People trust kids more, you know? Makes them lower their guard."

"And your father?"

"The bottle became his only companion. He'd ramble about Mom coming back, how he couldn't live without her." His chest rises with a deep breath. "Found him one morning, just a week before my sixteenth birthday. He'd drank himself to death."

I tighten my grip around his waist. "What did you do?"

"Ran. There was no way I was letting them put me into foster care. Ended up here at the carnival. The old ringmaster, Gary, took me under his wing and taught me everything about running this place—both the legitimate side and..." He trails off, but I understand what he means. "He handed me the reins when he was ready to retire."

The pain in his voice matches the ache I feel for my mother. We're both products of parents who couldn't handle their worlds—his father destroyed by love, my mother crushed by duty. Yet here we stand, choosing to fight instead of surrender.

36

TYSON

I stand in the abandoned warehouse, my crew strategically positioned around me. The setting sun casts long shadows through the broken windows, but our surveillance covers every corner. Phoenix's voice crackles in my earpiece, confirming that the feds are in position.

I pull Sofia closer, her body trembling. Her warmth is a stark contrast to the cold metal walls surrounding us.

"What if this doesn't work?" Her fingers grip my shirt. "What if someone gets hurt?"

I cup her face, tilting it to meet my gaze. "Your father has hurt enough people. It's time someone stood up to him."

"I know, but—"

"No buts." I brush my thumb across her cheek. "Remember what he did to your mother?"

Tears well in her green eyes. "He'll never forgive me for this."

"His forgiveness isn't worth having." My jaw tightens. "A man who forces his daughter into an arranged marriage, who locks her away when she dares to choose her own path? That's not love, Sofia. That's control."

"I'm just scared." She presses her face into my chest.

"Don't be. I've got you." I kiss the top of her head, breathing in the vanilla scent of her hair. "Your father needs to answer for what he's done. To you, your mother, and everyone he's stepped on climbing his way to the top."

"Boss, they're here," Lars mutters from my left.

Jimmy's convoy pulls up outside, black SUVs forming a semi-circle. He steps out, flanked by his goons. His face is twisted with rage when he spots Sofia standing beside me.

"You dare show your face here with my daughter?" Jimmy's voice echoes.

"It's over, Jimmy. The feds have enough to put you away already."

He laughs. "You think I care about recordings? About evidence? I own this city!"

"Not anymore," I say calmly. "Your empire's crumbling. Your suppliers have turned. Your protection's gone."

"You ungrateful little bitch." Jimmy turns on Sofia, his mask finally slipping. "I gave you everything! And this is how you repay me? By running off with carnival trash and spilling my secrets?"

Sofia stands taller. "You gave me a prison, Dad."

"Everything I did was for this family!" Jimmy roars. "Every person I killed, every cop I bought, every shipment of drugs I moved—it was all to build something for you!"

Phoenix's voice comes through my earpiece: "I got it all, boss. The feds are moving in."

I smile. "That confession just sealed your fate, Jimmy."

His eyes widen as sirens wail in the distance. He reaches for his weapon, but Lars and Nash are faster, their guns trained on his men.

"You destroyed everything," Jimmy spits at me. "My empire, my family—"

"No, Dad," Sofia interrupts. "You did that yourself."

I watch Jimmy's face contort as his daughter's words hit home. His fingers twitch, and I catch that telltale shift in his stance. The same one I've seen countless times before violence erupts.

"You ungrateful whore," he snarls, lunging forward with surprising speed for a man his age.

The flash of metal catches my gaze briefly before Jimmy pulls the trigger. I dive forward, shoving Sofia behind me as pain explodes through my left shoulder. Thankfully, it only clips the flesh and zooms past me, not embedding itself in me. I stay upright, my body a shield between Jimmy and his daughter.

"Ty! Oh god, you're bleeding!" Sofia's hands press against my back, trying to see the wound.

I push her further behind me with my good arm. "Stay back. It's a scratch."

Blood seeps through my shirt, hot and sticky, but the pain is nothing compared to the rage coursing through my veins. Jimmy's face twists with frustration as he realizes he missed his target.

"Please," she begs, her fingers clutching my shirt. "Let me look at it."

"I said stay back!" I growl, keeping my eyes locked on Jimmy. His gun remains trained on us. My guys are itching for their guns, but part of the feds' rules was that we bring no weapons and leave it down to them.

Where the fuck are they?

Jimmy is beyond caring about his own safety. His eyes are wild, fixed solely on his daughter cowering behind me.

"You think a bullet will stop me from protecting her?" I spit blood from my mouth where I'd bitten my tongue. "Try again, old man."

"Dad, please stop!" Sofia sobs, but I keep her firmly in place despite her struggles.

I step toward him, noticing that his men are all lowering their weapons. They're wondering what the fuck is going on with their leader as he's acting like a lunatic.

Jimmy's face twists into an arrogant smirk as he turns to Lars and Nash. "Apprehend them both. Now."

Lars and Nash exchange glances before bursting into laughter. Nash actually doubles over, clutching his stomach.

Jimmy's face reddens, his jaw clenching. The gun in his hand trembles with barely contained rage.

"I said grab them!" he barks.

"You really thought my most loyal men would turn like that?" I shake my head, fighting through the pain in my shoulder. "Shows how little you understand about loyalty, Jimmy. These guys aren't bought—they're family."

Lars wipes tears of mirth from his eyes. "Sorry, boss. Didn't mean to laugh. But the old man thinking we'd choose him over you..."

"Especially after everything we've seen him do to his daughter," Nash adds, his expression hardening.

Blood continues seeping through my shirt, but I move forward with Sofia caged behind me. Once I'm close enough to the bastard, I disarm him and punch him in the face, sending him sprawling across the concrete floor. His men raise their weapons, but they don't shoot.

"Try to hurt Sofia again," I growl, standing over him, "and I'll break more than your pride."

Jimmy spits blood onto the warehouse floor. "You think you're better than me? Running your little carnival drug ring?" He pushes himself up to his knees. "I built this city from nothing!"

"And now you'll watch it slip through your fingers," Sofia says, her voice steady despite the tremor I feel in her hand as she grips my arm. "All because you couldn't let go of control."

"Control?" Jimmy laughs, a manic edge creeping into his voice. "You want to talk about control? Ask your boyfriend here about the drugs he's trafficked through his carnival. Ask him about—"

"Shut your mouth," I cut him off. "We both know who runs the trafficking rings in Dawsbury. Phoenix has the paper trail to prove it."

Jimmy's face pales.

"It's over, Dad," Sofia says. "Just stop fighting."

I watch as federal agents flood the warehouse, their weapons trained on Jimmy and his men. The look of defeat on his face as they slap the cuffs on him is worth all the trouble he's caused us.

"Jimmy Moretti, you're under arrest for drug trafficking, racketeering, conspiracy to commit murder..." The list goes on as they read him his rights.

Sofia grips my hand, and I pull her close against my side. She doesn't need to watch this part.

"Mr. Kendall." Agent Cooper approaches me, holstering his weapon. "The Bureau appreciates your cooperation in bringing down the Moretti organization. The evidence you provided was instrumental."

I nod, keeping my expression neutral. "Just doing what any concerned citizen would do."

"The carnival's background check came back clean," he continues. "Looks like you run a legitimate business after all, and Moretti was trying to pass the blame."

Phoenix did his job well—every trace of our less savory operations has been scrubbed clean. The carnival stands pristine under scrutiny, thanks to years of careful planning. We always had a contingency for the shit hitting the fan.

"I'll get someone to take a look at that bullet wound," he says before walking away.

I unbutton my shirt, wincing as the fabric pulls away from the wound. The paramedic approaches with his kit, his expression professional as he examines my shoulder.

"You're one lucky son of a gun," he says, probing the area with gloved hands. "Bullet only clipped you."

I grunt as he cleans the wound. The sting of antiseptic is nothing compared to the burning rage I'd felt when Jimmy pulled that trigger. If he'd aimed a few inches to the right...

"No major damage," the paramedic continues. "Didn't hit bone or any arteries. It's really just a flesh wound—it will hurt for a couple weeks, but that's about it."

Sofia hovers nearby, her face pale. I catch her eye and wink, trying to ease her worry.

The paramedic applies a clean dressing, making his movements quick. "Won't even need stitches. The bullet barely caught you. Just keep this bandage clean and dry. Change it in a couple of days."

He tapes the edges down securely. "You should have full range of motion, but take it easy for a few days. If you notice any signs of infection—redness, swelling, fever—get yourself to a doctor."

I nod, rolling my shoulder experimentally. It hurts, but I've had worse.

"All set," he says, stripping off his gloves. "Just remember to change that bandage."

Sofia's fingers flutter over my bandaged shoulder the moment the paramedic is gone. "Are you sure you're okay? That looks painful."

I catch her hands in mine. "It's nothing. Just have to take it easy for a few days."

Her bottom lip trembles. "He could have killed you."

"But he didn't." I press a kiss on her forehead. "Come on, let's get out of here. I've had enough of this warehouse."

"Agreed," Phoenix says, tucking his laptop under his arm. "Our work here is done."

I scan the group—Lars is already straddling his motorcycle, adjusting his gloves. Nash, Colt, and Remy head toward the van they brought while Gage silently waits for direction.

"Let's head back to the carnival," I announce, fishing my keys from my pocket. "Time to get back to business."

We walk to my Mustang, the chrome gleaming under the warehouse lights. Sofia pauses before opening the back door.

"Gage, why don't you take the front?" she offers. "You'll have more legroom."

Gage's massive frame dwarfs the passenger seat as he folds himself in without a word. Sofia slides into the back with Phoenix, who's already typing on his phone.

I ease behind the wheel, careful not to jar my shoulder. The engine roars to life, and I catch Lars's nod in my rearview mirror as he revs his bike. The van pulls out behind us, and we leave the warehouse and Jimmy Moretti's broken empire in our dust.

37

SOFIA

The hot coffee cup in my hands does little to ease my nerves. I sit at Nonna's kitchen table, the familiar scent of her homemade biscotti filling the air. As I explain my plans to leave with Tyson and the carnival, Sasha sits across from me, eyes wide.

"You're joking, right?" Sasha leans forward. "This is the same guy who stalked you through your webcam."

"I know how it sounds." I trace the rim of my cup. "But he's different than what you think. He saved me from becoming like my mother."

Nonna remains quiet, her weathered hands folded in her lap. The silence stretches between us, broken only by the ticking of her ancient wall clock.

"Nonna?" I reach for her hand. "You could come with us. There's plenty of room, and—"

She shakes her head, a soft smile playing on her lips. "No, tesoro. I'm too old to be running around with carnival folk. My bones need rest, and my garden needs tending."

"But after everything that's happened with Dad—"

"Your father made his choices." She squeezes my hand. "Now, you must make yours."

Sasha shifts in her seat. "I still think this is crazy, but..." She sighs, running a hand through her hair. "If you want this, I'll support you."

"It is." I straighten my shoulders. "Ty might have pursued me aggressively initially, but he's shown me what real love feels like. What freedom feels like."

The kitchen falls quiet, save for the ticking clock. My coffee grows cold, untouched, as I watch these two women who have been my anchors process the news of my departure.

Nonna's eyes mist over as she releases my hand. "Your mother..." She pauses, collecting herself. "Maria was so much like you, tesoro. Beautiful, strong-willed. But your grandfather—" She shakes her head. "He wouldn't listen when I begged him not to force her into marriage with Jimmy."

My throat tightens. "You tried to stop it?"

"Of course I did. I saw how the arranged engagement was killing her spirit." Nonna's voice breaks. "The depression started right after the wedding. She'd sit for hours, staring out windows, barely eating. Jimmy kept her like a bird in a gilded cage, just as your grandfather wanted. Exactly what he did to you, too."

I grip my coffee cup tighter, the ceramic cool against my palms. "Did she ever talk about... about ending it?"

"No." Nonna dabs at her eyes. "That's what made it worse. She just... faded away, piece by piece. I watched my daughter disappear into nothing, and I couldn't save her."

"When you came to me about Paulie," Nonna's voice turns soft, "I was terrified. The same look in your eyes—I saw your mother in you that day."

I squeeze her hand. "But?"

"But you..." She smiles through her tears. "You fought back. Your mother just accepted her fate. Like a flower wilting in the shade, she stopped reaching for the sun. But you?" Nonna cups my cheek. "You broke free. You found your own path."

"I didn't want to end up like her." My voice catches. "Sometimes, I'd find old photos of her before she married Dad. She looked so alive, so full of joy."

"She was." Nonna nods. "But when your grandfather arranged the marriage, she just... gave up. No resistance, no tears. She walked down that aisle like a ghost." She takes a shaky breath. "But you, my Sofia—you have her spark but your own strength. When you told me about not wanting to marry Paulie, I saw that same despair in your eyes. But underneath? Steel. Pure steel."

Sasha takes my other hand. "Your mom would be proud of you, you know? For choosing your own happiness."

"She would," Nonna agrees. "Your mother couldn't find the courage to fight, but you've shown more bravery than any of us expected."

Tears stream down my face as I throw my arms around Nonna, breathing in her familiar scent of lavender and fresh bread. Her small frame trembles against mine as she holds me tight.

"I'll come back," I whisper. "Every time we're near Dawsbury, I'll stay with you. We can cook together, tend your garden—"

"Shh, tesoro." She strokes my hair like she did when I was little. "I know you will. The carnival moves, but your heart knows the way home."

Sasha joins our embrace, her own tears falling. "And I'll keep an eye on Nonna when you're away. Make sure she doesn't get too lonely."

"You're both acting like I'm dying." I try to laugh through my tears. "I'm just traveling with the carnival. Ty already promised we'd come through here regularly."

Nonna cups my face in her weathered hands. "Your mother never had this choice. To come and go as she pleased. To love freely." She wipes my tears with her thumbs. "You'll always have a home here, Sofia. Whether it's for a night or a month or a year."

"I know." I squeeze her hands. "And you'll always be my Nonna. Distance won't change that."

"Promise you'll call?" Sasha's voice breaks. "Even from the road?"

"Every week." I pull her into another hug. "And you can visit us at the carnival whenever you want. Ty already said you're both welcome anytime."

Nonna presses something into my palm—her silver St. Christopher medal. "For safe travels, tesoro."

Fresh tears spill as I clutch the precious necklace. "Nonna, I can't take this—"

"You can and you will." She closes my fingers around it. "It protected me through many journeys in life and belonged to my mother. Now it's your turn."

My heart aches as I say my last goodbyes. I clutch Nonna's St. Christopher medal as I walk to my car, the weight of it grounding me in this moment of change. The afternoon sun catches on the silver, reminding me of all the times I'd seen it gleaming at Nonna's throat while she cooked or gardened.

My chest aches with the bittersweet pain of goodbye, but underneath burns something brighter—hope. I'm choosing my own path for the first time in my life. No arranged marriages, no suffocating expectations, no living in fear of disappointing my father.

Leaving Nonna and Sasha behind hurts, but they'll always be my connection to home. Unlike my mother, who was trapped in a marriage that slowly killed her spirit, I get to write my own story. I will love freely, travel widely, and return whenever I choose.

The medal warms against my palm as I slip it over my head. Its weight settles against my chest like a promise—not just of safe travels, but of the courage to forge my own path. My mother never had this chance, but I do. And I'm going to grab it with both hands.

38

TYSON

One week later...

We're in our next town, Burlington. Sofia still feels sad about leaving her grandmother and best friend behind in Dawsbury. It's after hours as I lead her through the darkened carnival, the rides silent and still. Her hand feels small in mine as we walk past the shuttered game stalls.

"Where are you taking me?" Sofia asks, her eyes darting around the empty carnival as we approach my trailer.

I chuckle, pulling her closer. "Back to our trailer. I plan to fuck you senseless all night, baby girl."

She stops abruptly, her eyes sparkling with excitement. "Oh?"

I step closer. "Is that a problem?"

She bites her lip, her breathing quickening. "No... it's just..."

"Just what?" I brush a strand of hair behind her ear, my fingers lingering on her cheek.

"I want you, Ty. But—" She pauses, and I sense the conflict within her.

"But what?" I prompt.

"I want to try something." She sinks her teeth into her full bottom lip. "Lily told me how Cade likes to chase her in the woods." Sofia's gaze moves to the woods surrounding the carnival.

"Oh?" I squeeze her hand, already intrigued by where this is going.

"Mmhmm." She steps closer, her curves pressing against my arm. "I kind of like that idea. Especially if you wear a mask."

Heat floods my body at her suggestion. "That sounds perfect."

I guide her to the costume storage tent, rifling through our stock until I find what I want—a black full-face mask studded with silver and two dark mesh eye holes that will hide my expression completely.

Sliding it over my face, I turn to her. The mask changes my voice as it's fitted with a voice distortion, making it deeper. "Run for me, baby girl. You've got thirty seconds before I come hunting."

Sofia's breath catches, her chest rising faster. Her green eyes darken with desire as she backs away from me.

"Better start counting," she whispers, then turns and disappears into the darkness.

I begin the count, my blood pumping faster at the

thought of pursuing her. My shoulder still aches a little, but the adrenaline makes it lessen.

I count to thirty slowly, drawing out the anticipation as I listen for her fleeing footsteps. My body is coiled tight, ready to spring after her. The night air is crisp.

I move, my footsteps purposeful, cutting through the carnival grounds toward the woods.

Sofia's scent reaches me first—that unique blend of vanilla and something distinctly hers. I follow the trace of it, moving with purpose, my heart pounding in my chest.

The rustle of her dress betrays her hiding spot, and I smile beneath the mask. She's chosen a dense cluster of trees, hoping to conceal herself in the shadows, but I see her with her back pressed against the thick trunk.

I close in, my footsteps silent, until I stand directly behind her, the curve of her hip brushing mine. She startles, a gasp escaping her, but I cover her mouth with one hand while the other curls around her waist, pulling her against me.

"No fair," I murmur, relishing how she shudders in my arms. "I caught you too quickly."

She squirms against me, and in a flash, she slips from my grasp, darting deeper into the woods.

"You didn't catch me!" Her voice echoes through the trees.

I smile, eyes scanning the dark trunks and the moonlight filtering through. I spot her again. She's hiding behind a thick oak, the pale skin of her shoulder visible, her dress caught on a branch.

I stalk toward her, keeping my movements slow and

deliberate. She watches me, her eyes glittering with fear and excitement.

Closing the distance between us, I slam her against the tree, my body pinning hers to the rough bark. One hand tangles in her hair, holding her head back as I press my thigh between her legs.

"Please, no!" Her voice is breathless, her words arousing me further.

"I'm going to take what I want," I growl.

"No, let me go," she begs. Her eyes shine with unspoken desire.

She knows the word that will stop this. Just one word and I'll release her. But she doesn't speak it. Instead, I see the longing in her eyes that matches mine.

"Be a good girl and take it," I order, my voice a low growl that vibrates through both of us.

She shakes her head in denial. I see the truth in how she melts against me, her body softening, inviting me in.

My hands are rough as I tear at the delicate fabric of her dress, exposing her breasts to the night air. Her nipples peak, begging for my touch. I pinch one between my fingers, twisting it until she whimpers.

"You like that?" I demand.

Her fingernails dig into my shoulders, leaving a trail of fiery pain as I press inside her. This fire spreads through my veins, sharpening my focus on her body and mine alone.

"That's it," I whisper against her ear as I thrust into her. "Fight me."

The words leave my mouth as I claim her with every inch of me. I move with purpose, watching her face twist in a mix of struggle and pleasure. Those emerald eyes shine with a defiance that only urges me on.

Her legs wrap around my waist, drawing me in, even as she protests.

"No!" she gasps. "Don't do this!"

Her body betrays her lies as she arches her back, urging me to go deeper. I lose myself in the sensation of her wet heat, the way she squeezes around me as if she never wants to let me go.

"Tell me you don't want this," I challenge, withdrawing almost entirely and then plunging back into her tight core.

"I—I don't—" Her words break as I sense her orgasm building, her inner walls clenching around me.

"Tell me, baby girl," I demand. "Say you don't want to come all over my cock."

Her jaw clenches, teeth biting down on her lower lip. "I—can't—"

I lean down, my breath hot against her ear. "Say the word, and I'll stop."

But she doesn't say our safe word. Instead, her body speaks for her as I thrust harder, pushing her toward the edge. Her fingers dig into my back, pulling me closer, urging me on as her muscles tighten around me. She lets out a strangled cry, her release washing over her, her body trembling in the aftermath.

I touch her face, slide my hand along her cheek, and thread my fingers into her hair. I pull her head back to expose her throat, easing my mask up to press my lips to the sensitive skin below her ear.

She tastes like sin and temptation. Mine.

"That's my good girl," I whisper. "You came so beautifully for me while I took you against your will, didn't you?"

Her breath comes in ragged gasps as I press hot, open-mouthed kisses along her neck. I'm not ready to let her go, not yet.

"Please, no more," she whispers, turning her face away, but her words hold no real conviction.

"We're not done." My voice is rough with desire as I nuzzle her ear. "You know you love every second of this."

She shakes her head, her hair brushing against my bare chest. "Please, it's too much."

"Too much?" I growl, grabbing her hips and forcing her onto all fours. "I'll be the judge of that."

I push her forward so that her shoulders are pressed to the ground, her ass raised in the air, presented to me like a gift. Gripping her hips, I slide back into her, filling her in one smooth stroke.

Her shoulders tense, her fingers curl into the dirt in a futile attempt to find purchase.

"So tight, baby girl," I murmur, withdrawing and thrusting back into her. "So perfect."

My grip tightens on her hips as I move with a relentless pace, each thrust harder than the last. Her moans fill the night air with a beautiful melody. I lean over her, my hands gripping her shoulders, tilting her body to the perfect angle to take me even deeper.

"Please, Master," she gasps, her voice breaking as I ram into her. "Oh, God, please."

She's begging me to keep going, to push her beyond the limits of what she's known.

Her body is a symphony beneath mine, every movement a new note, a new chord that fills the night air with a song only we can hear. I thrust into her, again and again, each movement deliberate, meant to elicit a response.

"You're perfect, baby girl," I growl, my voice deeper than I've ever heard. I wonder if it's the mask transforming my voice or how she makes me feel—powerful, primal, in control. "You're everything I want, everything I need." I punctuate my words with each stroke of my cock. "Look at me."

She looks at me over her shoulder. Her eyes shine like emeralds in the darkness, burning with a passion that matches mine.

"You're my good girl," I tell her, watching her face as I say the words. "My perfect submissive."

With each movement, her moans echo through the woods, music that emboldens me, urging me to take her harder, make her feel even more.

My hands trail down her spine, over the curve of her hips, to the soft skin of her thighs. My fingers dip lower until I brush her clit. A strangled cry escapes her, and her body jerks at the contact. Her walls clench around me as she struggles to find purchase.

"You like that?" I whisper into the night air. "When I touch you there?"

She nods, eyes forward. "Y-yes."

"Do you like it when I make you come?" I continue

to rub her clit in slow, torturous circles, my hips slamming into her. "Let me hear your voice, Sofia."

"I—I like when you touch me." Her words are choppy, broken by her erratic breaths. "Please, Ty, I—"

"You what?" I stop my movements. "Tell me what you want."

She gasps, her body trembling. "I want—I want you to keep touching me. Please."

"Like this?" I tease, rubbing her slowly.

"Yes—please." Her hips roll in time with my thrusts. "More."

"Do you want to come for me?" I ask, my voice low and gravelly. My fingers still work their magic as my hips piston. "Beg me for it."

"Please, Ty," she whimpers. "Please, let me come."

"Not until you admit it." I pull out almost entirely, then slide back into her heat. "Not until you say that you want me to breed you. That you want to feel me pumping my cum deep inside that tight cunt."

My thighs slap against her ass with each plunge. "Say it," I order, quickening my pace. "Let me know how much you want me to breed you."

"I want—oh, God—" She breaks off with a cry, her walls clenching around me as her orgasm builds. "I want you to breed me, Ty. Fill me up and make me come at the same time."

"That's my good girl." I thrust with abandon, her words reverberating through me. My fingers working her clit even faster. "Come for me, baby. Come all over my cock and clench me so tight that I fill you with cum."

As her orgasm crashes over her, her walls clenching

and releasing in waves, I release my own pent-up desire, filling her with my release, branding her as mine.

"That's it," I whisper. "Take my cum, baby girl."

Together, we ride the waves of our climaxes, our bodies entwined in the darkness of the woods. At last, I slow my movements, easing her down from her high. She collapses against the forest floor, her breathing ragged, her body relaxed in the aftermath of her release.

Easing my dick out of her, I roll onto my side and push up on one arm, using my free hand to slide the mask up and off my face, tossing it to the side. Her eyes open, a question in their emerald depths.

Brushing the hair from her face, I see everything I never knew I wanted until I met her.

"I love you, Ty," she whispers. "I know it's crazy to say, with everything that's happened and only knowing you for such a short time. I love you so much it scares me sometimes."

My heart pounds against my ribs. For years, I've kept everyone at arm's length, convinced that love was a weakness I couldn't afford. But Sofia... she changed everything.

"I love you, too." The words come easier than I expected, as natural as breathing. "You're everything to me."

She reaches up, her fingers tracing the line of my jaw. "Really?"

"Really." I lean down, pressing my forehead to hers. "You make me want to be better. To be worthy of you."

"You already are worthy of me," she whispers, her

lips brushing mine. "You saved me, Ty. Not just from my father or Paulie, but from a life without love. Without passion."

I kiss her, pouring all my feelings into that gentle touch. When I pull back, her eyes are shining with tears.

"Don't cry." I wipe them away. "I've got you. Always will."

She smiles through her tears. "Promise?"

"Promise." I gather her closer, cradling her against my chest.

She's mine. And I'm hers. Nothing is ever going to change that. I want to build her up and erase any insecurity she's ever felt. And that's exactly what I plan to do for the rest of our lives.

39

EPILOGUE

SOFIA

One year later...

I adjust the sequins on my emerald costume, smiling as I catch my reflection in the mirror. I would've cringed at wearing something so form-fitting a year ago, but now I wear it with pride. The carnival lights dance across the fabric, making me sparkle like a jewel.

"Five minutes until showtime," I call out, striding through the backstage area of the main tent. The familiar buzz of pre-show energy fills the air.

Flora stretches near the rigging, her blonde hair in a tight bun. She joined us last Christmas Eve, and watching her soar through the air with Colt and Nash still takes my breath away. The three share something special—a connection I don't quite understand, but it works for them. They're inseparable both in and out of the ring.

"Everything set for the finale?" I ask, checking off items on my clipboard.

"Ready to fly," Flora says with a confident grin. She's far from the scared girl who showed up at our door that winter night.

Ty appears behind me, wrapping his arms around my waist. "My gorgeous girl," he murmurs against my neck. "Running the show like you were born for it."

I lean back into his embrace, savoring his warmth. "I was meant for this life—for you." My old insecurities have faded like morning mist under the sun of his love.

The tent fills with the excited chatter of the gathering crowd. I feel at home among the sawdust and sequins, the bright lights and bold dreams. This world that once seemed so foreign has become my sanctuary, and the man who rules it is my heart's true north. Sure, there's still the darker side of the carnival. Ty's true money maker is still running, but I don't get involved.

"Places, everyone!" I call out, stepping into my role as show coordinator with practiced ease. Ty squeezes my hand before heading to his position as ringmaster.

And then the show runs as smoothly as it does every night. The crowd's roar fades to silence when finished, but my heart still pounds with post-show adrenaline. Sawdust swirls in the spotlights as the last audience members filter out the big top. I clutch my clipboard, reviewing tomorrow's schedule when strong arms encircle my waist from behind.

"You were incredible tonight." Ty's deep voice sends shivers down my spine. His hands slide over my sequined costume, tracing my curves with possessive intent. "Watching you command the show... Fuck, baby girl, it made me so hard."

I melt into his touch, tilting my head as his lips find my neck. The clipboard slips from my fingers, clattering to the ground. His firm chest presses against my back, and I can feel how much the show affected him.

"I love seeing you take charge," he growls, nipping my earlobe. "The way everyone jumps to follow your orders. But we both know who's in control, right?"

My breath catches as one hand slides up to cup my breast through the thin material of my dress. "Yes," I whisper.

The empty tent feels charged with electricity, remnants of the night's magic mixing with our growing desire.

"Say it," he demands, his other hand gripping my hip tight enough to bruise.

"You are," I gasp as his fingers pinch my nipple. "You're in control, Master."

Ty growls, forcing me to face him and claiming my mouth in a searing kiss. Our passion ignites as we devour each other, hands tugging and pulling at our clothes. The fabric of his shirt rips beneath my eager hands, and he laughs. I need to feel his skin against mine.

He lays me down on the floor, our gazes locked. His eyes smolder with desire. "You're so fucking beautiful," he whispers, his lips never breaking contact with my skin as he trails kisses down my neck.

His mouth travels lower, worshipping the curve of my breasts, the swell of my hips, his tongue swirling over my navel. He teases me with gentle bites, making me squirm as I crave more.

"Please," I whimper, my breath hitching as he nuzzles the sensitive skin of my inner thigh.

He chuckles, looking up at me with a wicked gleam. "Not yet."

With nimble fingers, he pulls my panties slowly down my legs. I lift my hips in offering, eager to feel his mouth on me. But instead of giving me what I crave, he kisses my thighs. I moan softly, arching my back as the sensation shoots straight to my core.

"You like that?" he teases.

"Yes," I whisper, biting my lip as he mouths the sensitive skin of my inner thigh.

Finally, he licks my pussy, and I cry out at the first touch of his tongue. He laps at my folds, teasing my clit with gentle flicks. His fingers join the dance, plunging inside me.

I tighten my grip on his hair, tangling my fingers in the soft strands as I arch off the rug, urging him on. "Ty, please... I need you inside me."

He chuckles against my sensitive flesh. "As you wish, my gorgeous girl."

In one smooth motion, he stands and kicks off his pants, freeing his thick, pierced length. I watch him in awe, my body throbbing with need. He steps closer, positioning himself at my entrance.

Ty teases my clit with his piercing, the magic cross sending electric shocks through my core. I ache for him to make me whole.

He slides inside, the piercing hitting all the right

spots. It's one of his bigger bars, with bigger barbells, and it's exactly what my body craves.

"Oh, God, yes," I moan, tilting my hips to take him deeper.

The stretch burns so sweetly, and I relish the slight pain as my body adjusts. "More," I beg, needing to feel every inch of him.

Ty obliges, pulling out entirely before thrusting back in. I cry out, my fingers digging into his muscular back as he moves relentlessly.

"You like that, baby girl?" His voice is thick with desire. "My cock marking you as mine?"

"Yes," I gasp. "It's perfect. More, Master. Harder."

He grunts, grasping my hips and lifting me to meet his powerful thrusts. The slap of our bodies fills the tent, mingling with my shameless moans.

I stare into his passionate eyes as we move together, caught in the frenzy of our need. The piercing ignites fireworks within me, threatening to push me over the edge.

"So close," I whisper. "Don't stop, Master."

"Never." His promise sends a rush of pleasure through me, and I shatter, crying out his name as my core clenches around him.

"Good girl," he purrs, but the look in his eyes tells me he's not done. Pulling out of me, he gently taps my hip letting me know he wants me on all fours. I bite my lip, anticipating the stretch, as he pulls out the butt plug embedded within me. I spent the whole show with it nestled inside, a delicious secret that made my movements more sensual.

As the thick silicone leaves my body, I sigh with a mix of pleasure and relief. But the respite is brief as Ty pulls out a small bottle of lube from his jacket, and I watch over my shoulder as he coats his hard length in it.

I brace myself on all fours, closing my eyes and waiting for the divine invasion—the sharp pleasure I yearn for.

The stretch comes suddenly as he pushes inside, filling me up. I cry out, my fingernails digging into the rug to anchor myself. Ty's hands grip my hips, holding me still as he starts fucking me.

The pressure is exquisite as he pushes deeper, each thrust waking nerve endings I never knew I had. "Fuck, baby, your ass is so tight." His grip on my hips bruising.

"It belongs to you, Master," I reply, breathless. I breathe through the intensity, relishing the stretch and burn.

I've grown to crave this—the way he takes what he wants, commanding my body to pleasure him. There's no room for hesitation anymore, only surrender.

"That's right, baby girl. You know who owns you." He pulls out almost entirely before slamming back into me.

I cry out, my head hanging down as my body shakes with the force. "Yes, Master. More, please! Claim me."

"Always, baby." He pulls my hair, forcing me to arch my back and push my ass higher. The position gives him deeper access, and he takes full advantage, pounding into me with primal need.

"You like that? You like being my filthy anal slut?" His voice is dark.

"Yes, Master. I'm your filthy slut. Always." My words come out in gasps, intermingled with little whimpers as his piercing rubs against my sensitive walls.

"That's it, take it all," he growls, his pace relentless. "You know this ass is mine, don't you?"

"Yes! All yours." I claw at the rug, desperate for more friction as pleasure coils within me. I squeeze my muscles around him, wanting to milk every inch of his impressive length.

He chuckles. "Such a good girl. I'm going to breed this tight ass."

I'm keenly aware of every inch of him, the exquisite burn sending shockwaves of pleasure through my body. Ty's thrusts become more urgent, his grip bruisingly tight on my hips.

"You're so close, aren't you?" he grunts. "I want to feel that sweet ass clench around my cock as you come for me."

I moan, my face pressed against the rug as his words send me spiraling closer to the edge. "Please, Master... I'm there... I need to—"

"Come for me, Sofia. Let it go." His command is like a match striking tinder-dry wood.

An explosion of pleasure rocks my body, and I cry out, my head falling forward as my core clenches around his cock. I ride the waves of my orgasm, feeling every pulse and thrust of his hard length inside me.

Ty growls, his fingers digging into my hips as he continues to pound into me. "Fuck, your ass clenching around my cock is too much. Take my cum, Sofia. Take it all."

His release bursts through him. He empties himself inside me, the hot rush of his seed marking me as his. "That's it, take all of my cum," he pants. Finally, he pulls out, his length slipping from my body with a slick pop. "Now show me, baby girl."

I push, and his cum dribbles out, warm and sticky. My cheeks heat at the feel.

"That's my good girl," he murmurs.

I watch him over my shoulder as he retrieves the butt plug with one hand, slicking it with more lube. "I want my cum to stay inside you as long as possible. I want you to feel it in you all night, baby."

I tremble at his words, still breathless from my orgasm as he slips the plug back inside, stretching me open once more and plugging my ass to stop the cum from escaping.

"There we go," he murmurs, his hands gently caressing my ass cheeks. "My cum is still deep inside you and buried in your ass. And that means I own this ass." He gives it a light spank.

Goosebumps rise on my skin at his words. "It's always yours."

I curl into Ty's warmth as he lies beside me and pulls me against his chest, my body tingling from our passionate encounter. His heartbeat thrums steady and strong beneath my ear, a rhythm I've come to associate with home. His fingers trace lazy patterns along my spine, and I feel more at peace than I ever thought possible.

"I love you," he whispers, kissing my head.

Tears prick at my eyes as the words wash over me.

After everything we've been through—the danger, the uncertainty, the battles with my father—here we are. Safe. Together. Free.

"I love you, too," I murmur against his skin, breathing in his familiar scent of leather and spice. "I never thought I'd find this kind of love. The kind that sees all of me—not just the perfect mob princess, but the real me underneath."

His arms tighten around me. "You're perfect exactly as you are. Every curve, every laugh, every stubborn argument." He chuckles softly. "Even when you drive me crazy, you're everything I never knew I needed."

I lift my head to meet his gaze. "Thank you for saving me."

"You saved yourself," he corrects me. "I showed you the door was unlocked."

The carnival sounds drift in from outside—distant laughter, music, the whir of rides. What once seemed like a world I could never belong to has become my sanctuary. He kisses me again, and I know with absolute certainty that this is where I belong—in his arms, world, and heart.

THANK you for reading *Carnival Master!* Did you enjoy it? If so, check out my other Carnival Books:

Cade & Lily's Book - Carnival Nightmare: A Dark Stalker Romance

Lars & Alice's Book - Carnival Obsession: A Dark Romance

Gage & Aurora's Book - Carnival Monster: A Dark Serial Killer Romance

Phoenix & Tilly's Book - Carnival Stalker: A Dark Stalker Romance

More books by me:

Forbidden Harvest: A Dark Taboo Romance

Hunted: A Dark Romance

Welcome to Carnage: A Dark Romance Novella

Stranded: A Dark Romance novella

Salvation: A Dark Stalker Romance

Carjacked: A Dark Hitchhiker Romance

ABOUT THE AUTHOR

I've always been drawn to the dark side of fiction. My stories? They're an exploration of that darkness, filled with mysterious masked men, fearless heroines, and spice that'll set your Kindles ablaze.

Ever since I can remember, I've been captivated by the darker side of romance. It's necessary to add I don't condone these kind of relationships in real life. However, the intoxicating chase, the deadly dance, the heart-racing fear, and an irresistible attraction I adore writing.

I exclusively publish on Amazon, providing a thrilling escape for those who dare to venture into the dark side of love and lust. If you've read my book and found yourself wanting more, follow me on Amazon or social media for updates on my next dark novella release. Your adventure is only a page flip away.

Printed in Great Britain
by Amazon